Praise for the Mys
Jeanne M. D

Agatha Award Winner

∾

"Hilda loves life, and the joy she takes in the simple pleasures of Sunday picnics and summer holidays and a loud, lusty hymn is treat enough."

—*New York Times*

"Acute glimpses of anti-Catholicism, upstairs/downstairs class distinctions, wardrobe upkeep, Swedish family dinners...and the romantic touch, circa 1903. Dams's more heavy-handed historical brethren would do well to emulate her light touch."

—*Kirkus Reviews*

"Hilda is an endearing character with Old World social values. Skillful."

—*Chicago Sun-Times*

★ "The latest Hilda Johansson mystery is a real corker.... In a genre with no shortage of amateur sleuths in period costume, Hilda is one of the most memorable.... The secret to Dams's success is in the details: she plunks us firmly down in early twentieth-century Indiana. We learn, without realizing we're being taught anything at all, about social customs, class divisions, even the day-to-day operations of a wealthy turn-of-the-century household. Great characters, fascinating history, compelling mystery: this series could go on forever."

—*Booklist* (starred review)

CRIMSON SNOW

Also by Jeanne M. Dams:

Crimson Snow

A Hilda Johansson Mystery

Jeanne M. Dams

PERSEVERANCE PRESS / JOHN DANIEL & COMPANY

PALO ALTO / MCKINLEYVILLE, CALIFORNIA / MMV

This is a work of fiction. Characters, places, and events are the product of the author's imagination or are used fictitiously. Any resemblance to real people, companies, institutions, organizations, or incidents is entirely coincidental.

A PERSEVERANCE PRESS BOOK
Published by John Daniel & Company
A division of Daniel & Daniel, Publishers, Inc.
Post Office Box 2790
McKinleyville, California 95519
www.danielpublishing.com/perseverance

Book design by Eric Larson, Studio E Books, Santa Barbara
www.studio-e-books.com

Cover painting: Linda Weatherly S.

10 9 8 7 6 5 4 3 2

LIBRARY OF CONGRESS CATALOGING-IN-PUBLICATION DATA
Dams, Jeanne M.
  Crimson snow : a Hilda Johansson mystery / by Jeanne M. Dams.
    p. cm.
  ISBN 1-880284-79-0 (pbk. : alk. paper)
  1. Johansson, Hilda (Fictitious character)—Fiction. 2. Women detectives—Indiana—South Bend—Fiction. 3. South Bend (Ind.)—Fiction. 4. Swedish Americans—Fiction. I. Title.
  PS3554.A498C75 2005
  813'.54—dc22
              2004027166

CRIMSON SNOW

*The more that I consider the affairs of
Home, the more am I impressed with the
importance of the servant's position.*

—Mrs. Julia McNair Wright
The Complete Home, 1879

1

N O! THE SPREAD MUST be the same on both sides, even, and pulled up *so!*" Hilda tugged the bedding into the proper position and plumped a pillow with a vigorous fist.

Young Janecska, the under-housemaid, watched with a sulky expression on her face. "You don't have to get mad about it! Anyhow, I've made beds before."

"Not at Tippecanoe Place, you have not. We are careful here. Everything must be just so. And you will not answer back! Now go, finish Colonel George's suite, and do the bed properly this time. I will dust and begin on the bathrooms."

Janecska flounced out of the room. Hilda uttered a few highly improper words in Swedish and began dusting, moving with a speed that would, in the hands of a less experienced maid, have meant disaster to the fragile tortoiseshell accessories on Mrs. Clem Studebaker's dressing table. Hilda had been handling them for years and had never broken a one. Her light hand with the precious ornaments scattered all over the great house was one reason she was head housemaid for the fabulously wealthy Studebaker family.

Another was that she got along well with the other servants, as a rule. She was fair with her underlings, careful not to ruffle the feathers of Mrs. Sullivan, the temperamental cook, and respectful (at least outwardly) toward Mr. Williams, the butler whose strict discipline often verged on the tyrannical.

Today, however, she was in a raging temper and taking it out on Janecska. Mr. Williams, this morning at servants' breakfast,

had severely reprimanded Maggie, the new waitress, for an incident at last night's dinner party. Maggie had blamed Hilda, and
Hilda had defended herself. It was not her fault the stupid girl
had handed the dessert dishes on the wrong side, thus running
into Hilda who was removing water glasses. Certainly it was unfortunate that the ice water had landed in Colonel George's lap,
but it was only a few drops, and he hadn't minded much, really.
Mr. Williams, uninterested in explanations, had threatened to
dismiss them both.

Hilda had held onto her temper, barely. She had bitten her
tongue and kept back the words that begged for expression.
Now, however, alone in Mrs. Clem's luxurious bedroom, she re-
played the scene in her mind, muttering under her breath the
things she would like to have said at the time.

"Dismiss me, Mr. Williams? You cannot run this household
without me! You will be sorry when I go, but I will go when I
choose, not when you choose. Mrs. Clem will not allow you to
dismiss me."

Mrs. Clem is no longer mistress of this house, retorted the butler
in her mind. *Mrs. George has never interfered with my decisions
about the staff.*

"No, and a great pity it is! Mrs. Clem would have let Norah
stay on, even after she married and couldn't live here anymore.
Mrs. Clem would never have hired that Maggie, who knows
nothing of work in a fine house. Mrs. Clem knows how to deal
with servants. She will be very, very annoyed when I tell her
what you have said."

To that, the imaginary Mr. Williams had no reply.

"And when I tell her your temper has been so bad that I may
decide to marry Patrick and leave this place, she will listen!"

Hilda really had no intention of telling Mrs. Clem any such
thing. For one thing, she didn't want to worry the frail elderly
lady. Since the death of Mr. Clem a little over two years ago, Mrs.
Clem had been beset by trials. Turning over the reins of the
household to her daughter-in-law, Mrs. George Studebaker,
hadn't been easy. The adage that there isn't room in a house for

two women held true even in a mansion the size of Tippecanoe
Place, with its thirty-odd rooms. Mrs. Clem had conceded gra-
ciously to the necessity, but she missed her husband sorely. She
loved her son, of course, but George couldn't fill his father's
shoes. His philosophy of business, even, was different. Mrs. Clem
had watched the Studebaker wagon and carriage factory begin to
experiment with automobiles, an experiment she viewed with
deep misgiving. Clement Studebaker had never been opposed to
progress, but like nearly every sensible man in the country, he
had viewed automobiles as a passing fad. Now the company was
manufacturing them, in a modest way, to be sure, but George
wanted to expand. He even owned one of the dratted things!

Hilda knew all this, of course. Servants know everything that
goes on in a big house, whether their masters are aware of the fact
or not. Hilda heartily agreed with Mrs. Clem about automobiles,
and wasn't going to upset her further by bringing to her a petty
quarrel with the butler.

She straightened the silver clock on the mantel, checked to
make sure the hearth had been properly cleaned and a new fire
laid, and then went on to the bathroom, sighing gustily. No, she
wouldn't take her troubles to Mrs. Clem. But she wished, oh,
with all her heart she wished, that Norah were still here to talk
to. She felt she would burst if she couldn't express her feelings to
someone. For the seven years Hilda Johansson had worked for
the Studebakers, beginning as a daily and working her way up
quickly to head housemaid, her best friend and confidante had
been Norah Murphy, who waited at table, Hilda sometimes
assisting when there was a big dinner party. Their bedrooms
were next door to one another, and they had chatted and giggled
and wept together at all hours of the day and night, even when
they were supposed to be in bed and asleep. Norah had abetted
Hilda in her rule-breaking and her occasional forays into the
investigation of distressing events, and had never once given her
away to Mr. Williams. They had been closer than sisters.

But last summer Norah had become engaged to Sean O'Neill,
with whom she had been walking out in what Hilda had thought

to be a casual friendship. And last month, at Christmas time, they had married. Norah had given up her live-in position for a job in a much smaller household, and Hilda was bereft.

She hadn't been able to attend the wedding. Swedish Lutherans did not attend the religious services of Irish Catholics. She had been invited to the party afterwards at the home of Norah's parents, but she hadn't felt really welcome, even with Patrick there, and she had scarcely seen Norah since that day. Mr. Williams's household had been disrupted, his temper had been frayed, and he was keeping an eagle eye on all the servants, especially Hilda.

She, of course, took every moment of her time off, even going out sometimes in her rest times, simply to remind the butler that her privileges were still hers, no matter what the domestic problems might be. But she couldn't interrupt Norah at her work, and by the time Norah was home, Hilda had to be back at Tippecanoe Place.

They had met twice on a Sunday, once to go ice skating on the pond in Leeper Park and once for hot chocolate at the Philadelphia, but with both Sean and Patrick there, the meetings lost their zest. Norah was more interested in Sean than in Hilda, and though that was right and proper, it made Hilda realize that something important was gone forever. Norah was a married woman and Hilda was not. The old intimacy could never be recaptured.

And Patrick...Hilda sighed again. Patrick wanted to marry Hilda. She wanted it, too, in a way. But it would mean leaving her job, leaving this house. She sat back on her heels and looked at the bathroom she was cleaning, the spotless tiled floor, the marble wash basin with the gold-plated faucets, the huge, elegant porcelain tub with its mahogany surround, the modern, sanitary water closet. The servants' bathroom wasn't as grand, but it had simpler versions of the same equipment.

She thought about her brother's house, with its pump in the backyard. Baths were taken in a tin hip bath, every drop of water having to be heated on the stove. Faces were washed in a basin, in cold water. Sanitary needs were dealt with in the backyard, too, in the shed with the half moon cut in the door.

She and Patrick wouldn't be able to afford even as nice a house as Sven's. She would have to find a job somewhere, doing something far more menial than her duties in this house. And when the babies came along, what then? Take in washing, like so many women in her position? Become a dressmaker, she who hated mending her petticoats and aprons?

She finished the bathrooms mechanically, not really seeing what she was doing, and chivvied Janecska out of the last bedroom. The family was coming upstairs from breakfast. Hilda's and Janecska's skirts disappeared around the bend of the back stairs just in time.

Hilda sent Janecska upstairs to deal with the servants' bedrooms. She herself went down to the ground floor to clean the servants' sitting room. Mr. Williams was very particular indeed about how that room was done.

She stopped in the kitchen on her way. Mrs. Sullivan was stirring a pot of soup and scolding Elsie, the scullery maid. "And if you'd done as I told you and soaked that porridge pot in *cold* water, you'd not have to waste time scrubbing it now. How many times—and what do *you* want?" she said, rounding to direct her wrath toward Hilda.

Hilda smiled sweetly. "The cinnamon buns you made for breakfast, they were so good, and I am hungry. Are there any left?"

"There are, and I'm saving them for our tea." Mrs. Sullivan scowled fiercely, and then relented as Hilda continued to look deferential. "Ah, well, one won't be missed, I reckon. You didn't eat much earlier."

"No. I could not," said Hilda briefly.

"You don't want to mind him, child." The cook reached for the basket of leftover buns and handed it to Hilda. "He has his moods. Like as not he'll have forgotten all about it by dinner time."

Hilda didn't reply. She took a roll, carefully smoothed the

napkin over the rest, and nodded her thanks to the cook as she left the kitchen. She didn't want to discuss the brouhaha, at least not with the cook. Mr. Williams might forget his threats. She, Hilda, would not.

The servants' room, where their meals were served and they relaxed in their rare times for relaxation, was right across the hall from the kitchen, but Hilda took her time getting there. She stopped in the alcove by the back door to eat her bun. Mr. Williams frowned on eating between meals, and at this time of day he would be in his pantry, right next to the servants' room.

She had taken only a bite when she was startled by a knock at the door. It wasn't loud, but Hilda, engaged as she was in an illicit snack, jumped. She thrust the bun into the capacious pocket of her petticoat, peered around the door jamb, and then opened the door with a suddenness that surprised the child standing outside.

"Erik! What is wrong? Why are you here? Why are you not in school?"

"Let me in, Hilda. I'm cold!"

A burst of frigid air entered with Erik. Hilda had not yet been outside and hadn't realized, in the centrally heated mansion, how bitter was the cold on this January day.

"You cannot stay here. This is not a time I can visit. And why are you not in school?"

"That's what I came to tell you!" His voice was loud, and cracking with strain.

"Hush! If Mr. Williams hears you he will…I do not know what he will do. So tell me, and be quick about it, but softly."

Erik lowered his voice, but the strain remained. "Miss Jacobs isn't there! She never let anyone know she wasn't coming, but she didn't come, and today is the examination in mathematics, and I'm ready, but the principal is taking the class, and she doesn't know where the test paper is, so the class isn't doing anything, so I left—"

"Erik! You ran away from school?" She didn't shout it, but she wanted to.

"I did *not* run away! Listen to me! I went to find Miss Jacobs, because nobody else was doing anything and I wanted to take the examination before I forgot everything, but she isn't at her rooming house and she wasn't there last night and nobody knows where she is and I think something bad has happened to her!" He stopped, out of breath, and despite his best efforts to repress them, two fat tears rolled down his cheek. His lip quivered.

Erik was sure he was too old to cry, so Hilda ignored his tears and tried to think what to do. Whatever it was, it had to be done quickly and Erik sent on his way.

But sent where? No one would be at home. Mama, Erik, and the two youngest girls had moved out of Sven's house into a tiny home of their own, but Mama and Elsa were working at Wilson's Shirt Factory, and Birgit was in school.

School, that was where he belonged. At least his sister could keep an eye on him. "Erik, your teacher has probably gone home to her parents," she said in a low, hurried voice. "She is from Elkhart, is she not? Her mother or father must be ill, or there is some other emergency, so that she did not have time to tell the principal. She will send word soon. You must not worry. Go back to school now, and tell the principal why you left. I think she will understand. Do not tell her you came here; she would not like that. And here." She reached in her pocket and pulled out the cinnamon bun. "One bite only I have taken. Eat it on your way back to school." She gave him a little push toward the door.

Erik stayed where he was, rock solid. "I don't want to go back to school. I want you to help me find my teacher."

"Erik, I cannot leave here! You know that!" Her voice was rising. She took a deep breath. "I know you like your teacher, and that is good. But it is not good that you leave school without permission. You will get into trouble if you do not go back *now*. And so will I have trouble if you do not leave here. Mr. Williams does not allow me to have visitors except in my time off."

"I'm not a visitor! I'm your brother, and I want you to find my teacher."

Hilda rolled her eyes. Erik had inherited just as much Swedish stubbornness as she had herself, perhaps even more. "And how do you think I could find your teacher?"

"You're good at finding out things. You solved all those crimes, when the police didn't do anything. You're smart."

Hilda was not swayed. "It is different now. Mr. Williams watches me all the time. And it is not a crime that your teacher is missing."

Erik opened his mouth. Hilda forestalled him. "Look, little one, it is Wednesday, my half day. So this afternoon when you are at the firehouse, after school, I will come to see you and we can talk. Now go!"

Erik glowered at her, but he went, finally. Hilda breathed a sigh of relief and trudged off, still hungry, to clean the servants' room.

That most knowing of persons—gossip.

—Seneca, 8 B.C.–A.D 65

2

ER RELIEF WAS PREMATURE. As she rounded the corner, she saw Mr. Williams standing in the doorway of his pantry. His face reminded Hilda of a prune. An angry prune.

"And dare I ask, Miss Johansson, to whom you were speaking just now? Or do you consider yourself too valuable an employee to be expected to follow the rules of this household?"

She held fast to her temper. When the butler called her *Miss Johansson* he was dangerously angry. "It was my little brother, sir. He—he came on an urgent errand. I sent him away as soon as I could. Now I must go and clean—"

"You will stay here and answer my questions. Why was your brother not in school? Or is he as ready to flout rules as you appear to be?"

Hilda clenched her jaw. "The matter was urgent, sir. He has gone back to school." She knew Mr. Williams would be even more incensed by the details of Erik's tale.

"I'm not at all satisfied, Hilda. You have not explained why he came here. What are you hiding from me? Is it that your caller was not your brother at all?"

If Mrs. George hadn't come into the servants' quarters just then, Hilda might have said a great many regrettable things.

"Oh, good morning, Hilda, Williams."

"Good morning, madam. Is there something you wish?" His manner was stiff. Not only did he hate being interrupted when he was dressing down a subordinate, but he did not approve of the mistress of the house venturing into the backstairs regions.

"No, no, I'm just going to show Mrs. Sullivan how to make a new soup I want to serve for dinner on Saturday."

"Very good, madam." His manner continued to show just what he thought of the idea. Mrs. Sullivan did not appreciate being shown anything, especially not by a member of the family, all of whom were supposed to have the sense to stay out of the kitchen.

Hilda, however, was profoundly grateful. Mr. Williams would have to accompany Mrs. George, in an attempt to keep the peace, and she, Hilda, could escape.

She went about her work the rest of the morning with great care to avoid the butler. Fortunately, he had extra work to do in preparation for Saturday's dinner party, a large affair for Colonel George's professional and political associates. Mrs. George wanted the big silver punchbowl polished, along with the punch cups, all six dozen of them, and Mr. Williams would trust no one else to do the work—not that anyone else wanted to.

Thus it was that, when the front doorbell rang at about ten-thirty, Hilda was sent to answer it. She knew the caller, an elderly attorney named Barrett who was a close associate of Colonel George. "Good morning, sir," she said with a curtsey.

"Good morning, Hilda." He handed her his coat and hat. "Is the colonel in?"

"Yes, sir." With most visitors she would have used the standard formula about not being sure, but Mr. Barrett was always admitted.

"Good. Would you tell him, please, that I apologize for calling without notice, but I would be very glad to see him for a few minutes, if I'm not interrupting."

"Of course, sir. Will you come and sit down?" She led him to the small reception room off the big hall. She walked slowly, because Mr. Barrett had a game leg. His limp was pronounced today, probably because of the cold. Hilda took a moment to stir up the fire. Mr. Barrett was shivering. "Excuse me, sir, but you look cold. Sit here by the fire and warm yourself. And would you like a cup of coffee, or tea? You look cold," she repeated.

In fact, he looked terrible. His hands shook, and his face looked as though he hadn't slept for days.

"Thank you, my dear, that's very kind of you, but I'll be fine. I am a little cold, but that's a splendid fire." Stiffly, he folded himself into a chair, crossed his long legs, and nodded a dismissal. Hilda went to find Colonel George. She did hope Mr. Barrett wasn't ill. He was a nice man. She wondered what his urgent business was. Probably something political. This was an election year, after all, although January was very early to begin thinking about such things.

Once she had delivered the guest to Colonel George's office, Hilda's next task was the fireplaces. There were twenty of them, and they were all Hilda's responsibility. Those in the bedrooms had been done earlier, of course, but the reception rooms, the dining rooms, Colonel George's office, all these had to be cleaned and new fires laid in the morning, when there were few callers and the servants would not be seen about their duties. It made, in Hilda's opinion, a lot of needless work. The big coal furnace in the cellar kept the house warm enough, at least for someone raised on a Swedish farm. And the fires in the rooms created soot that had to be dusted away, every single day, from tables and carpets and windowsills and ornaments and draperies and lamps.

Hilda didn't actually do all the work, of course. There weren't enough hours in the morning. She supervised Janecska and the other daily maids, with Anton, the footman, carrying the heavy coal bucket from room to room.

This morning the dailies seemed even slower than usual. Having looked over the drawing room and grudgingly approved what had been done, Hilda whisked into the library, to find Janecska and the two other maids huddled in a corner, whispering.

"And why are you not doing your work?" Hilda demanded.

"Haven't you heard the news?" asked Sarah, the oldest and sauciest of the three. "I'd've thought you'd know all about it, being so much smarter than the rest of us."

Hilda tapped her foot. "I do not know what you are talking about, and I do not care. The ashes will not clean themselves out of that fireplace."

"Don't you even care that a girl about your age is missing, maybe dead? Or no, beg pardon, a little younger than you, I guess. Miss Jacobs is only twenty-two."

Hilda was quite sensitive about her age, and Sarah knew it. Twenty-three was getting well up into old-maid status, and marriage seemed a remote possibility unless several miracles occurred. Today, however, she didn't respond to the insult. "Miss Jacobs! What do you know about Miss Jacobs?"

"Only what everyone's saying. She's a teacher at Colfax School, and—"

"Of course I know that!" said Hilda, interrupting. "She teaches my brother Erik."

"Ooh! Then what do you know about her?"

"I know only that she is a very good teacher, and she did not come to school this morning. I think her parents needed her help. They live in Elkhart. Now you must—"

"People are saying she was in trouble," whispered Anna, at sixteen the youngest of the maids. "They say maybe she went home to—to have a baby."

"Or not to have it," said Sarah in a meaningful voice.

"That is enough!" Hilda stamped her foot. "Miss Jacobs is a respectable girl, and this is a respectable house, and Mr. Williams does not allow that kind of talk. If you do not have that grate cleaned and a new fire laid in five minutes, I will ask him to come up and talk to you, and he will not be happy about it."

The threat silenced them momentarily, but as Hilda turned her back to dust the windowsills, she heard Janecska whisper to Sarah, "The boy who brought the groceries said she had a big fight with her gentleman friend yesterday. And he thinks the man is somebody important."

After that Hilda stood over them until the job was done, and gossip was curtailed.

❧

After lunch Hilda climbed the fifty-odd steps from the kitchen level to her third-floor bedroom to change her clothes. She was going out, and she wanted to look pretty.

Her drab uniform dress was exchanged for a smart dark blue woolen skirt and her new white waist with the plaid taffeta ribbon trim. She arranged her blond braids in a careful coronet and topped them with a fearful and wonderful hat that her sister, Birgit, had concocted at the millinery shop where she worked after school. Hilda would never have been able to afford such a confection of feather and ribbon, but Birgit had made it of scraps and it was really very beautiful. At least Hilda thought so.

It was a pity she had to cover up her finery with her old black cloak, but it was the only warm one she had, and the day was still bitter cold. The weather had been bad for nearly a month. Just after Christmas an iron frost had gripped South Bend, to the despair of farmers whose livestock were in danger of freezing to death. "At least it's too cold to snow," said the weather-wise, but they were wrong. It had snowed, and snowed again, and thawed a little, and snowed still more, so that now the streets were uneven with packed snow and ice, rutted by carriage wheels and pockmarked by the hooves of horses. The sidewalks were just as bad, making one's footing uncertain at best.

Hilda walked down all the steps again, but before she left by the back door, she found her storm rubbers in the boot box and put them on, sighing a little. Decidedly it was not easy to look smart when going out in South Bend, Indiana, in the winter. Her scarf and gloves, pulled out of a cloak pocket, were of thick wool, knitted by her mother. They were not beautiful, but they were warm.

Hilda was not fond of these garments, but she was a Swede. Swedes learn early to be practical about winter dress.

She wasn't meeting Patrick Cavanaugh today, which was unusual. A veteran fireman, he could usually choose the shifts he wanted to work, and he always tried to be free on Hilda's afternoon off. This week, though, several men were ill with the respiratory ailments brought on by fighting fires in desperately cold weather, so the healthy members of the fire brigade were working double shifts.

Hilda had decided to do a little shopping of the kind she could certainly not do with Patrick at her side. She needed a new corset and had decided also to indulge herself with a ready-made petticoat. She hated fine sewing, or any kind of sewing for that matter, and she wanted a pretty petticoat with several flounces to give her skirts the proper shape (and show a little when she walked). Even the cheapest kind would cost over a dollar, and she felt guilty about spending so much on herself, but Mama and the younger children didn't need her help so much nowadays, and she had the money.

Her shopping took some time. Ellsworth's Department Store had everything she wanted, but fitting a corset was a fussy business, which Hilda's impatience didn't make any easier. Once that purchase was made, she looked at nearly every petticoat in the store before choosing one that suited her. Her next purchase was some fine white wool to knit into a warm corset cover. She wouldn't do the knitting, of course. Mama was a very good knitter who thought it her plain duty to keep all her children in warm garments. Hilda decided to buy a lace-trimmed handkerchief as a present for Mama. She would think it a wicked extravagance, but Hilda knew she would treasure it even though the lace was machine-made.

Finally, her shopping completed and her parcels ready to be sent home, she stopped at the candy counter and bought a penny's worth of sourballs for Erik. Then she made her way—cautiously on the slippery sidewalk—to the central firehouse, where Erik should now be working at his job as stable boy. With any luck Patrick would be there, too, and they might be able to talk a little.

The newsboys were on the streets crying the early editions of the South Bend *Tribune* and the South Bend *Times*. Hilda had just two cents left in her purse, the cost of the newspaper. Mr. Williams forbade Hilda to read the newspaper, and though she did so anyway, at Tippecanoe Place she had to be stealthy about it. It was often the next day or even two days later before she could pull one out of the trash and sneak it up to her room. By that time the news was new no longer. She was torn now. Should she spend the very last of her money on something she could read soon anyway?

Thrift was her watchword, always. It had to be. Even though she had few expenses, living at her place of employment, she tried to save every penny she could. But she wanted to learn all she could, as well. There had to be, someday, a way out of servanthood.

She heard the newsboys more clearly as she turned a corner. "Miss Jacobs found!" one of them was shouting. "Sensational development in Jacobs disappearance!"

Hilda hurried over, gave the boy two cents, and took a copy of the *Times*.

MURDER OF POPULAR TEACHER read the headline of the biggest story on the front page. Then in smaller type, *Body of Miss Sophie Jacobs Discovered in Shed.*

BY HAND OF A FIEND

—South Bend *Tribune*
January 22, 1904

3

ROOTED TO THE SPOT, heedless of the cold or the annoyed pedestrians swirling around her, Hilda read the account.

The body of a young woman had been found very early that morning in a cab shed not far from her rooming house. A cabman had come to hitch up his horses for the first business of the day and had found the body lying in a pool of blood. The face was so badly disfigured that the police had been unable for some time to identify the body as that of the popular young teacher. She had been dead for many hours, probably since shortly after supper the night before.

It seemed that Mrs. Schmidt, Miss Jacobs's landlady, did not provide board for her roomers, so the young teacher had taken her meals down the street at Mrs. Gibbs's. After supper, Miss Jacobs started off for her home only two blocks away, accompanied for part of her walk by Mr. Robert Barrett, a local attorney.

Hilda gasped. Mr. Barrett! Had he come to tell Colonel George something about the murder? Maybe that was why he looked so ill and distraught. Surely he couldn't... Hilda wouldn't let herself finish the thought. Respectable men like Mr. Barrett didn't kill young women.

The paper went on to say that Mr. Barrett had bidden Miss Jacobs good night and turned off toward his own home when she was but a half block from her door. She had gone only a few steps more when, at the entrance to an alley, she had been accosted, dragged into the alley, and beaten so severely that her skull was fractured in three places. Her clothing had been torn, and there was—Hilda shuddered—a large, bloody handprint on the bodice of her dress.

According to the evidence in the snow, she had not died in the alley, but had been dragged, still living and still struggling, to the cab shed at the far end. There she had lain, bleeding profusely, while the final death blows had been struck.

There was more to the story, much more, but Hilda was too sickened to continue. There was only one thought in her mind now. She must reach Erik before he heard of this. He would need her now.

She nearly ran to the firehouse, but when she half stumbled, half slid into the stable, she saw she was too late. Erik was sitting on a bucket, scanning a copy of the *Tribune*. A tear trickled slowly down one cheek. When he saw Hilda, he swiped his sleeve across his face and jumped up, knocking over the bucket.

"I told you! I said she was hurt and you didn't believe me! You wouldn't do anything, and *now* look!"

There was no answer to that, not just yet. Things would have to be said, but for now she simply enfolded her baby brother in her arms, murmuring words of comfort in Swedish.

He was in fact no longer a baby, and this was not the peaceful farm they had known years ago, when his worst hurts were scrapes and bruises that could be easily soothed with kisses and soft words. He clung to her for a moment, accepting the solace of her love and presence, but he wasn't ready to let his grief overcome his anger. He pushed her away.

"Hush," she said, as he opened his mouth to rail at her again. "This is very bad, yes, it is terrible, but now it is time to try to be sensible. You have read the story?"

"Not all of it. You know I'm not so good at reading English yet!" His voice rose to a shout.

"Hush," she said again. "You will frighten the horses."

"Huh! They're never scared of me." He lowered his voice, all the same. His love for the horses was deep.

"Then sit, little one, and let me tell you everything." She gestured toward the bucket. Erik put it upside down on the floor again and sat, though with rebellion implicit in every line of his body.

Hilda stayed on her feet. "That is better. I must tell you, first, that your teacher died long before you knew she was missing. Yesterday evening, the police think. So you see, I could have done nothing even if I had gone with you this morning."

Erik played with a piece of straw and looked at the floor.

"I am sorry, little one. It is a terrible thing."

"I am *not* little," said Erik, still looking at the floor. "I'm thirteen, and I'm almost as big as you."

"Yes. I will have to think of a new way to talk to you." She didn't smile, but her voice was warm.

Erik looked at her, his face set hard. "Don't laugh at me."

"I did not laugh, little—my brother. It is not a time to laugh."

"I liked my teacher." He sniffled and ran his sleeve across his face again. "And she liked me. She was teaching me to read and write English, really good, and she didn't think I was stupid. She was the best teacher in the whole world, and somebody's killed her, and I want you to find out who!" His voice cracked on the last word, and that embarrassment was, finally, too much. He broke down in sobs.

Hilda knelt beside him and held him. In a year, perhaps in a few months, as Erik grew to man's estate, he would no longer allow her embraces. They embarrassed him now, if there was an audience. Here, with only the horses to see, she could still ease his hurt as she had his baby troubles.

When his storm seemed nearly to have blown over, and his stiffening showed that his self-consciousness was taking hold, Hilda walked over to one of the horses and stroked its velvety nose. The horse whinnied softly. It seemed to Hilda that he questioned her about his young friend's distress. She murmured reassurances in Swedish. If they reached Erik's ears as well, they would do no harm.

When she could hear no more sobs, she turned to Erik and fished in her pocket for a clean handkerchief. Erik never remembered about things like handkerchiefs.

He blew his nose and stuffed the handkerchief into his pocket. Hilda reached into her petticoat again and pulled out the bag of sourballs. "Here. I bought these for you."

Erik took them suspiciously. "Candy won't make up for—"

"That is not why I give it to you. No, it is not enough, but it is something, and it will make you feel better. And if you will give me one, I would like to feel better, too."

It is difficult to talk with a lump of hard candy in one's mouth. Hilda pulled up another bucket and the two of them sat in a silence broken by the snufflings and stampings of the horses in the stable and the traffic sounds of a bustling city outside. Someone had a sleigh out; its harness bells jingled merrily. Farther away, probably on Michigan Street, the horn of one of the new electric buggies sounded. The horses stirred uneasily. They knew what that sound meant, and they didn't like those uncanny machines that moved by themselves.

The silence was companionable, but Hilda and Erik grew cold, sitting still. The stable, though heated somewhat by the bodies of the horses, was certainly not warm. Erik was the first to stand. He moved to one of the stalls and began to curry the horse.

"What are you going to do about it?" he asked, a challenge in his voice.

That was the question Hilda had feared. She swallowed hard. "Erik, I cannot do anything. The police—"

"Huh!"

The syllable summed up Erik's opinion of the South Bend police. Hilda felt much the same way, but she couldn't say so now. "They are better now, under Mayor Fogarty. They will do all they can. This kind of crime—" She stopped, suddenly aware that she had said too much. She wanted, if possible, to keep the sordid details from Erik.

He was sharp. "What kind of crime?" he asked instantly. "What do you mean?"

Well, he would hear from others, anyway. Perhaps it was better that it come from her. She would tell him as much as she could. "It was—very violent. I am sorry, Erik. I did not want you to know. Miss Jacobs was badly beaten. Probably some man had too much to drink and—and saw her and tried to make her talk to him. She was pretty, was she not?"

Erik nodded and moved to the next stall. He didn't look at Hilda.

"He must have wanted her to—to walk with him. And when she would not," Hilda continued hurriedly, "he became angry, because he had been drinking, and hit her. Perhaps he was a tramp or some such person. The police are good at solving that kind of crime. That is what I meant."

Erik ignored most of what she had said. "I like tramps," he said. "They're nice to me. They wouldn't do a thing like this."

It was certainly true that some hoboes had once been kind to Erik. "Some of them are good, but not all are like the ones you knew. And when a man has been drinking, he may do anything."

"Patrick drinks," retorted Erik. "He doesn't do bad things."

"Patrick is Irish. He—"

"Sure, and I'm from the good auld sod, and what of it?" said a genial voice in stage Irish.

"Patrick!" Hilda jumped to her feet. "I am glad to see you! Erik and I have been talking about Miss Jacobs. I told him it was probably a drunken man who thought she was pretty and wanted to walk with her." She put the slightest of stresses on the last few words and looked warningly at Patrick. "I am sure that the police will soon find him."

"It's to be hoped they will," said Patrick soberly. "It's a sad day in South Bend when a respectable young woman can't walk a few blocks of a winter's night without being struck down by some scum of a man." He hesitated a moment. "Hilda, I know you don't like me tellin' you what to do, but you'll be careful, won't you? The dark comes early in winter."

"I will, I promise, Patrick. I am almost never out at night. You know how strict Mr. Williams is about the rules."

"I do, and it's glad I am of it at a time like this. No decent woman is safe while a man like that walks the streets."

Hilda shook her head slightly and flicked her eyes toward

Erik. Patrick grimaced and nodded. Erik probably knew exactly what they meant. He was thirteen, after all, and a farm boy was no stranger to the facts of life. But there were things one did not talk about.

"Hilda breaks the rules all the time," said Erik, sticking to his point. "She can get away from that Mr. Williams any time she wants."

"But I cannot, Erik. Not anymore. I told you, he watches me day and night. Now that Norah is gone and the new waitress is bad at her duties, he is in a terrible temper. I dare not disobey him."

"You're out now," Erik pointed out. "And you're seeing Patrick. The old stick-in-the-mud wouldn't like that, and neither would Mama."

"It is my half day. He cannot object. As for Mama, she does not dislike Patrick as much as she did. She knows how much he did for you."

"Oh, she's grateful to him, but you should hear what she says about you maybe marrying him. She'd turn over in her grave, she says."

"She is not *in* her grave," said Hilda impatiently.

"Anyway, I don't know why you don't just marry him and leave that old Williams. You don't like your job anymore. And if you left, you could do what you wanted, and find out who killed my teacher!"

They were back to that. Hilda shook her head wearily. "Erik, I maybe helped the police a few times before, but it is different now. No, my job is not as good now, and I do not always like it, but I cannot leave. I need the money. And I cannot marry Patrick, as you well know, and I cannot become involved in a murder. Mama would really be upset if I did that, and Mr. Williams would discharge me." She sneezed twice, and sniffled. Erik had her handkerchief.

"Here, me girl, you have to get in out of the cold. Erik, Gray Boy's been favoring his right foreleg. Likely he's picked up a stone and all this ice has packed it in under his shoe. You'd best

see to it before he goes lame. And after they're all fed, come in
and have some supper yourself. I'm going to see your sister
home."

"Huh! You're not supposed to leave the firehouse when you're
on duty. You just want to talk to her alone."

"I want to see that she's safe! Do as you're told, me boy, and
less lip from you, now." He gave Hilda his arm and led her from
the stable.

The new firehouse had a visitor's parlor, a rather bare, com-
fortless apartment, but a place where the mothers, wives, and sisters of the firemen might be entertained. Patrick stretched a
point in Hilda's favor that cold afternoon and led her into the
parlor.

"The fire's not much, but it's warmer in here than out there, at
any rate," he said. "I think we need to talk a little before you go.
Sit you down and tell me what Erik knows. This is a bad business, me girl."

"It is," she said gravely. "He has not yet read everything the
paper said, and he may not. The print is small and the words are
big, some of them, and he does not yet read English easily. I do
not want him to know—everything. At least not yet."

"He'll know soon enough," said Patrick. He sighed for the
loss of innocence, but forgot Erik with his next breath. He looked
at Hilda, his face set in an expression foreign to his cheerful nature. "I meant it, Hilda, what I said back there. It's not safe for
you to be out alone, at least not after dark. If there's someone
goin' about preyin' on women, I want you inside out of harm's
way."

"Yes, but Patrick! I am safe enough at Tippecanoe Place, but
what about my mother and my sisters? They do not live where
they work, not any of them. Mama and Elsa, they work at the
shirt factory together and can come home together, but Birgit
and Freya and Gudrun, they all work different places. Birgit, she
is very young yet, and maybe safe, but Freya and Gudrun…and
it gets dark so early, these winter months."

"Erik could see Birgit home."

"Erik is only a child himself! And—and sometimes it is also bad for boys—"

"Erik has good reason to know about boys being preyed upon by some men. He's wary."

"I know. It is a great pity."

"It is that. But Sven—couldn't he see to the other girls?"

"I do not see how. He works late hours at the paint shop. Now that Studebaker's have begun to make automobiles, they need skilled painters even more than before. He cannot leave his work to see his sisters home."

"Then we'll have to do something. Us firemen, I mean. One of us could leave, maybe take several girls home. And the police— they'd have to help, too. Off-duty policemen, maybe."

"Oh, Patrick, it cannot be done! There are many, many young woman working in South Bend. This is a big city! And they do not all live in the same part of town. No, the only way they will be safe is when this man is caught, when he is safe in jail."

Patrick sighed. He knew Hilda was right. "And if it's some tramp, just passin' through, they may never catch him."

Hilda nodded. "But Patrick, it is almost better to think that it might have been a tramp. For if it was someone who knew Miss Jacobs…then it might be almost anyone. Someone we know."

In her mind was the image of Mr. Barrett, standing gray and shaking at the front door of Tippecanoe Place.

4

THEY HURRIED WHEN they left the firehouse. It was no weather for a leisurely stroll. The wind blew them along, cutting through their garments like a knife and causing them to slide and stumble over the rough, icy sidewalks. "Goin' to snow again," shouted Patrick over the wind. Hilda, out of breath, simply nodded.

The sky had been dark with clouds all day, and by the time Patrick delivered Hilda to the back door of Tippecanoe Place night had fallen, though it was barely five o'clock. "I hate to leave you," said Patrick, taking her hand.

"I, too," said Hilda. She would usually have made a sharp retort about both of them needing to tend to business. Tonight she would have liked to cling to Patrick, regardless of propriety or her pride. She looked up at him, her expression so soft that Patrick would have kissed her then and there if the back door had not opened.

"Hilda! It's after nightfall. You know the rules. Come inside at once!"

"She's safe with me, sir," said Patrick, his uncompromising tone at variance with the deference of his words. "I'll come in for a moment, by your leave. We've still a little time, I'm thinkin', before Hilda must go back to work." He gave the butler a determined look and held Hilda's arm close at his side.

Mr. Williams conceded with bad grace. "Come in, then, if you must. For five minutes. And mind you behave yourselves, the both of you." He stomped away muttering under his breath about what the world was coming to. Patrick grinned and followed Hilda into the servants' room, where a fire blazed in the grate.

Mrs. Sullivan, who also had Wednesday afternoons off and always served a cold buffet supper on that evening, was snoring in her rocking chair, the kitchen cat asleep on her lap. Mr. Williams's bulldog, Rex, slumbered near the fire, his paws working as he chased something in his dreams. Elsie, the scullery maid, was mending one of her aprons while Anton sat at the table working on the ship model he was building out of toothpicks and other oddments. He raised his head and nodded in greeting, then bent back to his absorbing task. Maggie, the new waitress, wasn't in the room.

"It doesn't look as if anything bad could ever happen," Hilda murmured to Patrick. "It looks safe."

"It's safe enough," said Patrick. "So's a cage."

Hilda sighed. "Yes. It is a cage, but it is comfortable."

"Hilda, I've somethin' to tell you," Patrick said in a low, urgent voice, leading her to the corner of the room. No one was paying any attention to them. "I didn't want to talk about it in front of Erik, and it was too blowy and wild on the way home. I might be gettin' a new job."

"Patrick! What?"

"Me Uncle Dan's offered me a place in his dry goods business. You know Sean died last year."

Hilda nodded. Daniel Malloy's older son, Sean, had succumbed to tuberculosis the previous winter.

"Cousin Mary lives in Chicago with her husband, and there's no hope me uncle can bring Clancy in. That boyo's left town and not likely to come back. So Uncle Dan's been thinkin' about it, he says, and I look a likely lad and willin' to work and—well, he's offered to make me a partner."

This was stunning news. "A partner! You mean—but you would have to buy your share of the business, yes? And where would you find the money?"

"He's givin' it to me, Hilda. Or—to us."

Hilda found herself without breath to speak.

"He says you and me together, we saved his life," Patrick went on. "And Aunt Molly says the same. You know they've been treatin' me pretty much like a son ever since that time he got kidnapped and you found him, and all, and..."

Patrick ran down. There was a great deal more he wanted to say, but not in front of other people, no matter how sleepy or preoccupied they might be.

As for Hilda, her mind was in too much of a whirl to know what to say. If this miracle was really true, the financial barrier to their marriage was gone. But there were still the prejudice of both families to be overcome, and the religious differences.

"Patrick, I can't—I don't—I must—"

The clock on the mantel gave a preliminary click, cleared its throat, and struck the half hour.

"Patrick, you must go! You've been away an hour, nearly. Mr. Williams will be angry, and the fire chief, also."

"We have to talk about this." His eyes, serious and determined, looked into hers.

"Yes. But not until I have had a little time. It is—Patrick, it is wonderful news, I t'ink, but it is too much. I must—" She waved her hands in the air, frustrated by her inability to express her complex feelings.

Patrick understood. It was only in moments of high stress that Hilda lost control of her accent. He dared not kiss her when Mr. Williams might walk in at any time, but he took her hand and gave it a hard squeeze before striding out of the room.

Hilda was never able, later, to remember anything she did for the rest of that evening. Presumably she went about her usual evening duties, checking the fires to make sure they had enough coal, tidying rooms, turning down beds. Probably she ate some supper, for Mrs. Sullivan would have been highly indignant if she had not.

Her mind was not at Tippecanoe Place at all. It wandered from the firehouse to the parks, Howard Park where she went with Patrick in the summer to picnic on the grass, Leeper Park where he sometimes rented a boat and took her on the river. They skated there in winter, too, on the duck pond. Then afterwards there were the long walks home, the talks, the arguments—for they were both stubborn and opinionated.

Would they argue when they were married? *Married.* Hilda could picture herself in wedding finery, perhaps a white gown, or perhaps traditional Swedish wedding garb, going into the church on the arm of her brother Sven...but there the image faded. What church? Her Lutheran church, or Patrick's Catholic one? She couldn't, no, she simply couldn't enter a Catholic church. They were idolaters, praying to saints...but they didn't act like bad people. Norah, and Patrick's aunt and uncle, they were just ordinary, nice people. And Patrick...her dreams grew rosy again. A house of their own, a neat little new house that she could keep clean with almost no effort. Children, pretty little girls with her blond hair and boys looking like Patrick —only without his dashing mustache, of course—and family meals...and her thoughts darkened. Would her family ever accept him? Would his family ever accept her?

Erik liked Patrick and didn't care about his religion. And Sven was coming around...but Mama was another story...and Patrick's mother...

She found herself, at the end of the day, in bed without remembering that she had climbed the stairs. She wanted, with a longing that was almost hunger, to talk everything over with Norah. In the old days they would have sat on the bed in Hilda's room and talked and giggled and made plans.

The grandfather clock in the great hall below had struck three before Hilda finally fell asleep.

~

She was awakened by a pounding on her door and Maggie's harsh voice. "It's past six. If you're sick you'd better say so. If you're gettin' up, you're half an hour late, and Old Sourpuss'll have your hide."

Hilda pushed aside the blankets, washed her face in the icy

water in her basin, and dressed as fast as she could. The room
was so cold she could see her breath. Anton had only just fired up
the furnace, and it took a long time for the heat to reach the top
story.

Shivering, yawning, and out of sorts, she hastened down the
long winding flights of stairs to begin her day's work.

Her first duty, before her breakfast, was to wash away the
ever-present soot in the reception rooms on the first floor: the
great hall, the morning room, the drawing room, and the rest.
Winter and summer, it was the same. Hilda could never decide
which was the worst culprit: the coal-burning furnace that
warmed the house, or the coal-burning power plants for the city's
many factories, or the coal fires in the fireplaces. The drawing
room, with its ivory paint and light-colored wallpaper, was the
biggest job. Every sooty speck showed. Hilda was usually particular about that room. She was proud of it, as she was proud of the
whole mansion.

This morning it got short shrift. Her mind dwelt on other
things, and most of them were not pleasant.

It wasn't fair of Patrick to drop such a bombshell and then just
leave, she thought as she beat a cushion furiously and returned it
to its place on a window seat. If there wasn't time to talk about it
properly, he should have kept his peace. How was a girl supposed
to get her work done when her mind was in such turmoil?

Of course it was all impossible. They both knew perfectly well
that they couldn't marry. Her thoughts started down the same
old dreary path: She would have to give up her job. But she didn't
like her job anymore. And if Patrick was making good money,
she might not need to work.

"Hah!" she said aloud. "An Irish immigrant never makes that
much money."

Some of them did, though. Daniel Malloy, Patrick's uncle, was
rich, and he'd been just as poor as anyone when he came to
America. Then there were the politicians she'd heard of in New
York, the organization called Tammany Hall. She'd read both

good and bad things about them in the newspapers (depending on which paper she was reading, the Republican *Tribune* or the Democratic *Times)*, but all agreed that they were rich.

What would it be like to be rich? She paused, duster in hand, and stared out the window. There was nothing to see. Dawn wouldn't come for at least another hour. But her mind's eye saw a house the size of Uncle Dan's, lush with handsome furnishings. She had never even imagined being mistress of such a house, as she had never imagined being mistress of Tippecanoe Place. Such grandeur was not for poor immigrants. How would it feel, sleeping as late as she wanted in the morning, having nothing to do but give orders to servants...?

"Hah!" she said again, blinking the vision away. She'd had enough of ordering servants about right here at Tippecanoe Place. It wasn't as easy as people thought. The under-housemaids almost never did exactly what she wanted. They arrived late and pleaded, on one pretext or another, to leave early. They broke things and skimped on the work. Hilda spent as much time checking their work and scolding them as she did on her own assigned tasks. In her own home she wanted none of that bother. Easier to do most things oneself, perhaps with a married couple to come in by day for gardening and laundry and the heaviest labor.

Her own home. Was it possible that she would ever have one? But Mama and Mrs. Cavanaugh—if they agreed on nothing else, they agreed that a marriage between Hilda and Patrick was *a bad thing*. And Hilda's mind was back on the same path again, endlessly treading the weary arguments she'd had with herself scores of times.

At breakfast she ate silently, too distracted to take part in the gossip of the other servants. But when she and Janecska had gone upstairs to do the family's bedrooms, the daily was eager to talk.

"Have you heard, Hilda?" she asked, as they made the big bed in the master bedroom.

"Heard what? The blanket, it must go down on your side. About an inch."

"About Miss Jacobs. They say she—"

"Not so far. And smooth it properly. And the pillow on your side must be plumped."

"Hilda, are you listening to me? Miss Jacobs met a man last night."

Hilda's attention was finally caught. "She could not have met a man last night. She was dead."

"I mean the night before last, the night she died. She left her boarding house—you know she boarded with Mrs. Gibbs."

"Yes. And roomed with Mrs. Schmidt."

Janecska nodded, the pillow in her arms. "Just down the street. Well, anyway, on her way home after supper, she met Mr. Barrett."

"Oh. I know that. It was in the paper."

"Colonel George knows him, doesn't he?"

"Yes, they know each other. Mr. Barrett visits here."

"He's an important man, isn't he?"

Hilda didn't like the way this conversation was going. "I suppose so. Most of the men who know Colonel George are important. Are you going to stand there all day hugging that pillow?"

Janecska beat it into shape and put it back on the bed. "Anyway, what I was going to tell you isn't about Mr. Barrett. He walked with her only a little way. He's lame, you know, so he walks slowly, and she caught up with him. They talked, only a few words, and then he went into his house and she went on. And what do you think happened then?"

"I will never know, if you do not hurry with your story!"

"Well, I thought you'd want to know, because of Erik and all, but if you don't care—"

"Janecska, we have work to do. Please tell me, but quickly."

Deprived of her dramatic moment, Janecska continued sullenly. "Well, she met another man, that's what."

Hilda shook her head impatiently. "Of course she met another man! The man who killed her. Everyone knows that!"

"Well, then, I suppose you know what he looks like!" Janecska tossed her head and went into the next room.

The temptation was too much for Hilda. She followed. "No, I do not know what he looks like. Have the police found that out already?"

"Someone saw him! A neighbor was looking out her window and saw a tall man wearing a long overcoat. And he had a light brown mustache. So there!"

*There was blood on the cab wheels,
the floor, the walls.*

—South Bend *Tribune*

January 23, 1904

5

H ILDA SPENT A MOMENT searching her memory for a tall man with a light brown mustache before common sense reasserted itself. "And how could she see all that? Miss Jacobs was going home after her supper. It must have been dark outside." She gestured to the bed and turned her attention to the dressing table.

Janecska frowned and ran her duster over the carved headboard. "I don't know…but she did. My cousin knows a woman who knows her, the woman who saw the man, I mean, and he said—my cousin, I mean—"

Hilda dismissed it with an impatient toss of her head. "I do not believe she saw anything at all. That alley, it runs from Colfax to Water Street, about halfway between Scott Street and LaPorte Avenue. There is no streetlight nearby. It is a very dark place to walk at night. If anyone saw anything, it might have been just the shape of a man, but not a mustache!"

"Well, that's what she *said* she saw!" Janecska was growing cross. Her sensation wasn't getting at all the reception she had hoped. She put the duster down and began to tug recklessly at the lace-edged sheets.

"Who is this woman who saw these things, or says she did?"

"I told you. A neighbor. She was looking out her window—"

"What window? Where? How near was she? And when did this happen?"

"How do you expect me to know all that! All I know is, that's what she saw, and if you don't believe it—well, you don't have to!"

"Janecska, do you not see that it matters where she was, this woman? If she was upstairs, looking out a second-story window, she would be looking down at the man. So how could she tell if he was tall? And it matters whether the streetlight was in the direction she was looking, or to her back—"

"So you *are* gonna find out who the killer is? They all said you was gonna try."

"I—who said?" Hilda stood with a silver-backed hairbrush in one hand and the polishing cloth in the other.

"Them, downstairs. Sarah and Anna and that Anton." Janecska tossed her head. She had an eye for Anton but wouldn't admit it, because he was German and she was Polish. "Anton says you're famous. He says you solve all the murders around here. Just like you found out who was killing those young boys last year."

Hilda recovered and began to polish the brush to within an inch of its life. "They are all wrong. I have no reason to try to find Miss Jacobs's killer. What are the police for? Janecska, you have not dusted in the cracks. Pay attention to your work!"

She could squelch the young maid, but she couldn't silence the conversation later on at the servants' luncheon table. Mr. Williams, afflicted with a bad cold, had left the table early, so tongues wagged freely.

Maggie had heard the same story Janecska had, but in more detail. "A Mrs. Bruggner," she said. "She lives just two doors east of the alley, at Mrs. Carpenter's. She has the second floor, but she was visiting with Mrs. Carpenter in the first-floor parlor after supper. The parlor has a bay window on the street. When they heard the scream—"

"Scream!" said Elsie, dropping her soupspoon into the fish chowder.

"There, now, look what you've gone and done," said Mrs. Sullivan. "Anyone would think you'd been brought up in a stable. You clean up that mess, girl. Not with your napkin! Go and get a cloth from the kitchen, and see you soak the tablecloth after we've finished eating."

"What scream?" asked Anton, keeping to the point.

"They heard a scream, the two women," said Maggie, "and looked out the window to see what it might be. And they saw a man stopped just at the end of the alley. He was tall and wore a long overcoat, and had a mustache."

Hilda had the same objections she'd had before. "How could they see all that? The streetlight is far away."

"But there was a full moon that night, remember? And there was fresh snow, and you know how that makes the night brighter. What with all that and the streetlight, they could see plain as plain, they said."

"I told you," murmured Janecska, but so quietly that Hilda wasn't quite sure she'd heard.

Hilda knew she shouldn't pursue the subject. She didn't want to add more fuel to the fire of speculation about her course of action. But her curiosity got the better of her. "Did they see Miss Jacobs, too?" It was the sort of question anyone might ask, after all.

"No. At least not that I heard," said Maggie. "They reckon she was already in the alley, running away from him."

"Oh, he was running? Then how could the women see him so plainly?"

"No, he was just standing there, I guess." Maggie scowled. "How do I know? I wasn't there! If you're so nosy, why don't you ask some of those police friends of yours? I thought you said you weren't going to get mixed up in it."

"I am not. I am worried, that is all. I have four sisters who must walk to work every morning and back home every night, and this time of year it is dark for both trips. Of course I want the police to find the man who did this, and in a hurry, so that women like us can be safe again! If you are not interested, why do you talk about it so much?"

She glared at Maggie. Mrs. Sullivan sighed and pushed her chair back from the table. "I'm sure I don't know why you two girls can't learn to get along. Help me clear, and then you can have your rests, but don't let me catch you taking advantage just because Mr. Williams isn't feeling well."

The gossip and rumor about the murder had kept Hilda from dwelling on her own problems most of the morning, but the moment she was alone in her room, they flooded back. After almost no sleep, she was tired and irritable, but she knew she was too edgy to rest. She looked longingly at her bed and then, with sudden resolution, flung her cloak over her uniform, pulled on her oldest hat, and ran back downstairs.

"I am going out for a few minutes, Mrs. Sullivan," she called into the kitchen as she passed. "I will be back soon."

"Where're you headed, then?" shouted the cook, but Hilda was gone.

She hadn't bothered with rubbers since her destination was only two blocks away. She was sorry before she was halfway down the back drive. Several inches of new snow had fallen overnight. It worked its way into her shoes and made the footing even more treacherous than the day before. She half slid the last few feet to the sidewalk and had to walk carefully the rest of the way, instead of running as she longed to do.

However, it was just as well. It meant that when she arrived at the Hibberd house she wasn't out of breath. She went around to the kitchen door and knocked decorously.

The door was answered by the butler, who happened to be passing. He knew Hilda. His face set in a frown.

"Please, Mr. Leslie, I am sorry to bother you, but I have a message for Norah. May I see her for a moment?"

"You may not. She is out on an errand for Mrs. Hibberd."

Hilda had prepared for this possibility. "Then would you ask her, please, sir, to stop at Tippecanoe Place on her way home? It is very important, or I would not ask."

The butler opened his mouth, probably to ask what was so all-fired important. Hilda smiled sweetly. "I must go, sir. They will be needing me. Thank you, sir." She turned and moved away as quickly as she could on the icy path. Mr. Leslie, she knew, was far too dignified to shout after her. She knew also that his pompous façade hid an indecisive mind. He would be almost certain that her message was frivolous, but the more he thought about it, the less certain he would become. With any luck, he'd deliver the message and she'd get to see Norah this evening.

She slipped and stumbled her way back to Tippecanoe Place, changed her stockings and dried her shoes as best she could, and went back to work, drooping with fatigue, but buoyed up by the evening's possibilities.

More news and rumors arrived with the afternoon deliveries of groceries and meat. The police had made an arrest. No, they hadn't, but they were looking for a college athlete with whom Miss Jacobs had quarreled. He was a Notre Dame student, a football star. No, he wasn't, he had already graduated. He had graduated from Indiana University, not Notre Dame, and he lived in South Bend. No, Elkhart, where Miss Jacobs had lived with her parents before coming to South Bend. No, a psychic had been consulted, and she said the man in the long, dark overcoat was the one, and he was a prominent South Bend businessman. No, that was wrong, she had said...

Hilda stopped listening. She wasn't interested in rumor. She wanted facts, and she might find a few of those later in the newspapers. Meanwhile she fixed her mind on what she was going to say to Norah, and how they could arrange a meeting to really talk.

Mr. Williams was still feeling poorly and keeping to his room when the papers arrived at the back door. The ground floor of Tippecanoe Place, which housed the dining rooms as well as the backstairs premises, was, rather oddly, a semi-basement. Since the great mansion was built into the side of a hill, the front rooms had large windows and a view, but the back door was at the bottom of a flight of steps leading down from the driveway above. One of Anton's jobs was to keep the steps clear of debris, and in winter, of snow. Today, with Mr. Williams ailing and not on the alert, Anton had "forgotten" the task. The bottom landing was six inches deep in snow, and both the *Times* and the *Tribune* were quite wet.

Hilda, rejoicing, collected the papers and took them to the laundry. It was plainly now her duty to take over Mr. Williams's task of ironing the papers and delivering them to Colonel George's study. It would take longer than usual, since they were so wet, but that hardly mattered. Colonel George barely glanced at the papers, anyway, except for the financial news. She could take her time, and if in the process she happened to read some of the stories, Mr. Williams could hardly blame her for that. She set the irons to heat on the laundry stove and began to read eagerly.

The murder case was the lead story in both papers. The *Tribune* was critical of the police, saying that a murder on a well-traveled street should surely have been solved by now. Hilda paid scant attention. The *Tribune* was always critical of the police. Ever since Mayor Fogarty, a Democrat, had been elected, the *Tribune* had taken the view that the city was going straight to the dogs. The *Times,* of course, laid any shortcomings in city departments to the deplorable state of affairs Mayor Fogarty had inherited from the previous Republican administration. Aside from being offended when the *Tribune* published scurrilous anti-Irish cartoons on the front page, Hilda made it a policy to ignore the political posturings. She tried to winnow out facts from opinion in the stories, and concentrated on what was really important.

The irons were hot. She applied one to the front page of the *Tribune* and continued to read. At least one of the rumors turned out to have some basis in fact, if the paper was to be believed. The police were indeed looking for a man, said to be a college athlete, who had recently called on Miss Jacobs at her rooming house and "made himself objectionable." There was no further information about who the man might be, or where he might be found, or indeed in what way he had offended the young teacher.

Hilda's imagination took flight at that. The man might have done any number of things. He might have brought her an unsuitable gift, perhaps a late Christmas gift, something too expensive or too personal. Of course, if they had been alone in the room (unlikely, but possible), he might have attempted liberties, verbally or even physically. It was a pity the police had been able to

learn no more, but apparently the incident had been reported in a
letter from Miss Jacobs to her mother in Elkhart, and the mother
was too prostrate with grief to be interviewed.

Hilda read on. Miss Jacobs had evidently struggled with her
attacker, for her hair pins were strewn the length of the alley.
One or two boards of the picket fence at the far end of the alley
were torn loose, apparently as Miss Jacobs made a desperate
attempt to prevent her captor from dragging her away. Blood
stained the snow everywhere. The police speculated that the attacker had struck Miss Jacobs a blow on the head that failed to
kill her or even render her unconscious, and that several more
blows were then struck in the cab shed, where blood was found
on cab wheels, floor, and walls. Her underclothing was torn, her
skirt was ripped from its belt, and there was a bloody handprint
on her bodice. It was assumed that assault had been the motive
for the murder.

Much of that was a repeat of yesterday's information, and Hilda stopped reading. Her mind was filled with horrified speculation. The newspaper stopped short of saying that she had been
raped, but then it probably wouldn't. Such words were not used
in a family publication. But torn underclothing?

A curl of smoke rose from under the iron. Hilda hurriedly removed it, pulled away the corner of paper that had been charred,
and went on to the *Times*.

The *Times* was slightly more sensational in its reporting style
than the *Tribune*. Its story listed many of the same details, but
made much of the report of a psychic from Elkhart, who claimed
to have handled some of Miss Jacobs's clothing and thus obtained
a clear vision of what had happened. The woman, who went by
the name of Madame Rosa, claimed that a tall man in a dark
overcoat was the murderer, and that he had a *red* mustache!

The man in the overcoat had not been mentioned yesterday in
either newspaper. Hilda frowned. How, then, could Madame
Rosa—or whatever her name really was—have known about
him in such detail? Hilda put no stock at all in psychics or medi-
ums or séances or any such supernatural claptrap, but how—

Then her brain took over again. The newspapers hadn't printed the prevalent rumors, but the so-called psychic had heard them, just as Hilda had, and hadn't scrupled to use them. Hilda snorted and removed the iron just in time to prevent another scorched page.

There wasn't a great deal more to be learned. Hilda skimmed rapidly, catching a few words here and there as she ironed. She stopped at a small heading: MISS JACOBS WAS AFRAID.

The *Times* reported that two days before she was killed, the young woman had been at home at her rooming house, entertaining a friend. As they sat in the front parlor, a step was heard on the porch outside. "She was frightened," the friend reported. "She turned pale and stood up, very agitated. She said, 'I wonder who can have come to see me.' I thought that was strange, for there was no reason to believe the person outside was calling on Miss Jacobs. She trembled as she went to the front door and opened it, shielding herself behind it as she did so."

The caller, it turned out, was no caller at all, but Mrs. Schmidt, the owner of the house, returning from an errand. Hilda thought about that as she finished ironing the papers and carefully folded them for Colonel George. Why had Miss Jacobs been so fearful that the footstep of her landlady, which should have been familiar, sent her into a nervous fit? What— or who—was she afraid of?

Whatever it was, it had caught her in the end.

The maid has a heart, the natural affections
of a young woman; she likes to be admired,
to think that there is someone who esteems
her above all the world.

    —*The Complete Home*

6

HILDA TOOK THE NEWSPAPERS up to Colonel George's office. He wasn't in, so she laid them on his desk and took a moment to look the room over and make sure it was in order, or as much order as she could produce. Her employer was not a tidy man, so letters and envelopes and scraps of paper were strewn all over the big desk, but Hilda knew she dared not disturb them. The colonel knew where everything was, as unlikely as that might seem, and would roar his displeasure at anyone who moved anything. At least the visible surfaces were free of dust and the few ornaments in the room were spotless. The door to the safe—a walk-in vault, really—was, of course, closed and locked. Hilda didn't know exactly what was kept in there, but she knew that a footman who ventured to peek in, one day when the door had been left open, had been sacked without a reference. "And lucky not to be sent to jail," Mr. Williams had said of the incident, which had happened before Hilda came to work at the house. "You remember, girl, that you are never, under any circumstances, to go near that safe."

Well, she was neither a thief nor a fool, she thought as she left the room. She had no wish to know what was in the safe. Or if she did, she acknowledged in a burst of inner honesty, she would control her curiosity. She couldn't afford to be thrown out on the street…and that brought her thoughts back around to the most important subject. What future lay ahead for her and Patrick?

She got through the rest of the afternoon's drudgery automatically. She performed tasks she could have done in her sleep, and chivvied the under-housemaids to perform theirs, without giving more than a quarter of her mind to the job. When at last five o'clock came, she pulled her cloak over her uniform and slipped out the back door and up the outside steps to wait for Norah.

Hilda saw Norah before Norah saw her, and Hilda's heart sank. This wasn't the Norah of the old days, this woman who trudged up the back drive, her body drooping with weariness. She, Hilda, was tired, too, but not bone-weary. Norah looked ready to drop, and the first thing Hilda said when her friend got close enough was, "Hurry! Come in and sit down. There is a good fire in the servants' room, and I can make you some coffee."

"Can't. Sean'll be gettin' home and expectin' his supper. Anyway, Mr. High-and-Mightiness would never allow it."

"He has taken to his bed. He is sick with something. And Sean can wait, for a change. Norah, you must sit down and get warm, even if you do not have coffee. You look terrible!"

"Always were the soul of tact, weren't you?" But Norah allowed herself to be taken inside, divested of her hat, cloak, and wet shoes, and installed in the most comfortable chair in the room, her feet propped up near the fire.

"If the old tyrant catches me in his chair—" Norah began.

"He will not. He is in bed, I told you. And he has no control over you, not anymore."

Norah sighed and wiggled her warming toes. "He does over you, though. Suppose somebody tells him?"

Hilda tossed her head. "Let them. I might not be here forever, anyway."

"Hilda!" Norah sat up straight and stared at her. "Do you have something to tell me?"

"To ask you. Oh, Norah, I need your advice—yes, Maggie, what is it?"

The waitress stood in the door, hands on hips. "Mrs. Sullivan said as I was to get you to help set the table for dinner tonight, as there's guests and Mr. Williams isn't fit for a thing, and *some* of us is run off our feet."

Hilda looked at the clock on the mantel. "Dinner is at eight, as usual, is it not?"

"Yes, but there's our supper, too—"

"I have finished with my work for the afternoon. Now I speak with my friend. I will help you when it is time."

"Well, of all the—it must be nice to be you, take time off whenever you please, entertain your friends, *and* in Mr. Williams's chair!"

She flounced off, and Norah raised an eyebrow. "Her face'd sour milk, that one. She'll make trouble if she can."

"She makes trouble all the time. She does not like me, nor I her. But Norah, maybe it does not matter. You see, Patrick wants to marry me."

"Tell me somethin' I don't know."

"I mean really. And now, or soon, anyway. He thinks there is a way."

"Ooh! Tell!"

"Patrick's Uncle Dan wants to make him a partner. With Cousin Clancy off to New York, and planning to stay there, Mr. Malloy has no son here to carry on the business when he retires. And he is not a young man, and he has always loved Patrick like a son. So he wants him to leave the fire department and come into the business, so he—Patrick, I mean—can take over one day."

"Glory be to God, you'll be rich!"

"Patrick will be rich. Well, he will be comfortable, at least. But I—nothing is settled about our marrying. I am still Swedish, and he is still Irish, and our families—"

"Now, you look here!" (It was an unnecessary command. Hilda was studying Norah's face earnestly.) "How old are you, anyway?"

Hilda did look down at that. "Twenty-three," she murmured. It was a fearful age to be unmarried.

"And Patrick's twenty-five. So you're both old enough to know your own minds, aren't you?"

"It is not that we do not know what we want to do. We—"

"I'd say it was," Norah retorted. "Do you want to please your families? Do you want to live here in the fanciest house in town?

Or do you want to grow up and marry the man you love and start a family?"

"Of course I want to marry Patrick!"

"Then it's time you stopped shilly-shallyin' and did it! I could see before why you didn't, with both of you so poor an' all, and you losin' your job if you couldn't live here. But if he's goin' to be a partner, you wouldn't need to work. You could hire servants of your own!"

"No, I have already decided I would not want to do that. I thought— "

"Hilda Johansson, you're already makin' plans! You're goin' to do it, you know you are! Ooh, I'm so excited!"

Norah jumped up out of her chair and gave Hilda a hug. But Hilda was not yet ready to stop talking about the matter. "Yes, yes," she said, extracting herself from Norah's embrace. "It is exciting to think about. But Norah, I am not sure I would even like marriage. It is true that I—am fond of Patrick. We are happy when we are together, even when we argue— "

"Which you do every time you say more'n two words to each other," Norah put in.

Hilda ignored her. "And I—well, I like it when he kisses me and—but look at you," she said, hurriedly changing the subject. "You are so tired, and you must hurry home now to cook Sean's dinner, not to rest. And we never see each other, you and I, and that is not good, not to have time for a friend. I do not think marriage is all fun and kisses."

"I'm tired because I have to work all day, an' then go home and work some more. At least until we save a little more money," said Norah. "And workin' in other houses isn't like workin' here. The work was different here, easier than housemaidin', and there were lots of people to help, and there was you to talk to. I miss that, too, Hilda. But it won't be this way forever. Sean's makin' good money now, and so am I. Soon we'll have enough to buy a little house, and then maybe…" Her eyes became dreamy and a becoming blush touched her cheeks.

"Yes," said Hilda gently. She didn't want to hurt Norah, to

destroy her dreams. But she had to talk this out. "Yes. It will be very nice when the babies come. If there are not too many of them, and if they do not come before you can afford to look after them. But Norah, babies have a way of coming when they will. What if you—well, what if one decides to come before you can afford to stop working? And then there are more, and more?"

She didn't have to spell it out. She and Norah both knew women, many women, who had grown old before their time bearing child after child, who had known the pain of losing infants to disease, who had drifted from the self-respecting working class into abject poverty because there were too many mouths to feed. Then there were the women who died in childbirth, or the ones who died simply because their bodies had been weakened by pregnancy after pregnancy. Most of these women were immigrants, or of immigrant backgrounds, so Norah and Hilda could both feel as sisters to them.

It was a bleak picture, but Hilda was a hard-headed Swede who liked to look facts in the face.

Norah sighed. "Yes, it can happen as you say, but..." She lowered her voice. "There are ways...you don't *have* to have babies you don't want, or can't afford."

"But..." It was Hilda's turn to blush.

"I can't—you don't want to know about these things until you're married, but believe me. There are ways."

"I am not a child, Norah! And I do read the newspapers, and sometimes the *Ladies' Home Journal*. I know about...things. I know, too, that the Catholic Church does not approve of...of the ways you speak of. And I am not a Catholic, but Patrick is, and you are."

"What the Holy Father doesn't know won't hurt him," said Norah defiantly.

Hilda was shocked. "But—you must do as your church says!"

Norah stuck out her lower lip. "Hilda, you've got to understand somethin'. I'm a good Catholic, and I wouldn't be anything else, ever. But that doesn't mean I think I have to do every single tiny thing the Church tells me to. Or not do every tiny thing they forbid, neither. I think the good Lord gave me a mind of my own and meant me to use it. And sometimes the Church makes me so mad I could spit. I never told you—we never told nobody—but a few years ago an uncle of mine hung himself, see."

Hilda's eyes grew wide.

"It was when times was so bad and he couldn't find work. And his family was gettin' poorer and poorer, and he couldn't figure out a way to feed them. And then he got sick, and he thought he was dyin' anyway, so…" She brushed away a tear. "He didn't want the family to have to buy medicine and pay doctor's bills, along with everything else, y'see. He thought he was doin' the best thing, and we all grieved, but we understood. And then the priest wouldn't bury him proper, because suicide's a sin. And that was when I decided the Church wasn't always right. I was that mad at the priest, I never went to Mass at all for a month. And I decided then and there I'd use me own head to decide what was right and what was wrong. And I don't think tryin' not to have babies every year is bad. So there!"

"But—oh, Norah, I understand, and I am sorry about your uncle, but—if the ways you talk about work so well, why do women sometimes have babies when they shouldn't? Even when they are not married?"

"Hilda!"

"It happens. You know that it does."

"Yes, well, when people are stupid—" Norah's face changed. "Jesus, Mary, and Joseph! Hilda, you're not tryin' to tell me—"

"I am not!" Hilda was highly indignant. "I am a respectable woman, and Patrick would never ask me to do something I ought not!"

"Patrick's an Irishman," said Norah with a small grin. "You might be surprised."

"I can manage Patrick," said Hilda shortly. She didn't like the turn the conversation had taken. "But what about his family? And mine?"

"Look, Hilda," said Norah, serious again. "I'm part of Patrick's family. Shirttail cousins, true, but still part of the family, and you're my best friend. Patrick's Uncle Dan and Aunt Molly think the sun rises and sets on you, you know they do. As for your family, your sisters are a little stuffy about us Irish, but Sven is coming around, and your little brother adores Patrick. Your mother—well, that generation's stuck back in the old country."

"It is not so long ago that Mama was *in* the old country," Hilda reminded Norah.

"That's what I mean. This is America. It's different here."

"We would have to be married by a priest, in a Catholic church. My family would not even come!"

"Yes, well, you didn't come to my weddin', did you, but you came to the party afterward, and we had a fine time."

You had a fine time, Hilda thought but did not say. "It's not the same thing. Mama would never forgive me if she could not see me married."

"Well, let her come, then!" Norah was growing impatient. "There's no law against it. It's only your own ideas keep you out of Catholic churches. Or else get married all over again in your church. Or have a judge marry you, if it's goin' to fret you so much."

"But—a Catholic cannot be married by a judge! Can he?"

Norah rolled her eyes. Hilda sighed and shook her head, and would have said more if Mrs. Sullivan hadn't sailed into the room in a full-blown temper. She was in charge of the household with Mr. Williams abed, and it wasn't a responsibility she relished.

"So there you are, Miss High-an'-Mighty! I've no time to wait for your pleasure, Your Majesty, what with tryin' to do two people's work, and company coming, and the soufflé sauce tryin' to curdle, and that Maggie no more use than a sick headache! You go an' set that table *now,* and then come back and help me in the kitchen. As for you, Norah, I'd think you'd know better than to keep Hilda from her work. And didn't you ought to be home cookin' supper for your man, as'll come home tired and hungry any time now?"

She stood in the doorway tapping her foot, her lower lip jutting out. Hilda sighed and shrugged. Norah got to her feet. "It's very nice to see you again, too, Mrs. Sullivan," she said as she pulled her shoes on. As she left the room, she stuck her tongue out at the cook's back.

Hilda went resentfully to the family dining room. There were only a few guests tonight, so there was no need to use the enormous state dining room, whose table would easily seat fifty. There was no need, either, for Maggie to ask for help with setting a table for a mere twelve people. But as Hilda made the rounds of the table, laying down silver, straightening glasses, and tossing scornful remarks Maggie's way, she wasn't really thinking about her grievances. She was thinking how profoundly unsatisfactory it was to have to talk to Norah in stolen moments. She wanted a private heart-to-heart, the kind they used to have and would never have again.

As long as you work at Tippecanoe Place, whispered a voice in her head.

*The servant girls marry...just as frequently
as their young mistresses.*

—*The Complete Home*

7

H ILDA WAS TOO TIRED to stay awake that night, but she woke up early the next morning and lay in bed for a few minutes, thinking about Patrick and marriage and families. When could she see him and talk things over sensibly?

It wasn't easy. In theory she could leave the house during her rest time, but the weather was far too cold to make an outside rendezvous practical and there was no other really private place they could meet.

Well, she'd just have to see if she couldn't run down to the firehouse for a few minutes this afternoon. There would be no time to talk, but at least she could make sure that they planned something for Sunday afternoon. This was Friday. It was a long time to wait, when she was bursting with things to say and to ask, but it would have to do.

Life doesn't always work out the way we plan. When Hilda finished her early-morning chores and went down for breakfast, she found Mrs. Sullivan in a state of total distraction.

"Mr. Williams can't get up at all this morning," the cook announced when all were seated at the breakfast table. "He's terrible bad. The doctor's been, and he says it's *la grippe,* not just a cold. He's afraid it may turn to pneumonia."

The servants were struck silent. Mr. Williams could be a hard taskmaster, but they had worked for him and lived under the same roof, some of them for a long time. He was never ill. This was a frightful and a frightening thing. He was not a young man. None of them had ever thought much about his age until now.

56 ᕈᕈ

They turned solemn faces to Mrs. Sullivan as she continued.

"You know there's a big dinner party tomorrow night. It's important, because it's something to do with politics. I've never understood politics and I never will, but I hope I know my duty in this household. It's up to us to make sure everything goes like clockwork, the more so since it's the first time we've entertained on a grand scale since Mr. Clem died, rest his soul." She crossed herself, took a deep breath, and continued.

"So it's extra work for everyone. I've tried to think what must be done, because Mr. Williams is too sick to give instructions. I'll have Janecska to nurse him this morning, Hilda. She has a nice way about her when she wants to, and a light step and hand. When Mrs. George is up, I'll ask if we should have a real nurse in. Meanwhile, Hilda, you'll have to see that Janecska's regular work gets done, and you'll have to see, yourself, to the silver Mr. Williams hasn't polished. Oh, there'll be no rest for any of us till this is over!"

Hilda wasn't sure whether the cook meant the dinner party or Mr. Williams's illness, and she didn't like to ask. One possible end to Mr. Williams's illness was too disturbing even to mention.

She was, however, quite clear about the most important matter. She wouldn't get out of the house today, nor tomorrow. So much for talking to Patrick.

But Hilda was due for another surprise that day.

Things went badly from the start. Everyone had extra duties, some of them unfamiliar, so the work went slowly. But worse than that was the feeling of unease about the house. A trained nurse took over from Janecska in midmorning, and came out of Mr. Williams's room from time to time looking grave. Even the family was worried. Mrs. Clem had known Mr. Williams ever since the family had moved into Tippecanoe Place fifteen years before, and she paid a call on him herself, taking him a little vase of hothouse roses from the bouquet in her own room.

Hilda took a moment to glance at the papers when they arrived. Wild speculation about the murder continued, but little new fact. Apparently Miss Jacobs had not actually been raped, after all. The *Tribune* conveyed, in delicate euphemism, the impression that she was a virgin still. Hilda shook her head, sighed, and left the papers to be dealt with later. There was no time for ironing them tonight.

At about five o'clock, Hilda was scurrying from the kitchen to the butler's pantry, carrying a tray full of the best china. (In the emergency conditions Elsie had, with threats of dire consequences if she damaged anything, been allowed to wash the Royal Crown Derby.) A loud knock sounded as Hilda passed the back door. She was so startled she nearly dropped the tray. She glanced at the shadow visible behind the glass in the door, and muttered Swedish imprecations under her breath as she called for Anton to see who was there.

But Anton was apparently out of earshot, so Hilda set the tray down on a table in an alcove and stomped to the door.

Patrick stood outside.

A wave of longing swept over her, so strong that she had to catch hold of the door for support. For an instant, she wanted nothing more than to be safe in Patrick's arms, shut away from turmoil and confusion and hard work forever.

Being Hilda, she refused to give in to her emotions. Anyway, she was being silly. No one could protect her from the world. She didn't need protection. She could look after herself.

Still, it was an effort for her to keep her voice stern. "I cannot come out, Patrick, and I have no time to talk. Family dinner is at seven, and we are in a hurry, all of us, because Mr. Williams—"

"I heard. Word about Tippecanoe Place gets around, you know," said Patrick, stepping inside and firmly closing the door after him. "Some of the men are back today, so I have the evenin' off. I thought the household would be in a rare taking, and you worked off your feet. I came to help."

"You? Help? But you do not know—"

"I know how to fetch and carry, and soothe the feelings of an irate Irish cook, and make people smile. Someone can teach me to hand round food at the table."

"Oh, you would never be allowed to do that! Even though it is just the family tonight. You do not know the rules, and you do not have on the right clothing."

Patrick's eyebrows rose almost into his tousled black hair. "It takes rules, and special clothes, to give folks their food?"

"You know it does, Patrick. There are rules about which side to offer things, and how, and besides that, butlers change their clothes all day long. Sometimes I think it is all they do. Plain trousers and an ordinary coat in the morning, striped trousers and a tail coat in the afternoon, a dress suit in the evening with black trousers."

Patrick grinned. "Then I expect me fireman's uniform won't do. Never mind, me girl, I was teasing you. I'll make meself useful behind the scenes. Now where's that tray you was carryin' when I peeked through the glass?"

"It is here, but Patrick, Mrs. Sullivan will not—"

He picked up the tray. "You let me worry about Mrs. Sullivan. Now, where're all these dishes goin'?"

She allowed him to carry the tray to the butler's pantry, but insisted on putting the china away herself. "Suit yourself," he said with a grin. Whistling, he went back to the kitchen.

Hilda didn't dare hurry with the china, but she ran to the kitchen as soon as she could. Standing just outside the door, she eavesdropped shamelessly.

"...and how did a colleen like yourself get to be such a fine cook, now tell me that? And without eating more of your own cookin' than'd keep a bird alive?"

(Mrs. Sullivan was many years the wrong side of forty, and weighed, Hilda guessed, not much less than two hundred pounds.)

"Ah, get away with ye! Sure, an' it's a fine line o' blarney ye spin, me lad." Her brogue, like Patrick's, had broadened so much that Hilda had some difficulty in following the conversation.

" 'Tis no blarney to say you're the finest cook in South Bend. Even me own blessed mother doesn't make as light a bread, and

her the best baker in all of County Kerry. It's honored I am to be
helpin' ye in yer hour of need. Only tell me what I can do. I'm yer
willin' slave!"

There was a rich chuckle, and Mrs. Sullivan sailed out of the
kitchen, looking positively kittenish. Hilda got away from the
doorway just in time.

"Sure, and it's a fine young man you've got for yourself,
Hilda! Givin' up his time off to help us, I call that downright
neighborly. Now mind the two of you keep your mind on your
work tonight!" But she said it with a coy smile. "You'll be servin',
Hilda, with Anton, so you'd best be goin' up and puttin' on a
clean apron. I'll keep Maggie in the kitchen to help me. When
you come down, you can have yourself a bite to eat before you
start your kitchen work. Patrick, you'll be eatin' with us. There's
plenty."

Hilda was so taken aback by the cook's attitude that she forgot
to grumble about being assigned Maggie's duties.

The evening's work, which Hilda had been dreading, was
made easier by Patrick's genial presence. He did whatever he was
asked to do and made a joke whenever possible. He kept the
backstairs atmosphere so pleasant that all the servants, over-
worked and tired though they were, stayed cheerful, even while
they were cleaning up in the kitchen afterwards.

Hilda, all evening, went about her duties in a sort of daze. She
knew her job, and Maggie's job, too. Never once did she hand the
vegetables on the wrong side of a diner; never once did she drop a
spoon or jostle anyone's elbow, even though she wasn't thinking
about what she was doing. In fact, she wasn't thinking about anything in particular. Her mind didn't seem to want to function.
Too many things had happened too quickly; too many ideas
sought her attention. It was good that she was kept busy with
menial chores. One doesn't have to think when one is concentrat-
ing on being deferential and filling coffee cups properly.

When the dishes were done, when the china and silver had
been put away (by Hilda; she would trust no one else), when the
table linen had been put in the bin for the laundress on Monday

and the crumbs swept up from under the table and the leftover food put away in the pantry or ice-box and the kitchen table and floor and sinks scrubbed and the servants' breakfast table set for the next morning, Anton and Elsie went home.

Mrs. Sullivan looked at Patrick and Hilda. "It's early yet, only just past nine. We've got along wonderful this evenin', thanks to Patrick. But I'm tired, all the same, and I'm goin' up. And just as soon as I've seen how Mr. Williams is feelin', I'm for me bed. And Maggie's comin' up, too, aren't you, Maggie?"

Maggie opened her mouth to argue, but she changed her mind after one look at Mrs. Sullivan's face. "Yes, ma'am. And Hilda, too, I suppose."

"No," Mrs. Sullivan snapped. "Hilda, I know you're tired, too, but somebody has to be ready to go to the door if anyone should come, and answer the telephone, and see to the bells if one of the family rings. I'm sorry, Hilda, but those are your jobs when Mr. Williams is busy. So now you'll have to take over. You can shut up the house and go to bed at eleven, unless the family needs you. And don't forget to turn off all the lamps!"

As if, Hilda thought, she was likely to forget. The house had burned nearly to the ground some years before, when it was only a few months old, and the first thing any servant in the house was taught, and reminded over and over, was to be careful about any kind of fire. The gas lamps and wall sconces and chandeliers were inspected regularly and kept in perfect repair, and were never left burning at night, nor were the servants allowed to take candles to bed. Hilda hated being the last up at night, for it meant climbing the three steep, narrow, twisting flights of the back stairs in pitch darkness.

Mrs. Sullivan pushed Maggie ahead of her and turned back to Hilda. "Don't keep Patrick too long, now. I ought to stay and chaperone you, but you're a sensible girl, Hilda." And with a wink she began to trudge up the steps.

Hilda *was* tired, but the wink brought her awake in an instant. "Why," she whispered to Patrick, "I believe she meant to leave us alone."

"She's a young Irish lass at heart, though you'd never think it to look at her," he whispered back. They listened as the cook's firm tread slowly moved out of earshot, and then Patrick took Hilda's hand.

"Come, girl. There's a fire still in your sittin' room, and we've things to talk about."

He sat down on the shabby old couch and patted the cushion beside him, but Hilda shook her head and turned to one of the wooden chairs around the table. "No, Patrick. Mrs. Sullivan has shown that she trusts us. We must not misbehave ourselves."

Patrick sighed. "Me girl, this is the first time in months I've had you alone anyplace where we wasn't freezin' to death. And you're tellin' me I can't even have you sit next to me?"

Into Hilda's mind swam Norah's comments. "Patrick's Irish. I wouldn't be so sure…"

"It would not stop at that, would it?" said Hilda primly. "No, we must talk, but it must be talk only. And Patrick, I am sorry, but we must not be too long. I am very tired."

"You work too hard." Patrick dropped his flirtatious tone and became serious. "Hilda, I watched you tonight. This was just an ordinary family dinner, but you was run off your feet."

"That was because Mr. Williams was not there. The work is not usually so hard."

"It's hard enough. How many times have we been out together when you was so tired you near fell asleep? How often have I heard you complain about old Williams bein' a tyrant, and a slave-driver, and—"

"No, Patrick! It is not right to talk about him when he is ill, when he is maybe…" She wouldn't say the word, but it hung in the air between them.

"All right, I won't talk about him. I'm sorry he's so bad sick, but I'm not wantin' to talk about him, anyway. I'm talkin' about us. I'm wantin' to take you out of this, give you a house of your own, servants of your own. Haven't you had enough of bein' ordered about?"

Hilda waited a long time before replying, so long that Patrick looked at her anxiously. "No, wait," she said. "I must say this the right way."

Patrick looked more anxious than ever.

She took a deep breath. "I have thought for a long time about this. Always I say to myself the same t'ings. *Things.* I say—I think to myself, you understand—that I want to marry you and have my own home and—and children. I say that I want to be my own mistress, not a servant anymore. I say that now, if you become Uncle Dan's partner, these things are possible. And then I remember about your family, and my family, and how much they would hate this."

She sounded so forlorn that Patrick longed to take her in his arms, but she saw the wish in his eyes and put out a forbidding hand. "No. Let me finish. Always I think the same things, and never do I come to an answer. But yesterday I talked to Norah."

At the "but," Patrick's eyes grew a little brighter.

"We did not have enough time, because she had to hurry home to cook supper. And she was very tired, and I had a new thought, that maybe marriage was not all fun, that it, too, was work. But," she hurried on to forestall him, "Norah said something else, something that made me think another new thought. All day today, when I could think at all, I thought about what she said. She asked me what I wanted most, to please my family or to marry the man—the man I loved." Hilda looked down and addressed her next remark to Patrick's shoes. "And I decided," she whispered, "that I do not know what our families will do, but I want to marry you."

This time she didn't try to stay Patrick from the joyful embrace that swept them both into another world, one built of pink clouds and inhabited by chubby cupids.

When he at last freed her, gently, reluctantly, he reached into his pocket. "I've had this for a while, darlin' girl, just hopin'," he whispered. "I've held your hand often enough to have an idea of the size. I hope it fits."

He slipped the ring on her finger. It was a little loose, but she didn't even notice. She gazed, awestruck with the beauty of the gold setting and the fire of the diamond. "Patrick! You—it must have cost—is it real?"

"It's not so big, and it's only from Sears, Roebuck, but it's real. One day I'll buy you a fine one, big as a hotel doorknob!"

"You will not. It is this one I love. Oh, Patrick!"

The embrace this time was more passionate. Despite Hilda's best intentions, there's no telling what might have happened if they had not, after a time, heard the insistent knocking at the back door.

"Ignore them," said Patrick, his lips against her cheek, his hand stroking her golden hair.

Hilda sighed. "I cannot, Patrick. I am on duty. And you are on call. It could be anyone."

Patrick came down to earth with a thump. "Yes, that it could be. And you're not goin' to the door, me girl. Not when there's murderers still runnin' loose. I'll go."

The pink clouds had not yet quite receded for Hilda. Someone to protect her. Someone to look after her. She sighed luxuriously and smiled at Patrick's retreating figure.

He was back in moments, bringing with him a tall, agitated man. Hilda blinked, and blinked again, but the man was still her brother Sven.

"Hilda, you've got to come," said Sven, ignoring Patrick completely. "Erik's run away again, and Mama says you're the only one who can find him."

8

*School was suspended...as the city is trying
to unravel the mystery of the crime.*

—South Bend *Tribune*
January 23, 1904

I T TOOK HILDA A MOMENT to gather her thoughts. "Erik...?"

"What is the matter with you?" said Sven impatiently. "You must come, I tell you. Erik is gone, and Mama is beside herself. I know it is hard for you to get away, but if I explain to Mr. Williams—" He looked around the room. "Where *is* Mr. Williams?"

"He is in bed. He is very ill. There have been nurses with him all day, and oh, Sven, he might—"

But Sven was not interested in Mr. Williams just then. He surveyed the empty servants' room. "Where are all the other servants, then?"

"They've gone home, the dailies, and Maggie and Mrs. Sullivan have gone to bed."

"Then what," roared Sven, "is *he* doing here?"

Sven was a good six inches taller than Patrick and looked, just then, a good deal like one of the more fearsome Scandinavian gods, Thor, perhaps.

Patrick grinned. "I came to help, and I stayed to talk to Hilda. I have the right." He ignored the frantic signals Hilda was making behind Sven's back. "She and I are engaged to be married."

"You are *what?*"

"Sven, there is no time for this," said Hilda firmly. "We must find Erik. You can tell me everything, later, and forbid me to marry Patrick, and whatever else you are thinking, but now, tell me: When did Mama last see Erik, and where?"

"That's my girl," said Patrick in an undertone, and the love and admiration in his voice made Hilda feel, suddenly, like a queen on a throne. Oh, she could tackle anything with Patrick at her side!

Sven frowned. "He was—but we must talk about—"

"Later, not now. *Erik.* Tell me." Hilda grasped Patrick's arm.

Sven glared at Patrick. "I—oh, *ja,* later, then. Erik was—you know there has been no school this week, ever since his teacher was found killed?"

Hilda nodded.

"So Erik has been going to work all day at the firehouse." Sven shot Patrick another angry look. "And today he saw a newspaper that said school would begin again a week from Monday, after Miss Jacobs's funeral. And when he came home, Mama says, he said at the supper table that he would not go back to school. He is very sad and angry about his teacher, Hilda."

Again she nodded.

"Of course Mama said he must go to school. She says Erik was very naughty, then, and talked back to her, and refused to go back to school, ever. She explained why he must, but he became more and more angry."

Hilda could well imagine. Sven was, of course, relating only Mama's side of the story, but Hilda could almost hear the shouts. Mama's "explaining" had probably not been phrased in terms of cool reason, and Erik—well, all the Johanssons had more than their share of Swedish stubbornness, but Erik was the worst. "Yes," she said. "They fought. What happened then?"

"Erik refused to say he would go to school, and at last he lost his temper completely and said he would run away. Mama sent him to his room then, without his supper, and she locked him in."

Hilda groaned. "And he got out the window."

"He did. When Mama went to see him later, and give him something to eat—for you know, Hilda, that Mama can be strict, but she is loving, too—when she went to his room and unlocked the door, he was not there, and the window was wide open, letting in the snow."

"It is snowing?" Hilda had been too busy all evening to look out the windows.

"It is snowing hard. It has been since nightfall."

Only then did Hilda notice that the rug was wet from Sven's boots, and his coat and hat were sodden.

"But Sven! This is bad! If he is out in a snowstorm, why do we stand here and talk?"

"But it was you—"

Patrick, who had stood by silently, broke in. "We can't go any quicker than now, but we must go. Hilda, should you tell Mrs. Sullivan you're leavin'?"

Hilda looked at the clock on the mantel. "It is after ten o'clock. She will be sleeping. I will tell Colonel George. He will still be in his office, or the library. I will be back in a moment."

Hilda would ordinarily have shied away from telling the master of the house that she was going out, especially at night. However, this was not an ordinary time. Events were falling about her head thick and fast, but the supreme event was that she had just committed herself to marriage. She was wearing Patrick's diamond ring on her finger. With calm step and utter confidence, she approached the open door of Colonel George's office, knocked, and went inside.

He looked up from what he was reading. "Yes, Hilda? I hope Mr. Williams hasn't taken a turn for the worse."

"No, sir. That is, I do not know, sir. I have heard nothing since the afternoon. I am sorry to disturb you, but someone had to be told that I am leaving the house, perhaps for the night. My little brother has run away again. He is distressed because it is his teacher who has been killed. It is snowing very hard; we are afraid for him. I will take a key to the back door, and I will turn off all the lamps downstairs, but there will be no one to answer bells or see to the rest of the lights when you go up. You will not forget to turn off the gas, will you, sir?"

And with a little curtsey, she turned and was gone.

Colonel George sat for a moment with his mouth open. Finding that he could no longer concentrate on the journal in front of him, a treatise on the automobile, he sighed, stood, and turned off the lamps in his office. Methodically he went around the main floor of the house, turning off every gas fixture, and then, stumbling in the dark, he groped his way to the upstairs hall, where the sconces were still lit. He turned those off, too, and went to his bedroom.

Mrs. George put aside the book she was reading. "You're retiring rather early, George. Are you not feeling well?"

He sat down on the bed, heavily. "I don't know what the world's coming to, Ada. Hilda just came to my office and announced she was taking off for the night. Going out in a blizzard to hunt for that rascally little brother of hers, who's gone missing again. Never a hint of 'May I?' or 'By your leave' or anything else. Told me I'd have to fend for myself, there's nobody to answer bells, and to be sure and turn off all the gas before I went to bed! I don't know why I keep a pack of servants around this place if I'm going to have to do the work myself!"

"Now, George. Hilda is very reliable. She'll come back when she can. Come to bed."

"It was her attitude, though!"

"Surely she wasn't disrespectful. She's always so correct."

"Not disrespectful, exactly," he grumbled, loosening his tie. "Just—I can't put a finger on it. Over-confident, maybe. That girl has changed, Ada, and not for the better." He took off his jacket and flung it over a chair.

Mrs. George said nothing more, but a suspicion arose in her mind. Hilda had been seeing a good deal of that fireman of hers, lately. Even the mistress of the house sometimes heard the servants' gossip. Surely Hilda wouldn't...no. Mrs. George let the uncomfortable idea drift away as she reached again for her book.

～

Hilda, meanwhile, had struggled out into the storm, which had grown much worse while Sven had been in the house. They had not been out five minutes before Hilda's skirts were heavy and sodden. Her face was numb. She could scarcely see where she was going, and she would have fallen several times had it not been for the sturdy arms of Sven on one side and Patrick on the other.

"Look here," Patrick shouted above the wind, "this won't do. Stop a minute."

He pulled her into the relative shelter of a house, and Sven, perforce, followed. Leaning against the wall of the building, they simply stood for a moment, catching their breath.

"Now listen to me, both of you," said Patrick when it was easier to speak. "It's a blizzard out here."

"It is nothing," Sven insisted. "In Sweden—"

"But we're not in Sweden, are we? We're in South Bend, Indiana, and we don't have the kind of clothes they wear in Sweden, and we could freeze to death out here tonight!"

The wind howled. Snowflakes swirled. Sven decided not to argue the point.

"So," Patrick went on with dogged persistence, "there's no point at all in us goin' off tryin' to find Erik in this. He could be three feet away and we'd not see him. And he's not a fool."

"But we go to Mama's house," said Hilda, "to talk to her, and try to get an idea where he is."

"We could die before we get there," retorted Patrick. "I'm serious. You can't see your hand in front of your face out here. So I figure we'd best do some thinkin'. Sven, when does your ma reckon he left home?"

"She does not know. Probably before the snow started to fall so hard. She did not think he would go out in a storm. But—"

"So he went, and he wouldn't have just run off. He would have gone to a place. Where, Hilda?"

"I am t'inking. A friend's house, maybe. Not a train. They do not run so late, I t'ink, and he would not have enough money. Or—Patrick, the firehouse! The stables!"

"That's what I'm thinkin'," said Patrick with satisfaction. "He loves the horses, and he'd be safe enough there. Nobody'd catch him, neither, if he hid when any fireman came in. It'd be cold, of course, but he could bed down in the straw and do well enough. And he could think things out while he was there, decide what he's goin' to do."

"Yes," said Hilda. "Yes, that is where he must be. That is where we should go."

"Where we're goin', my girl, is back home. Your home, I mean. Tippecanoe Place. If I can find it, that is."

"But we cannot abandon Erik!"

"I should say not!" said Sven furiously.

"I don't mean to abandon him. Have you forgotten, darlin' girl, that the firehouse has a telephone?"

Hilda *had* forgotten. She was never allowed to use the instrument at the Studebaker mansion, except on rare occasions to answer it if it rang when Mr. Williams wasn't around the house. She had never in her life placed a telephone call, but there was a first time for everything.

She took Patrick's arm again. "The snow is not falling so hard now. The house is that way, I t'ink. Let us hurry, before the storm is worse again."

They struggled back. The streets and sidewalks were deeply drifted. Walking was treacherous.

Clinging tightly to Patrick's arm, Hilda rounded a corner and saw the great house looming on the next corner. The nearby arc light lit up the snow, but couldn't reach across the broad lawn to the house itself. It brooded on its hill like a dark mountain, the blackness relieved only by one pale rectangle high in the tower—Colonel and Mrs. George's bedroom. There was probably a light in Mr. Williams's sickroom, too, but it was on the other side of the great, dark house. Hilda shivered, and not just from the cold. This house that had sheltered her for years seemed suddenly ominous. As they approached, the one pale light went out.

In the basement entryway the darkness was complete, until Patrick found a match and kindled the gaslight. Then shadows dispersed and familiarity returned, but still Hilda shivered.

"Cold, darlin' girl?"

Hilda saw Sven frown at the endearment. She ignored him. "A little cold," she replied. "John will have damped down the furnace for the night, and I am very wet."

Patrick grimaced at the mention of John's name. John Bolton, the coachman and general handyman, had for years been a casual rival for Hilda's attentions. Patrick pulled her closer. "You'd best get out of your wet things and then into bed. It's nearly eleven. Just show me where the telephone is. I can talk to the firehouse and make certain Erik is safe and sound."

"No, Patrick. I mean, yes, I will show you the telephone, and I will be happy if you will make the call. I do not know how. But I must know, before I can go to bed, that he is safe. And I must lock the door after you."

"I, too, must know!" Sven tried to make it a roar, but the effect was spoiled by a sneeze at the end.

"Of course!" Patrick smiled at them both, to Sven's obvious annoyance. "That's what we'll do. Hilda, go on up and get yourself into warm things while I make the call. Then I'll leave Sven here to tell you the good news, and I'll be off."

"Oh, that is good, Patrick," said Hilda, starting up the back stairs before Sven could object to the plan. "The telephone, it is in Colonel George's office. I will go to my room and change my clothes."

She heard the *ting* as the receiver was raised from the hook, and Patrick shouting at the operator, and then she went on up the stairs. She wanted to listen to what was said, but it was more important to leave Sven and Patrick alone. Sven was going to have to get used to the idea that Patrick was now one of the men of the family.

She was exhausted, she found as she reached her room. Not only was she up later than usual, not only had her work been exacting all day, but she had been through so many emotional peaks and valleys that she felt wrung dry. She would have preferred to shed her wet clothing and fall into bed, but there were duties yet to be done.

She dropped her apron, skirt, and outer petticoat on the floor, where they lay in sodden puddles. She simply could not muster the energy to hang them up properly, and Mrs. Sullivan would be too busy tomorrow to scold her for her carelessness. There was a clean uniform skirt in her drawer, and Hilda could wash and iron the apron early in the morning, before she had to put it on. For now she pulled the clean skirt on over the thin inner petticoat. It clung to her figure in a most improper way, but she was far too tired to worry about that. Her wet boots and stockings cast aside, she thrust her feet into worn crocheted slippers and wearily trudged downstairs again.

Patrick was still there, just hanging the ear-piece back on the hook.

"Is he there? What did he say? Is he all right?"

"He's there. They let us talk to him. I gave him an earful, and so did Sven—in Swedish. I told him to stay where he was till the mornin' or I'd skelp him, and I reckon Sven said much the same." Patrick grinned reassuringly at Hilda. "Not that what we said would keep him where he was, but it's snowing hard again, and they've given him a proper bed. They'll keep an eye on him, so you've no need to worry. Then tomorrow—"

His tone of voice boded no good for Erik on the morrow.

Hilda's worry gave way instantly to anger. "Oh! I wish he were here! I would turn him over my knee. I do not care how big and grown-up he is."

"I expect Sven'll do that for you," said Patrick, and yawned. "We'll be gettin' along now, so's you can lock up and get to bed, but there's one more thing."

Hilda sighed. "What is that?"

"Well, you'll not be likin' it, but I reckon I'd better tell you, so you can be thinkin' some about it."

"Patrick! *What?*"

"It's only that the young imp says he'll run away again unless you agree to start lookin' into Miss Jacobs's murder."

He tipped his hat and hurried downstairs before she could muster her wits for a reply.

A short distance in front of her as she left [her boarding house] was...a leading attorney, who is lame, and was walking slowly.

—South Bend *Tribune*
January 23, 1904

9

S VEN WATCHED PATRICK GO with mixed feelings. On the one hand, he was glad to be rid of him. Patrick had no business to be here in the house with Hilda, unchaperoned, indeed alone for all practical purposes until he, Sven, had come.

On the other hand, Patrick had been useful over the Erik business. And he appeared to be able to handle Hilda, something Sven was no longer sure he could do.

Sven looked at Hilda, hoping to read her face. Would he find anger there? Stubbornness? That ridiculous lovesick look he had caught more than once this evening?

He saw none of those things. Hilda's face was wiped clean of expression, but two tears rolled down her cheek.

"Hilda! Little sister!" The words were in Swedish, and he continued in that language. "What is the matter?"

"I do not know," she said dully. "I am crying. I do not know why. I am very tired, Sven. I must go to bed."

"I—yes. Of course. Erik—in the morning—"

"I cannot go to bed until you leave, Sven. I must lock the door."

She spoke in that same toneless voice. Sven had never heard her sound like that before. He opened his mouth, closed it again, opened it once more. "Yes. I go now. Do not— try not to worry. In the morning..."

He trailed off and went down the stairs. Hilda followed. He dared not offer any parting words. Her behavior was too strange; he was too afraid of provoking some sort of storm. He kissed her on the cheek, said, "Good night" in Swedish, and left.

Hilda locked the door, turned off the gas, and climbed the stairs to bed. She locked her bedroom door and lay down to rest for a moment before undressing.

The next thing she knew, someone was pounding on her door and shouting.

"Hilda! Maggie couldn't wake you! Are you well? Hilda! It's past six-thirty!"

She roused herself. She was still in her clothes, and she was stiff all over. She made an instant decision. "No, Mrs. Sullivan. I am not well. I have a headache. I must sleep until it goes away."

And she turned over and put the pillow over her head, ignoring the further shouts and poundings. There was work to be done. Let someone else do it. For once in her life, she was going to do as she pleased. And what she pleased, just now, was to sleep for hours. Everyone in the household, including Mrs. George, knew about Hilda's terrible sick headaches, and knew that she was utterly useless when she was in the grip of one. The other servants would complain resentfully, but no one would disturb her.

But sleep wouldn't come. The upheavals of the day before had left her drained and spent, but once awakened she found that the problems began immediately to assault her mind.

What was she to do about Erik?

You have troubles enough of your own, a voice in her mind said. *Erik is not your problem.*

He was, though. Hilda was an accomplished liar, when lies were necessary, but she was basically honest. And honesty compelled her to acknowledge that she, of all the family, understood Erik best. Mama still thought of him as a baby, and Sven was overly harsh with him. Hilda and Erik had always been the best of friends. If anyone could deal with Erik, it was going to be Hilda.

But he wants you to investigate that murder. And with Mr. Williams ill, you have no time.

She turned restlessly to her other side, with a creak of bed-

springs. That was another thing. Her job. When she married
Patrick, she would lose her job.

When she married Patrick. She closed her eyes and allowed a
tide of joy to wash over her. Patrick's kiss…his arms warm
around her…

She lost herself in rosy daydreams that turned to real dreams.

When she woke again, she could tell that it was very late. The
sun had come out, a watery, wintry sun, but strong enough to
make a small pool of light on her floor, almost directly below her
south window.

Reluctantly Hilda abandoned her dreams and got out of bed.
Someday she would be mistress of a house and could arrange her
work to suit herself, but for now she had responsibilities. Including—she bit back an improper Swedish expression as she remembered—including preparations for a dinner party tonight.
She shed her wrinkled skirt and waist and dressed in the freshest
uniform she could find. She also took off her ring and hung it on
a chain around her neck, hidden under her clothes. She wasn't
ready yet to talk about her future, especially not to the family.

"You're a sight, girl," was the cook's sour greeting when Hilda
hurried into the kitchen.

"I know. I am sorry. I will wash my apron as soon as I can.
How is Mr. Williams feeling?"

Mrs. Sullivan shook her head. "No better. He can't hardly eat.
What with him sick and you sick, this house is goin' to rack and
ruin. If you'd got to bed at a decent hour last night, you'd not
have had to lie abed this mornin'. As if we didn't have enough
troubles…"

The cook went on in the same vein for some time. Hilda
didn't listen. She'd expected the tirade, and she had to admit she
deserved it, especially since she'd lied about the headache. She
tried to look properly penitent, and when Mrs. Sullivan finally
ran down, Hilda nodded. "I am sorry," she said again. "I will
work extra hard to make up for it. Do you have orders for me?"

"Girl, I've trouble enough runnin' me own kitchen, what with
cookin' for forty people and makin' trays for upstairs that come

down untouched." She raised her arms to the sky in a gesture of despair. "See what needs to be done and do it. And if ye get hungry come and find somethin' to eat. There's no time today for servants' meals."

Hilda nodded. "Is Mrs. George going to hire a butler for tonight? I don't see how we are to serve without Mr. Williams."

The cook nodded, her mind obviously back on the tarts she was preparing. Hilda hoped the pastry wouldn't be tough, but from the way Mrs. Sullivan was thumping down the rolling pin she had her doubts.

For the rest of the afternoon Hilda had no time to think about anything except work. The dailies were upset by the change in routine and had to be alternately scolded and cajoled into doing their jobs. Anton, who was doing many of the butler's jobs in the emergency, was pale and nervous. Mrs. Czeszewski, the laundress who came in twice weekly, resented Hilda's intrusion when she went into the laundry to wash her apron. Of course, Mrs. Czeszewski was always inclined to surliness, so Hilda didn't pay much attention, but it was an additional stress she didn't need on that stressful day.

Hilda hung the apron outside to dry. The air was very cold, but what with the sunshine and a stiff breeze Hilda thought it would dry better than inside. At sundown she threw on her cloak and ran out to retrieve the apron. It still had to be ironed before she could help serve dinner.

The clothesline was tucked away behind the carriage house. John Bolton, the coachman, stood in the drive, unhitching the horses from the sleigh. "Bit chilly for you to be out, dressed in no more than that, isn't it?" he said to Hilda as she hurried by. "Don't you want to come in for a warm?"

He made it sound like the most improper of invitations. Hilda tossed her head. "No, I do not. I am in a hurry."

"Huh! And too high 'n' mighty to talk to the likes of me, now you're to be married and a fine lady."

"How did you know…" She stopped short. She had no wish to be drawn into conversation.

John shrugged. "I heard. That Irishman of yours talks nineteen to the dozen. Shouldn't think there's anyone in town doesn't know by now. And speakin' of talk, have you heard the latest?"

"No, and I must—"

"They've got new evidence in the Jacobs case." He led the horses into the carriage house and began to curry Star, whistling tunelessly. "Thought you was in a hurry."

"New evidence?" Hilda stayed where she was, her hurry forgotten.

"They're sayin' a big man in town, an important man, knows a lot more about this than he ought to. And they're lookin' at a fella stayin' at the Oliver, too."

"But who—"

"Hilda! Get in here this minute!" It was Mrs. Sullivan, calling from the back door, and her tone left Hilda no choice. She snatched the apron from the line and scurried back to the house.

John chuckled and led the horses into their stalls.

After a hasty conference with Anton and the hired butler, it was decided that Hilda would answer the door and admit guests while Anton took their coats. Janecska, pressed into staying on for the evening, would show the ladies upstairs to freshen their gowns and hair before descending the grand staircase in their finery.

When Hilda opened the door to Mr. Barrett and his wife, she was shocked at their appearance. Smiling and curtseying, Hilda tried to keep dismay out of her face. Mr. Barrett looked extremely ill, much worse than he had a few days before. Mrs. Barrett, a usually handsome woman in her fifties, had deep lines in her face and bags under her eyes that Hilda had never seen before.

"Good evening, Hilda," said Mrs. Barrett. "Williams is still ill, then?"

"Yes, madam. He is very ill. We are quite worried about him. Thank you for asking, madam. Janecska will take you up to the powder room, if you would like to sit here for a moment until she returns."

"Thank you, Hilda, but I know my way." She touched her

husband's arm for a moment and looked him in the eye. The look said much, but Hilda was unable to interpret it. Then Mrs. Barrett gave Anton her velvet cloak and made her way, slowly, up the stairs that wound around the elevator.

Mr. Barrett, leaning heavily on his cane, allowed himself to be divested of his coat and hat and then tried to smile at Hilda. He didn't quite succeed. "My dear, I need to have a private word with the colonel for a moment, and my leg is not so well this evening. Do you think you could find him for me?"

"Of course, sir. Sit down, and I will bring him to you." She raised her eyebrows at Anton, who shrugged and tacitly agreed to cope with new arrivals until she came back.

It wasn't easy to find Colonel George among the swirl of guests, but Hilda finally tracked him down in the library, where he was enjoying a preprandial cigar with several of the gentlemen. Hilda murmured in his ear. He excused himself and followed her, and after a word with Mr. Barrett, the two men disappeared into Colonel George's office and shut the door. Hilda looked at the door, her mind full of questions, but a large party of guests arrived just then and she resumed her duties.

The dinner went well enough, she supposed. The hired butler was competent but slow, because he didn't know the routines of the house nor the layout of the pantry. Hilda, Anton, and Janecska all helped Maggie and the butler serve. Few ate all of their tarts, Hilda noticed. Evidently Mrs. Sullivan's light hand at pastry had, indeed, failed her.

The evening dragged on. After the meal was over, Hilda and the butler served coffee for the ladies in the drawing room and the gentlemen in the library. In this teetotal household there was no lingering over brandy or port for the men, but they did enjoy their cigars and even the occasional cigarette.

The ladies had finished their coffee and bonbons, and Hilda was ready to go downstairs and tackle the mountain of tasks that awaited her there, when the butler slipped into the drawing room and beckoned to her.

"Mr. Studebaker would like to speak to you," he whispered.

"His name is *Colonel* Studebaker," she corrected impatiently. "What does he want?"

"How would I know? He asked me to find you. No, not that way," as Hilda turned toward the library. "He's in his office waiting for you."

"His office? When there are guests?" Hilda's eyebrows rose, but she went as directed to the office.

Colonel George was sitting at his desk, Mr. Barrett once more closeted with him. Hilda tapped on the open door and went in.

"Sit down, Hilda," said the colonel, gesturing to a chair.

Hilda did as she was bidden, but uneasily. This was not at all the correct thing. She looked from one face to the other. Neither was informative, though her employer shifted restlessly in his chair. Neither spoke.

"Sir," said Hilda at last, "there is much work in the kitchen. I must "

"Yes," said the colonel. He sighed and toyed with a pen, then tossed it back on the desk. "Hilda, I—that is, Mr. Barrett—we have—oh, the fact is, I Iilda, Robert here finds himself in a bit of a mess, and wants your help." He spread his hands in a gesture of impatience.

"Mine, sir?"

Mr. Barrett spoke. "You see, Hilda, your reputation has spread."

"My *reputation,* sir? I am a respectable woman, sir!"

"Yes, yes," said the colonel. "We don't mean that kind of reputation. It's this confounded habit you have of nosing into criminal matters. I'm not at all sure it's becoming to a housemaid, but my wife doesn't seem to mind, and the household is her affair, after all." He sighed once more.

"I scc, sir." She was beginning to.

"Yes, well, it's this nasty business of the schoolteacher. I think you said she was your brother's teacher?"

"Yes, sir, my brother Erik. He is very much upset. She was a good teacher and he loved her."

"Hmph. Well, the police seem to have some doubts about how

good she was in some ways—but never mind that. The police have made a lot of blunders in this matter. As usual. And their chief mistake is that they are looking at Mr. Barrett. They've implied that since he was the last person to see her alive, he might just have been the first person to see her dead, as well."

Hilda looked at Mr. Barrett, her face full of pity. "Yes, sir. I thought they might think that. Myself, I do not believe it. You are a good man, sir. Not the sort who could—do those things."

The old man spoke. "I'm glad you think so, Hilda, because I'd like you to look into the matter for me."

"But, sir, I—"

Mr. Barrett held up his hand. "You see, Daniel Malloy is a good friend of mine. I've been his lawyer for many years, and I know the family well. He told me all about what you did in that unfortunate business a couple of years ago, how you, virtually unaided, solved the crimes of which he had been wrongly accused." He waited while Hilda took that in, and then continued. "The police brought Pinkerton's men in for this business, from the time they first found the body, but they seem to be doing nothing but making a lot of fuss and learning nothing new. I—my wife is suffering a good deal over this. Would you be willing to—to do whatever it is you do, to winnow out the facts of the matter?"

Again Hilda looked from one man to the other. "I do not know, sir. The other times, I knew the people, or some of them. I was able to talk to my family, other servants…" She moved her hands in distress. "I know none of the people connected to Miss Jacobs. I do not know if I could help. And there is my work here. Mr. Williams is ill, and I am needed."

"We can hire another housemaid, Hilda," said the colonel. "I had thought of one of your sisters, perhaps. We have no plans to entertain again for some time, so there shouldn't be all that much to do."

Hilda kept a straight face. Men never had the slightest idea how much routine work was needed to keep a large house clean and running smoothly.

Mr. Barrett spoke. "I'm not expecting miracles, child. I only know that I have no faith in the South Bend police, who may be corrupt and are certainly incompetent. And from what I've seen of the Pinkertons so far, they're not much better. You are apparently able to talk to people, get them to tell you things, and you have a good head on your shoulders. Will you do what you can, as a favor to me?"

Hilda turned to the colonel. "If I do this, may I stay on here and do what work I am able to? I have no other place to live, sir."

"Of course, of course. My wife would have my hide if I let you go permanently."

The colonel had obviously not tuned in to the servants' gossip about Hilda and Patrick. That was good. She wanted to tell Mrs. George herself, and in her own good time. She took a deep breath. "Then—then yes, I will do it. For perhaps a week. If I cannot learn anything in a week, I will know that I can be of no help. Will you tell Mrs. Sullivan, sir? She will not be pleased. "

"I'll leave that to Mrs. Studebaker," he said hastily. "Er—starting tomorrow, then?"

"On Monday, sir. Tomorrow I will bring one of my sisters here and show her what is to be done. Thank you, sir. Good night, sir. Good night, Mr. Barrett."

And she escaped to the kitchen.

The interest in this remarkable crime
and the horror of it have not abated....

—South Bend *Tribune*
January 27, 1904

10

HILDA THOUGHT IT BEST the next morning to get up at her usual time and do her usual duties before breakfast. They were few, for Sunday was nominally a holiday, but Mrs. George had undoubtedly not yet notified the cook about Hilda's new status. Mrs. Sullivan was going to lose her temper when she heard about it, and since she didn't dare take out her outraged feelings on her employer, it was Hilda who would bear the brunt of them. Well, she, Hilda intended to give no offense in the meantime. With luck she'd be out of the house before the storm broke.

Chores done and breakfast eaten, Hilda hurried to church. The day was bitter cold; her family had not waited outside the church for her. She stopped for a moment just inside the door, to calm her rapid breathing and let her eyes accustom themselves to the relative dimness, and then slipped into the pew beside her sister Gudrun just as the pastor entered.

Since the congregation was between pastors and was therefore sharing one with an Elkhart church, the service was brief. Too brief for Hilda's liking. There was going to be unpleasantness afterwards.

When church was over, no one foregathered around the door. It was too cold. Civil greetings were exchanged, hats were tipped, and then every family hurried back to its own fireside, its own good Sunday dinner.

The kitchen at Sven's house, where the family always ate on Sundays, was small, far too small for three women. At last Gudrun shooed Hilda and Mama out to set the table. The three younger girls were huddled around the fire in the tiny parlor, enjoying a little rare leisure. Erik and Sven were outside gathering more wood. Mama and Hilda were essentially alone.

Mama had said nothing to Hilda all morning, indeed had scarcely looked at her. Now they spread the embroidered Sunday cloth across the table in silence. Hilda set out plates on her side of the table, carefully positioning them over the darned places, and then passed the plates to Mama for her side, all in silence. They laid out cutlery in the same fashion. Hilda knew what was coming, but she was determined not to speak first. Mama was the one who was angry. Let Mama raise the subject.

When they had folded the last threadbare napkin and set the last glass in place, Mama could no longer contain herself. "So," she said. "You act like a member of the family now. But you are no longer my daughter." She spoke in Swedish, and her voice was colder than the air outside.

Hilda was stung, even though she had thought she was ready. But she had her answer. "Then I will no longer have to go out in a blizzard and look for Erik?" Hilda asked, also in Swedish. "Good. I do not know who else will do it, but if he is not my brother, why should I freeze for him?"

Mama had expected tears or fury. She changed her tactics. "Why do you break my heart this way? Are there no Swedish boys in this town? I wish I had never come to America. This is a terrible place, where young boys are molested and young women killed, and my daughter chooses to marry a Papist."

"A Papist who saved Erik's life last year. Whose uncle paid for you and Erik and the girls to come here, and in luxury, too." Uncle Dan had paid the passage for the last four Johanssons to join the older siblings, and had done it in style, buying second-class tickets rather than the usual steerage. "Mama, I have no wish to hurt you. That is one reason I have said no to Patrick for years. But he is a good man, and he will be rich, and I love him. This is America. The world is changing. Mama, I hope you will give us your blessing. But I will marry Patrick even if you do not."

Tears began to gather in Mama's eyes.

Hilda hurried on with the rest of what she had to say. "I have other news, Mama. We will speak of Patrick later, but I have exciting news. Colonel George has given me leave to find out what I can about Miss Jacobs. That will please Erik, and he will not run away anymore." Hilda crossed her fingers at the last words, but behind her back.

"And," she went on, "Mrs. George will have to have someone to take my place while I am doing this other thing. Colonel George wants one of my sisters, he said. Just think of that! Would that not be a grand opportunity for Elsa? She would make much more money than at the shirt factory and she would stay with me at Tippecanoe Place. You would not have to feed her and there would be more room in your house."

Mama was not to be swept away by the change of subject. "And when you go back to work, what then? She will have no job, because Wilson's will not keep the job for her, and we will be poorer than ever."

"I think Mrs. George will keep her on," said Hilda, crossing the fingers on her other hand. "Because one day soon she will need someone to take my place for good."

Mama started to cry in earnest.

The Sunday meal was a dismal affair. Even Erik, usually irrepressible, picked at his food and asked to be excused at the first possible moment.

Hilda went with him, pulling him up the stairs. "Erik, I have news, and I must not speak about it in front of Mama. She is very angry with me."

Erik made a face. "She's mad at everybody, because of you."

"I know, and I am sorry. She will be better in time. But Erik, I must tell you. I am to investigate Miss Jacobs's murder! Colonel George himself has asked me to. And I will need your help."

"Mama will not let me."

"Erik, you are thirteen years old. You are almost grown. It is time you stopped acting like a little boy. You run away when you are angry. You sulk. You must learn some sense, learn to do what you think is best."

"Everybody yells at me when I do what I want."

"I did not say, what you want. I said, what is best. There is a difference. You know the difference quite well."

She looked at him steadily, two pairs of blue eyes locked in an intense gaze. Erik's eyes dropped first. "I guess so," he mumbled.

"Of course you do. Now tell me what you will do about Miss Jacobs."

He thought for a moment, and then shrugged. "I don't know. What you tell me to, I guess."

Hilda nodded. "And if you think of something that I have not, you will tell me, and we will talk about it together. And what will you say to Mama?"

"Well…she'll be at work. I could sneak out…." He stopped at the look on Hilda's face. "No. I guess that's no good. I'd better tell her I'll be helping you. She'll be mad."

"Yes. But if you want, I will be with you when you tell her. Then she will be angry with two of us, which is better than just with you."

Erik sighed. "I don't think it's such fun growing up."

Hilda smiled and gave him a quick hug. "You will be surprised. It is more fun than you think. Now I must go and talk to Elsa about a job at Tippecanoe Place."

By the end of the afternoon, all was arranged. Mama had stormed and wept, but Gudrun and (surprisingly) Sven had been on Hilda's side. Sven's point of view was that, since Erik had no school for a week, he would be better off helping Hilda than left to his own devices. Gudrun thought that Elsa, though young, could learn the duties of a housemaid quickly, and if the job turned into a permanency, she would be well fixed.

Freya was a little jealous. She was older than Elsa, and an experienced maid. "Why can I not go instead?" she asked with a frown.

"Because you have a good job, much better than Elsa's," said Gudrun.

"She could take my place, instead of Hilda's."

"You are the only maid in that house," said Hilda. "There

would be no one to train Elsa except that cross butler. I will have time to train her, and Mr. Williams will not trouble her for a while, because he is so ill. Besides, Freya, you are old enough to marry, and there is Gunnar Borglund, who spoke to you after church this morning, even in the cold."

Freya colored and lowered her eyes.

"And when you marry Gunnar and leave your job, what would Mrs. George do then? No, it is better for Elsa."

"And I want to go," said Elsa, who had remained dutifully quiet until then, letting her elders settle her fate.

Mama raised her hands and rolled her eyes, but the matter was settled. When Hilda returned to Tippecanoe Place just before sundown, she brought Elsa with her and introduced her to Mrs. Sullivan.

The cook was over her first anger at the plan Mrs. George had announced to her that morning, and Elsa was careful to curtsey prettily and speak softly. "Hmm," said Mrs. Sullivan. "Looks all right. Nice manners. Does she know anything?"

"She knows how to work hard. I will teach her the rest. She will be no trouble, I promise you."

"Better not be. You'll have to take her to see Mrs. George, you know. Though with things the way they are, she'd likely take anybody who came in off the street. I don't suppose you care how Mr. Williams is doin'."

Hilda's hand flew to her mouth. "Oh! He is not worse?"

"They took him off to the hospital this afternoon. It's pneumonia, and the doctor said he needs round-the-clock nursin'." Mrs. Sullivan wiped away a tear. "So we're havin' to keep on that temporary man, and how he'll work out I don't know. We're all at sixes and sevens, and I'm sure you'll do your best, child, but I don't know what we're to do about clothes for you."

Hilda pointed to the carpetbag Elsa had set on the floor. "She brought a plain black dress, and she can use my caps and aprons for now. She will be no trouble," Hilda said again. "I am sorry about Mr. Williams. Elsa and I will say a prayer for him before we go to sleep tonight. Come, Elsa, I will take you to Mrs.

George. You must remember to call her Mrs. Studebaker. Then I will show you our room, and then teach you what you must do in the morning."

Mrs. George was in the drawing room, reading a book of sermons, the only reading thought appropriate for a Sunday. She set it aside to look Elsa over, and sighed. "Hilda, I hope you understand that we need you back at work as soon as possible. Now that we are entertaining again, we can't do without proper service. Are you sure your sister can cope?"

Elsa, though intimidated by the house and so great a lady, was getting tired of being referred to as if she weren't there. "I will work hard, madam," she said with some spirit. "I am careful and quick. With Hilda to teach me, and to help sometimes, I will give satisfaction."

Mrs. George looked amused. "You're like your sister, I see. Very well, you'll do. Tomorrow we'll see about uniforms for you. Thank you, Hilda."

Dismissed, the two girls went off to explore Elsa's new home.

Patrick came for a visit after supper. Hilda was too busy to sit down with him, but she allowed him to trail along as she took Elsa from room to room, explaining her duties.

"This is the drawing room. It is very hard to keep clean because of the soot. You must use a wet cloth here; a dry one makes smears. There is a closet on each floor where cleaning supplies are kept; I will show you."

"So you're in the thick of this thing, are you? And Erik is going to help you?" said Patrick. He frowned. "I'm not sure I approve of any of this. It isn't right, puttin' a girl in harm's way like this. I'd like to give that Mr. Barrett a piece of my mind!"

"I will be careful. And Elsa, make sure you brush down the draperies every day, and the walls once a week. The draperies need a hard brush, the walls a soft one, so you do not scratch the wallpaper. Then the chandeliers—you do not clean them, the dailies do that, but you must know how. There is a new paste that is much better than the old way, but you must be sure that the girls do not leave any in the cracks."

"Hilda, are you listenin' to me? This man you're lookin' for, he kills young women! Are you thinkin' of that?"

"Patrick, I am busy! And yes, I think of the danger. Do you not understand that I have been *told* to do this?"

"You could've said no," said Patrick. "Why do you kowtow to these people? You don't have to, not anymore. When we're married—"

"But we are not married yet, and Colonel George is my employer still! And I feel sorry for Mr. Barrett. And I must do this, so why do you argue?"

"Because I care what happens to you," said Patrick softly, and Hilda's anger evaporated.

"I will be careful, Patrick. I promise. I will not do stupid things. I go only to talk to people, to learn what I can. Then I tell Mr. Barrett everything and I come back to my usual duties."

"You've said that sort of thing before," said Patrick gloomily.

"And I have always been all right in the end!" said Hilda, annoyed again.

The two glared at each other, and Elsa giggled. "The way you two fight, anyone would think you were married already."

"We do not fight," said Hilda with dignity. "We argue." Then she smiled at Patrick, her dimple showing, and he grinned back. "And we like it."

The officers and detectives have not yet talked with [the victim's friend] because her physician says...any excitement might be injurious to her.

—South Bend *Tribune*
    February 3, 1904

11

HILDA DIDN'T SLEEP WELL that night. Her bed was narrow and she was used to the luxury of having it to herself. Elsa wasn't a large person, but she wiggled a lot in her sleep. Sometime after four o'clock Hilda gave it up. She would have to rise in a little over an hour anyway. She might just as well get up and dress and spend some time planning her day. She crept down the back stairs in the pitch darkness and felt her way to the kitchen.

When she had stirred up the banked fire in the kitchen range and made herself a pot of coffee, she sat at the kitchen table and did some serious thinking.

Her first obligation today was to get Elsa properly started in her job. It was important, for everyone's sake, that Elsa do well. Someday...no, Hilda wouldn't let herself think about that. Not now. There were too many things to be done.

After Elsa was well launched and Hilda could get away, what then?

The obvious thing was to find friends of Miss Jacobs and listen to what they had to say. Of course, the police would already have done that, but they probably had not talked to the maids who worked in the friends' houses. Servants always knew far more about what went on than their employers ever suspected. So— where to start?

There was the school, of course. Miss Jacobs must have had friends among the teachers. But the school was closed for the week.

Her boarding house, then. And her rooming house. Hilda

knew where both of those were. They weren't far away, an easy
walk in the summer. In the winter—well, she'd just have to wait
until daylight and see how much she'd have to bundle up. She'd
go, anyway, and talk to the servants there, and see what she could
find out.

Then there was the funeral. That would be attended by lots of
people who knew Miss Jacobs, almost certainly including some
servants. The newspaper today should say when it would be held.
It would be in Elkhart, of course, where the poor woman's family
lived. Hilda had never been to Elkhart, but there would be train
service. She would have to ask Mr. Barrett for some money to
spend on that sort of thing. She did not intend to spend her own
good money on trips for his benefit. She was a frugal Swede, even
if she was going to be rich someday.

Hilda glanced at the clock. She had nearly a quarter of an
hour before she had to wake Elsa at five-thirty. She abandoned
herself to the luxury of daydreaming. Pretty clothes. A big house,
with room for lots of children...

She poked herself, mentally, finished her coffee, and stood up.
Pretty, fashionable clothes required corsets, which Hilda detest-
ed. Houses and children required hard work. Probably there
were other perils for the rich, as well. Better to do what she had
to do today and let all the tomorrows take care of themselves.

She went upstairs to roust Elsa out of bed.

By the time the family sat down to breakfast, Hilda had
launched Elsa on her day and was ready to leave the house. The
temperature had not moderated, but at least the sun was shining
and there was no fresh snow to contend with. She sought out her
warmest apparel, wishing Mama had had time to knit that new
corset cover. She put on two flannel petticoats, her oldest flannel
waist and the wool skirt, and finally a thick sweater her mother
had made her for Christmas. It was meant for skating and looked
odd over the other garments, but Hilda meant to spend the
morning talking to servants. It didn't matter how she looked.

Before Hilda left the house, she peeped in to see how her sister
was getting along. Elsa was doing Mrs. Clem's bedroom, talking

animatedly to Janecska, but getting the work done. Janecska looked sulky. She probably resented the new girl being put in authority over her. Hilda closed the door gently. Elsa could fend for herself.

Hilda's first stop was at Mama's house, to pick up Erik. She had no idea at this point how Erik might be able to help, but he needed to be kept out of mischief.

"Where are we going?" he asked, as they hurried back toward the center of town.

"To Mrs. Gibbs's boarding house. It was where Miss Jacobs took her meals. I thought the servants there might know who Miss Jacobs's best friends were."

"Huh! I know that! Everyone at school knows that!"

"Erik! You did not tell me!"

"You never asked," he said reasonably. "Can't you walk slower? I have a stitch in my side."

"You ate too much for breakfast, then. And it is too cold to dawdle." But she slowed her pace a little. "Now tell me about the friends."

"She had a lot of friends, but her *best* friend, her name is Miss Lewis. She's a teacher, too, only at the high school. But she and Miss Jacobs live in the same rooming house. Lived, I mean." His voice faded.

Hilda ignored his distress. A brisk approach was better than sympathy. "Yes, very well, and has this Miss Lewis talked to the police, do you know?"

"If she has I don't know about it. She's not here."

Hilda frowned. "What do you mean, not here?"

"She went away. Some of the kids said she was sick and had to go home to stay with her mother for a while."

"And where is home? Elkhart?"

"I don't think so. I don't think Miss Lewis is from there. Indianapolis, maybe? Somewhere far away."

"Very well. You say they were good friends, she and Miss Jacobs."

"They ate their lunches together most days, the two of them.

Mostly Miss Lewis would come to our classroom and they would eat at Miss Jacobs's desk. And they walked home together almost every day, until Miss Lewis went home at Christmas and didn't come back."

"Does she plan to come back, do you think?"

Erik shrugged. "Don't know. Mrs. Schmidt would maybe know, her landlady."

"We go there next."

"I have an idea, Hilda," said Erik after a few more steps.

"And what is that, little—my brother?"

"I don't know anybody at Mrs. Gibbs's house, or Mrs. Schmidt's. But I do know some of the boys who work at the Oliver Hotel. Have you heard about the man who disappeared from there?"

"No! Oh, but yes, Erik. I heard a little. John Bolton started to say something to me, but Mrs. Sullivan called me in. Tell me what you know."

"Nothin' except there was a man stayin' there for a couple of nights, the night before everything happened and then the night of—the awful night—and then he left without payin' his bill, or so the talk goes. I could go there and find out a lot! Kurt works there, and Andy, and lots of boys I know."

His voice was full of pleading. Hilda considered. "You will go straight there and only there?"

Erik made a face. "I'm not a baby! Even Mama lets me go where I want when I don't have work to do."

"I don't mean that. I know you are almost grown. If you have money and want to stop for an ice cream or buy some candy, that is your business. What I mean is, if you find out something, you will not go somewhere else and try to find out more. You will come back to me and consult. You promised yesterday, Erik. This is dangerous, and Mama is trusting me to keep you safe."

Erik stood up straighter. "I won't break my promise. But what if one of the boys wants to take me and show me something?"

Hilda sighed. "If it is at the boy's house or in the hotel you may go. If it is anywhere else you must come to me first. If I do not see you at Mrs. Gibbs's I will come to you at the hotel when I am finished."

Erik frowned and kicked at a clump of ice, shattering it into glittering shards. "Anybody'd think I didn't have any gumption."

"And what is that?"

"Good sense. Horse sense. You order me around, and you don't even speak English as well as I do!"

"I order you around," said Hilda furiously, "because you do *not* always show good sense. As for my English, I do not use slang, if that is what you mean." Her English was a point of pride, and it annoyed her that Erik did, in fact, speak more idiomatically than she.

She stopped to take him by the shoulders and glare at him. The glare in his face was so exactly like the one she felt on her own face that her sense of humor took over. She clapped him on the back and started walking again. "I believe that when I marry Patrick and we quarrel, it will be no different from what I have done all my life with you. If ever I knew a stubborn Swede, it is you."

"You oughta know," said Erik, but he said it under his breath. His sister could be pushed only so far.

They parted at the door of Mrs. Gibbs's boarding house. Erik went on downtown to the hotel, while Hilda took the path around to the kitchen door and knocked.

A large woman answered the door. She was wearing a white apron and had flour on her hands. "Good morning, ma'am," said Hilda with a polite nod. "I can see that you are busy, but may I come in and speak with the housemaid for a minute? I work at Tippecanoe Place, and I need to talk to her, for a little time only."

"Come in, then, and shut the door. You're lettin' in all the cold air. Come in to the kitchen with you."

Hilda followed meekly. The cook led the way down a dark passage to a small kitchen. Almost all the space was taken up with a huge kitchen range. The coal fire at the heart of the monster made the room stiflingly hot; Hilda unfastened her cloak and loosened her scarf. The cook turned to her breadboard, took a portion of the large lump of dough, and began to shape it into a loaf.

"Now, you'll not be wantin' to take away our Kathleen, will you? You'd be that Swedish maid that's pantin' to marry Daniel Malloy's nephew, wouldn't you? A bit above yourself, my friend Mrs. Sullivan says."

Hilda bit back a retort and said simply, "Yes, I am Hilda Johansson, and no, we have no need of more maids at Tippecanoe Place. But if I could speak to her? I will not interfere with her work."

The cook gave her a sharp look. "Give yourself airs, don't you? Well, it's none of my business. Kathleen's doin' the parlor, if she's where she's supposed to be. You'll find it easy enough. I've no time to be showin' the likes of you around."

Hilda couldn't trust herself to reply. She nodded to the cook's back and got out of the kitchen, stopping in the hall to take a few deep breaths and think of the things she would have liked to say to the cook.

The house was not a large one, nothing like as fine as Uncle Dan's. Hilda found the parlor with no trouble, and sure enough, a young woman with an unmistakably Irish face was dusting the wooden curlicues on the arms of the old-fashioned sofa.

"Excuse me," said Hilda.

"Oh! I didn't hear you come in. If you was wantin' to board here, you'll have to speak to Mrs. Gibbs. Not but what she has a vacancy at the table, now that…" The maid's speech trailed off.

"No, I do not need a place to board. My name is Hilda Johansson, and I think you must be Kathleen, and I want to talk to you for a few minutes."

"To me? Mrs. O'Leary won't like that."

"I have spoken to Mrs. O'Leary, if that is the cook. And I hope her cooking is better than her manners!"

Kathleen giggled. "She's a tartar, that one, but she cooks fit for the angels in heaven, and she can stretch a piece of stewing beef farther than anyone in town. It's the only reason Mrs. Gibbs keeps her on. We wouldn't keep a full table here without Mrs. Gibbs puttin' such tasty fare on it."

"You have many people board here, then?"

"A full table, like I said." The maid turned to the windows, giving the lace curtains a shake and running her duster idly along the sills. "Only I suppose you heard about what happened to one of the boarders here, such a nice lady."

"That is why I am here," said Hilda.

"Ooh!" said Kathleen, waving her duster in agitated fashion. A cloud of dust rose; Hilda coughed. "Sorry, but I just figgered out who you are. You're the one as saved Daniel Malloy's bacon that time!"

"Yes, and now a friend of his has asked me to find out what I can about Miss Jacobs. And I thought you would know a lot about her, so I came to ask you. If you have another duster, I can help while we talk. Then Mrs. O'Leary will not be able to say I kept you from your duties."

"Oh, she never leaves her kitchen, except when she has to talk to Mrs. Gibbs about food. But take off your things and sit down."

"Mrs. Gibbs will not mind?"

"She's not home. She's gone out to do some shoppin'. So make yerself comfortable."

Hilda was glad to rid herself of her outer garments. She sat down and began.

"What kind of person was Miss Jacobs? I know she was a good teacher. My little brother Erik was in her class at Colfax School and loved her."

"Near everybody loved her," Kathleen declared. "She was a happy, cheerful sort of person, and treated people right. There's some as treats servants like dirt under their feet, but not her. It was always, 'Thank you, Kathleen,' and 'Good evening, Kathleen,' and 'You look pretty tonight, Kathleen.' Never ordered me about, always said please, never made extra work."

"Did she have friends here?"

Kathleen nodded vigorously. "There was a lady teacher boarded here that was her special friend, Miss Lewis. She taught at the high school. The two of 'em went about together a lot. Until Christmas, anyway. Then Miss Lewis got sick and had to go home."

"I had heard that. What is the matter with Miss Lewis?"

The maid picked up her duster and turned to the mantel. "I couldn't say, I'm sure."

*Evidence that the dead girl believed she had been marked for assault was given the police today by...
a substitute school teacher.*

—South Bend *Tribune*
January 27, 1904

12

HILDA'S EARS PERKED UP. "Oh, you must have some idea," she coaxed. "You hear people talk, do you not? Always they talk in front of us maids as if we are not there."

"I shouldn't say. I don't know if it's true or not."

"But if you tell me, I can find out. And then if it is not true, you can make sure no one spreads lies about Miss Lewis." By now Hilda had a good idea of what was coming.

"Well—I know for a fact that she'd gone off her food, from about Thanksgivin' on. She didn't take her breakfast here, o' course, just supper, but even then sometimes, when she smelled the food, she'd turn green and have to leave the room. And her face looked different, just like my sister Brenda when she was first married. And once I heard her and Miss Jacobs arguin' to beat the band. They stopped talkin' when I came in the room, so I know they was talkin' about somethin' real private. But I heard Miss Jacobs say, 'You didn't ought to do that. He'll do the right thing by you.' And Miss Lewis, she was cryin'."

"So you think Miss Lewis was going home to have a baby."

"No, miss." Kathleen took a deep breath. "What people are sayin' is that she was goin' home to get rid of a baby."

Hilda was shocked, but not really surprised. These things happened. Proper ladies might not know about them, but women of Hilda's class did. "Do you think that was true?"

"Oh, miss, I don't know what to think!" Now that the terrible secret was out, the maid was eager to talk. "I'd hate to believe it of her. She's a nice lady, Miss Lewis. Not like Miss Jacobs, not as easy-goin'. Miss Jacobs was sort of gentle and kind. Miss Lewis, she's quicker, more pert and saucy-like, with an eye for the gentlemen. She's as pretty a lady as you'd ever want to see, real dark hair done up in poufs, with little curls loose here and there. And a beautiful complexion, all rosy-cheeked, and snappy blue eyes.

"She could have had any man she wanted, I reckon, but I heard her say to Miss Jacobs that they were all too young and silly, that she wanted an older man, or someone from a big city. She's from Indianapolis, you know, and I guess that's a really big city, three, four times the size of South Bend. Miss Lewis sort of turned up her nose at the gentlemen around here."

"Was there any particular man she rejected?"

"Oh, I don't know as any of 'em had got round to proposin' marriage. They'd call on her—"

"Here? Why not at Mrs. Schmidt's?"

"Well, they'd come here to take her home after supper, see. And in summer they'd maybe take her for an ice cream, or a walk in the park or whatnot, before seein' her home."

"In summer? She had lived in South Bend longer than Miss Jacobs, then? Because Miss Jacobs came only last fall, is that not right?"

"Yes, Miss Jacobs started at the school then, but Miss Lewis, she'd been teachin' at the high school for three years. She was a little older than Miss Jacobs, but as soon as Miss Jacobs came to town, the two of 'em was thick as thieves."

"Hmm. And of all Miss Lewis's callers—all the ones you know about, anyway—do you have any idea which of them…?" Hilda, out of delicacy, let the sentence trail off.

"Honest, I don't. I can't imagine her lettin' any of 'em…I mean, she liked walkin' out with 'em, but she didn't like one more than another, and there was nothin' serious. That *I* saw, anyway."

Hilda filed the information away in her mind, but at first glance it seemed to provide no clue to Miss Jacobs's murderer. She changed tack. "And what about Miss Jacobs? Did she have any particular gentlemen friends, that you knew about?"

"I don't think she had any at all, particular or not. Her friends were other ladies. Oh, and the men who lived here, but they were friends, not nothin' more. Like I said, she was different from Miss Lewis. Miss Jacobs was more serious-like in her ways. Or no, that's not the right word. She was happy and cheerful, but she didn't go about much. I don't think she had very much money. Her clothes was always neat and proper, but not fancy. She liked music. Sometimes she'd stay in the parlor here after supper for a little while and play the organ for people to sing to. Or she'd sing when Mr. Delaney would play his mandolin."

"Who is Mr. Delaney?"

"Mr. Clay Delaney. He's a teacher at the high school, and he boards here. A very nice gentleman."

Kathleen smoothed back her hair and looked away. Hilda smiled to herself. So Kathleen had an eye for one of the boarders, did she? Well, that was normal. And Delaney sounded like an Irish name. Very suitable.

Stray thoughts about the problems looming ahead for her and Patrick sought her attention. She brushed them away.

"Did Mr. Delaney like Miss Jacobs?"

"No more than he liked anyone else. He's poor, too. Never even paid much attention to Miss Lewis." Kathleen spoke with great satisfaction, and then blushed when she caught Hilda's eye.

This time Hilda smiled outright. "You like Mr. Delaney, do you not?"

Kathleen scowled. "I know I'm thinkin' outside me station in life. But a cat can look at a king."

"At least he is Irish, and you are Irish. That is better than a Swede marrying an Irishman, but I am going to marry Patrick Cavanaugh."

Kathleen's mouth dropped open, and then she smacked her forehead. "And him me fourth cousin once removed, and I never thought about it bein' you! Well, fancy that!" She looked at Hilda with frank curiosity.

"You wonder what he sees in me," said Hilda. "I wonder, too, sometimes. I am not at all like a pretty Irish lass. But—" she shrugged "—we go well together. So you see, anything can happen."

A dreamy look came into Kathleen's eyes.

Hilda saw it and hurried back into questions. "Kathleen, the newspapers say Miss Jacobs acted afraid of someone, or something, the last few days of her life. Do you know anything about that?"

"Now you mention it, miss—"

"You had better call me Hilda, if we are to be cousins."

"Hilda, then," said Kathleen with a broad grin, "I did see somethin' like that, though I didn't think nothin' of it at the time. It was about a week before it happened. She had come from school a bit before supper time. School lets out at four, you know, and the teachers are supposed to stay until five at least to get their work done. Sometimes it was a lot later for Miss Jacobs. She worked hard. It's no wonder the kids loved her.

"Anyway, this day—it would have been about the first week of school after the Christmas holidays, and I guess there wasn't quite as much work to do as later—she came in about quarter past five, and supper isn't till six, so she sat in the parlor with some of the other boarders, talkin' and readin' the evenin' papers, and at maybe a quarter to six someone knocked on the door. I was vexed, because I was just rushin' to get to the kitchen and help with the dishin' up, and I was late, and I knew Mrs. O'Leary'd skelp me. But Mrs. Gibbs was upstairs, so I had to answer the door, and it was a man wantin' to know about boardin' here.

"I let him in, o' course, for it was perishin' cold outside, but I had to tell him it was no good, we were full up. So we stood and talked a minute in the hall, and after I'd showed him out, Miss Jacobs came up to me, and bless me if she wasn't tremblin.' 'Who was that?' she says, all nervous-like. So I says it was just some man, and she wanted to know what he looked like and how old he was, and all. I told her I hadn't noticed, and then I rushed back to the kitchen, and Mrs. O'Leary was in such a state I forgot all about it till I read that in the paper about her bein' scared."

"Did you really not notice, or did you just say that because you were in a hurry?"

"Well, I don't know, and that's the truth. I've tried and tried to remember anything about him, but all I can say is, he was a man. Well, a gentleman; at least he talked like one."

"Do you remember what kind of overcoat he had on?"

"After all this time? He had one, or he'd have died of the cold, but all I know is, it was bundled up around him, and no wonder."

"All bundled up. Did he wear a scarf?"

"I can't remember, I tell you! I've tried till me head aches!"

"Try again," Hilda insisted. "Close your eyes. Yes, good. Now you are in the hall, and you are late, and Mrs. O'Leary will be angry at you. There is a knock on the door. You do not want to stop and answer it, but you do. Can you see yourself opening the door?"

"Ye-es," said Kathleen doubtfully.

"Who is at the door?"

Kathleen seemed to stare intently with her closed eyes. "I can't hardly see nothin'. It's nearly six, and it's dark."

"Is there a lamp in the hall?"

"Yes, and it's lit, for I just lit it myself."

"So when the man comes in, you can see him."

Kathleen opened her eyes. "But that's just what I can't do," she said. "I remember now, he was so bundled up in hat and coat and scarf, I couldn't hardly see his face at all. Only his nose and eyes, and don't ask me what color they was, for I didn't take the time to notice."

"So you see, you did remember," said Hilda. "It is a good trick, that, closing the eyes and trying to be back where you were."

"But it didn't do no good, for I still can't tell you anything about him."

"You have told me one thing, and it is very important. You have told me that his face could not be seen. Could it be, do you think, that he did not want anyone to see it?"

*...the mysterious tall man who disap-
peared the morning after the murder
without settling his bill.*

—South Bend *Tribune*
February 5, 1904

13

HILDA COULD THINK of no further questions to put to Kathleen, so she left after securing her firm promise to let her, Hilda, know if anything else came to mind or if anything important happened. Hilda was well satisfied with her work so far. She had learned a few things, though she wasn't sure how helpful they would be. She had also established a secure foothold at Mrs. Gibbs's. Kathleen would be a faithful reporter.

The day had warmed a little. Perhaps the January thaw would begin soon. Hilda welcomed the idea of warmer weather, but she hated the thought of the mess. The streets in the part of town where her family lived were not paved, and when the snow and ice melted, the frozen ruts turned into furrows of mud and horse manure. A woman had to raise her skirts high if she were to cross the street without soiling her clothes.

The streets in the downtown area, however, were all paved, and though they had begun to turn slushy, they were navigable. In front of the fine Oliver Hotel they had been shoveled clean, and as Hilda neared the hotel she saw Erik and another boy leaning on shovels, talking.

"Did you do all this?" she said, when she had crossed the beautifully clean street.

"Well," said Erik, "Andy did most of it. I helped, though."

"You did a very good job, both of you. It is nice to see you, Andy." For Andy was an old friend. A year or two older than Erik, he had helped him out of a number of scrapes and a few instances of serious trouble. "But you are not in school? Or no, it is not open."

"High school's open. Just Colfax is closed still. But I'm finished with school," said Andy. "I'm fifteen. I work here at the hotel now, and for good money, too." He held his head a little higher, and Hilda realized his jaunty round cap was part of a bellboy's uniform.

"But that is fine! Your family must be very proud of you."

Andy shuffled his feet. "My ma is."

Hilda shot Erik a look. He glowered at her. She nodded. She would ask him later about Andy's father. So many immigrant families were without one parent, the other lost to disease or accident or, in some cases, to drunkenness or even jail. America was not, for many of her new residents, all that they had hoped.

Erik spoke. "Hilda, we've found out a lot! I was waitin' for you to come. What took you so long?"

"I, too, have learned things. But it is too cold out here to talk about them. Andy, is there a place where we could go to talk?"

"Sure thing! I've got an office!"

He led them into the hotel to a cubicle behind the front desk. Few of the hotel's luxurious appointments could be seen here, but the floor was of marble and the electric light fixture was shaded with beautiful amber glass.

Andy pointed to the three wooden chairs taking up most of the space in the tiny room. "See, this is where us bellboys wait until we're needed. The others are busy now, I guess, and if a bell rings I'll have to go, but this is mostly a slow time. The guests as was leavin' early has left, and them that's leavin' late are havin' their breakfast, and nobody much comes in before afternoon. So unless there's somethin' else for me to do, like Erik and me just cleaned the street, I'm a gentleman of leisure." He gestured grandly. "Take a seat."

They shed their outer garments and sat. Erik got straight to the point. "Tell her about the man."

"Well." Andy sat down, wrapped his legs around the front

legs of the chair, and took a deep breath. "Erik says he's told you about the guy who skipped out."

Hilda frowned.

"Left without paying," said Erik impatiently. "Go *on,* Andy. Get to the good part."

"Well, see, I was the one took care of him when he came in. A week ago today, that'd be."

"What did he look like?" asked Hilda, interrupting.

Andy shrugged. "Ordinary. Rich. He had on good clothes."

"I don't mean his clothes. His face, eyes, hair?"

"Didn't notice much. Oh, except he had a mustache. Sort of orangey-colored." He waited for Hilda to ask other questions. She tucked away the satisfying detail of the mustache and nodded for him to go on.

"Well, he come in just about supper time, but he didn't want no supper. Not then, anyway. Just wanted to go up to his room. So I took him up in the elevator and carried his valise for him. A good piece of leather, and not worn much. You can tell a lot about customers by their bags. This fella looked rich, like I said. Not just the valise, but a nice suit, nice overcoat, expensive shoes. He'd just had a shine, too, at the station prob'ly."

"Which station?" Hilda asked, leaning forward eagerly.

"Dunno. Coulda been any of 'em. I tried to get him talkin' some. Mostly if you can get 'em to talk to you, you get a bigger tip, and I reckoned this fella had lots of money to give away. Well, he gave me a quarter, all right, but he didn't want to talk. So I just figgered he was tired, and maybe if I was the one to take him down again when he left, I'd get more. He was gonna stay a week, so I'd have lots of chances to see him around, tip my hat to him, maybe take messages. Little things like that, we're supposed to do 'em anyways, 'cause this is a swell hotel."

"Classy," Erik interpreted in response to Hilda's furrowed brow. "Elegant."

"So you coulda knocked me over with a feather when I went up to his room with a message on Wednesday morning, and he was gone. Bag an' all. I figgered maybe he was in a hurry, like, and didn't want to wait for help. Didn't need it, really, the valise wasn't real heavy. But it was kinda funny, all the same, 'cause he was on the fourth floor, and mostly people want to take the elevator—and who would've run it for him?

"So that's why I said somethin' to the manager, and that's when I found out the fella'd skipped out. Owed the hotel twelve dollars, 'cause he'd had one o' the best rooms and he ate dinner here both nights. Well, that's a lot of money, so the manager, he was riled, and he sent a telegram to the police in Fort Wayne, the fella's hometown. And come to find out there's no such address in the town, and no such person!"

Hilda's eyes grew big. "But Andy, what—?"

The bell at the front desk rang in clamorous summons. Someone shouted, "Front!" Andy jumped up.

"Gotta go. Don't know where the other boys are. Wait here." He ran out the door.

Hilda stood up and began to pace. "Erik, this could be very important! Do the police know about this?"

Erik shrugged. "I guess they know about the guy skippin' out and givin' a made-up name."

"And what are they doing about it?"

He just looked at her.

"Oh. You would not know, of course. But they should be trying to trace this man!"

"I guess they are. But they don't know everything." Erik had a sly grin on his face.

"Erik Johansson! Do you mean there is something Andy is hiding from the police? That is very, very serious."

"Not hiding exactly. He doesn't like the police. And they never asked him anything."

Hilda remembered Andy's dislike of the police. It was mutual. When he was a little younger Andy had run with a rowdy gang of boys whom the police tended to blame for most small crimes in the city. Some of the group, Hilda knew, did in fact stoop to petty theft now and again, but most of them were decent kids, immigrants trying to get along in a strange and sometimes hostile environment.

"But what does he know that he hasn't told?"

"It's just something he found. It may not mean anything." And Erik refused to say any more until Andy returned.

Meanwhile Hilda had taken time to organize her thoughts, and the first question she asked when Andy stepped into the room was the one she had started before he left. "Andy, what was the message you tried to deliver to—what was the name he gave?"

"Perkins. Mr. Harold Perkins. And I dunno what it was. The desk clerk gave it to me, sealed in an envelope, said to take it up to room four-seventeen. And when he wasn't there, I took it back to the desk."

"Does the desk clerk still have it?"

"I think he gave it to the manager, on account of it might have told who Mr. Perkins really was, or where he was from, or some way to get him to pay his bill."

"Then I must talk to the manager. Now, Andy, Erik says you found something that might be important. Why have you not taken it to the police?"

Andy's expression changed from affable to defiant. "Don't want nothin' to do with the police."

"Yes, but—oh, never mind. Will you show it to me?"

He reached into the pocket of his tight-fitting trousers. A handkerchief, a piece of string, some lint, several coins, and a dirty, ragged scrap of paper appeared. He handed Hilda the paper and stuffed the rest back into the pocket.

She looked at it with distaste, holding it with thumb and one finger. "What is it?"

"It's a piece of a train ticket. I found it on the floor of his room. I reckon maybe it'd stuck to the bottom of his shoe, and that's how it got so dirty. That's another reason I didn't say anything about it, see. It might not have anything to do with him, just somethin' he happened to step on."

Hilda looked more closely at the repellent object, with Erik peering over her shoulder. Under close scrutiny she could make out parts of a few words: *ary 1904* it read at the top end, *ia RR* in the middle, and *apolis* at the bottom.

"This month's ticket," said Erik.

"And the Vandalia Railroad," said Hilda. "But what's *apolis?*"

"Indianapolis, of course," Erik replied with scorn. He had recently learned to spell the name of the state capital.

"But the Vandalia Railroad doesn't go there."

"It does now," said Andy. "I heard some men talking about it at the hotel. I didn't understand it all, but the Pennsylvania line bought up a lot of little railroads, only in Indiana they call it the Vandalia, and it goes to a lot of places it didn't use to. Now you can go straight to Indianapolis from here."

"Then this man is from Indianapolis!" said Hilda triumphantly.

"If the ticket belonged to him," said Andy.

"How many people live in Indianapolis?" asked Erik.

"A lot," Hilda answered. She was deflating rapidly. "I don't know, but many, many more than in South Bend. A hundred thousand, maybe?"

The three looked at each other. Hilda sighed. "We will have to find him some other way. Did you find anything else in the room, Andy?"

He shook his head. "It was clean. He'd even made the bed."

"Or never slept in it, maybe. Did you talk to the maid?"

"Mr. James did. He's the manager. I guess she didn't see anything unusual. Or anything with his real name on it."

"What is her name?"

"Nellie. I dunno her last name. She's Polish." Andy was German. There was a hint of condescension in his voice.

"Is she working today?"

"Dunno. The maids work six days a week, but they've got different days off, see, 'cause somebody's got to be on duty all the time."

"Yes, well, I will have to find her. That will be my job. A maid can talk to a maid. You, Andy, and you, Erik, you will try to find out where the man who called himself Mr. Perkins went while he was in South Bend. He came to the hotel when, Andy—at what time on the Monday, I mean?"

"Near supper time, like I said. Six, maybe? Somewhere around then. I remember 'cause I was just about to go off duty."

"From six last Monday evening, then, until he left town— well, I suppose on the first train to Indianapolis on Wednesday. I can ask at the Vandalia station."

"We'll do that, miss," said Andy. "And I'll ask all the boys who work at the hotel what they seen. And Erik can try to follow the trail."

"Yes, that is good," said Hilda with a sharp little nod. "But remember. Report what you find to me. Do *not* try to catch the man yourself, somehow. He is probably a murderer. Do you understand?"

They nodded solemnly, but there was a strong current of excitement in the room. With deep misgivings, Hilda stood to leave, just as two boys rushed into the room, wearing the same uniform as Andy.

"We had to unpack a trunk for a rich old lady," one of them said. "It took a long time and she was really particular and she only gave us a dime each!"

"Never mind," said Andy grandly. "There's something much more important for you to do now."

Hilda shook her head and left the room.

She had no trouble finding the manager, nor did she find him uncooperative, once she had told him who she was and what she was trying to find out. "Believe me, miss," he said, gesturing her to a seat in his office, "I want to find that man as much as the police do. I don't know if he's a killer, but he's for sure a thief, and I want him caught. But I've told the police all I know."

"I wondered if you still have the message that was left for him."

"Some message!" He reached into his desk drawer, pulled out an envelope, and tossed it across the desk to Hilda. The envelope had the hotel's name and address in the upper left-hand corner. It had been slit open; she pulled out the contents, three sheets of stiff, expensive hotel stationery.

"But—I do not understand. There is no message here, only stationery with nothing written on it."

"And that's all there was when I opened it. Now, who would go to the trouble of leaving an envelope full of blank paper for a man who was already gone?"

14

The sheriff believes that the finding of this man will go a long way toward solving the mystery.

—South Bend *Tribune*
February 5, 1904

HILDA SHOOK HER HEAD. "I do not know. It is foolish. And it gives us no clue to who the man is, or where he lives. Unless—maybe he knows one of the people who work for the hotel? Because of the paper." She gave the envelope back.

The manager shook his head. "Anyone could get that stationery. It's available in all the bedrooms and in the writing desks in the lounges. Anyone could come in off the street and pull a stunt like this." He threw the envelope onto his desk.

"Oh." Hilda sat back, discouraged. "Well, do not throw it away. I may think of something. Also, I need to talk to the maid who served Mr. Perkins while he was here. Andy says her name is Nellie."

"And that's another thing!" said Mr. James, throwing up his hands in disgust. "Seems like there's no limit to what can go wrong in a hotel. Nellie hasn't come in today, so the other maids are having to do extra duty. Fortunately the hotel isn't full, so we'll manage, but she'll find herself without a job when she does show up. If she's sick she should've sent a note."

"Perhaps she cannot write English," suggested Hilda, ever sympathetic to immigrants.

"Possible, I suppose. But she could've sent someone to tell us."

"If you will give me her address, sir, I will talk to her and find out what is the matter. Has she been a good worker until now?"

"One of the best, my housekeeper tells me. Reliable, works hard, never complains. Of course, her English isn't so good, but that doesn't matter much. She hardly ever has to talk to a hotel guest."

"Then please give her another chance. It is not so easy to get a good job, and I do not think she would risk hers without a good reason. I will find her and then tell you what has happened."

"And how's that going to help me get my money back?" he demanded.

"That is why I want to talk to her." Hilda held onto her patience. "She may know something she has not told. If she cannot speak English well, it would be hard for her, maybe. Or maybe she has remembered something since you talked to her."

"And I suppose you speak Polish?"

"No, but I have friends who do." She stood. She was growing tired of this man. "May I have the address, please?"

Mr. James grinned. "Might as well, I suppose. You're a determined young woman, aren't you?"

Hilda lifted her chin. "Yes, sir. That is why I am good at what I do."

"Hmm. And pretty, too. You ever want to change jobs, you come to me. I could use a bright go-getter like you."

Hilda simply nodded. She couldn't afford to offend the man, but her temper was rising.

The manager took her to the front desk, told the clerk to direct her to the housekeeper's office, and finally went back to his own work. Hilda breathed a sigh of relief and found the housekeeper, who gave her Nellie's address. "And I hope she's all right, I'm sure," said the woman. "It's not like her to miss work, and it's been several days, now."

"Several days! Mr. James only said today."

The housekeeper sighed. "It's been since the middle of last week. She worked the late shift on Tuesday. That'd let her off at close to midnight. I worry about girls like her walkin' home that late at night, but the trolley goes close to her house. Then her day off was Wednesday, but she never came in on Thursday and I haven't seen her since. I let it go till today. She has troubles at home—her mother has the rheumatics somethin' fierce and gets sick a lot. I hated to tell Mr. James, but when it went into a new week, I had to. It's over my dead body he'll fire her, though. She'll have a good reason for bein' away. She's a good worker, and they're not so easy to get nowadays."

Neither Andy nor Erik was in sight when Hilda left the hotel. She hesitated for a moment and then decided they were both old enough to look after themselves. Mama might baby Erik, but Hilda didn't intend to. She had work to do.

The sun was high in the sky. Hilda walked through increasingly thick mud toward the Polish part of town. Most of the Poles lived in a section of the west side not far in distance from Tippecanoe Place. In character it might have been a different world. The streets were unpaved, the houses tiny and close together. The snow here was left to be trodden into ice or slush. Most of the residents made heroic efforts to keep their curtains and their children clean, but they had no money to paint the houses, and the landlords didn't bother. Some people had given up the struggle. Gray rags hung at the windows, and in summer one could see filthy, half-starved children playing in the streets.

Hilda was struck, as always when she came here, with a mixture of pity and fury. How could employers pay their workers so little? And why did these women go on having baby after baby, ruining their health and stretching family finances to the breaking point and beyond?

Hilda thought of her conversation with Norah. The memory bought a hot flush to her cheeks. Perhaps these women did not know that there were ways to avoid huge families. Someone should tell them.

But they were all Catholic. And the Church forbade such practices. And when she married Patrick...well, she and Patrick would have to talk seriously one day.

She found the house number she was seeking, negotiated the muddy path, and knocked firmly on the door.

A woman opened it. Her gray hair was tied back with a cotton scarf, once printed in gay colors, now faded and patched, but clean. She wore a black dress with many petticoats and a white apron—darned, its lace missing, but again, spotless. Her figure was stooped and bent, and she moved with difficulty.

Her expression, eager when she opened the door, faded at once. *"Tak?"* she said.

Hilda remembered, too late, about the language problem. Did *"tak"* mean yes?

"Do you speak English?" she asked, without much hope.

The woman shook her head and unleashed a torrent of Polish, of which Hilda understood not a word except the repeated "Nelka."

Nelka. Nellie? "Nellie. Is she here?" Hilda gestured, hoping she was understood.

More Polish, accompanied by tears and gesticulations. The woman shook her head vigorously from time to time and lifted her arms and shoulders in the universal "I don't know" gesture.

"Nellie not here?" said Hilda, using gestures of her own to try to convey her meaning.

It became apparent that Nellie was not at home, and that the woman, her mother presumably, was upset.

"I come back," said Hilda, pointing to herself, then away from the house, then back to the house.

The woman looked confused.

"Do not worry. I will be back." On impulse Hilda put a hand in her pocket. It was difficult, wearing mittens, but she pulled out a few coins and gave them to the woman. "For you. I will be back."

She fled as fast as she could before she could see if the woman took offense.

Something was seriously wrong. That was apparent. Hilda needed to find one of her bilingual Polish friends and come back as soon as she could. But lunch was becoming an urgent matter, and home was nearer than any of the other places she needed to go, so she slipped and slid back to the neighborhood where there were paved streets and sidewalks that were always kept clear. She scraped her boots carefully at the back door. Mrs. Sullivan would not take kindly to mud on the floor.

The midday meal for servants and family had been served and cleared away, and the house lay in the lethargy of early afternoon. Some of the dailies were at work, but the live-in servants were taking their well-earned rest. Hilda found some bread and butter and cold ham in the larder and made herself a sandwich.

She ate it in the servants' room, sitting at the table with its spotlessly clean cloth. The fire in the grate burned with a cheerful warmth. The clock on the mantel ticked. The only other sounds were the snores of Mr. Williams's bulldog, asleep on the hearth, and the gentle creaks and groans of a great house at peace.

Hilda sighed, tidied up after her quick meal, and then tiptoed up to her room to change her clothes.

Elsa was asleep on Hilda's bed, but she woke when Hilda came in.

"Oh! I didn't expect you until supper time!"

"Shh!" said Hilda. "Speak quietly. I do not want to wake the household. How did your work go this morning, my sister?"

"We-ell—I don't like that Janecska. She got mad at me when I couldn't say her name right, and then she tried to make fun of me to the other girls. But they didn't like that any more than I did, so she stopped. The work isn't hard. Easier than the shirt factory, only I don't know how to do everything."

"You will learn. It is hard when there are big parties, but not too bad most of the time. How is Mr. Williams, did anyone say?"

"No better. But no worse, I guess. Everyone is worried about him. That's funny, Hilda. You always say what a mean man he is."

"He can be. But he can be kind, sometimes. And we have all known him for a long time. We will not say bad things about him while he is ill."

Elsa was glad to change the subject. "So what did you do this morning? Was it exciting?"

"Not very. I will tell you all about it tonight. Rest now, little sister. I will be back before nightfall."

She had better be, she thought. It was not safe out there after dark.

Hilda's best Polish friend was a young policeman, Sergeant Lefkowicz. She had met him on a dreadful occasion when she had discovered a dead body in the shrubbery, and he had been kind and pleasant to her, unlike his boss, who had bullied her. She hurried now to the police station to see if he was on duty.

She hated visiting the station. The men there were often rude to her, and today was no exception, but she had learned to ignore their innuendos and persist in getting what she wanted. Persistence was one of her specialties.

She was out of luck today. Sergeant Lefkowicz was not working. And just what did Hilda want with him anyway? Hadn't they heard she was engaged to that Irishman? Paddy wouldn't take kindly to her going around with a Polack.

And so on. Hilda waited it out and then asked if they knew where the sergeant was, which caused more hilarity. She gritted her teeth and said nothing, but stalked out of the station with the information that she'd probably find him at home.

She had been to the sergeant's house once before, and knew more or less where it was, not far from Nellie's house. Hilda could have saved herself many steps if she had known earlier that Mr. Lefkowicz was at home. She hadn't known, and that was that.

The sergeant wasn't yet married, so he lived at home with his mother. When Hilda walked up, he was busy clearing the front path of snow and mud.

"Why, Miss Johansson! How nice to see you. I'm sorry, my mother is at work right now."

He meant, Hilda understood, that he could not invite her into the house. It would be most improper for them to be alone together, unchaperoned.

"It is all right. I came to ask for your help, if you can come with me. There is a Polish lady I need to speak to, and she speaks no English."

He put aside his broom and wooden shovel and bowed. "I am at your service."

Nellie's house was in the next block. Hilda explained the

situation as they went, and why she needed to talk to Nellie. "Something is wrong, but I could not understand what. I think perhaps Nellie is very ill, in the hospital maybe, but I do not know. The woman we will see is probably her mother. Maybe her grandmother. She looks very old."

"People grow old early when they are poor and worked to death," replied the sergeant soberly.

The woman answered the door of the shabby house at their first knock. Her look of expectation was replaced by one of despair.

Sergeant Lefkowicz spoke a few words, and the woman asked them both in, speaking volubly as they entered.

The sergeant turned to Hilda. "It is more serious than you thought. This lady is Mrs. Chudzik, Nelka's mother. She has been afraid to go to the police—and I have not yet told her that I am a policeman—but Nelka has been missing from home for nearly a week."

For the issuing of a dispensation for a mixed marriage, the Church requires three conditions; that the Catholic party be allowed free exercise of religion, that all the offspring are to be brought up Catholics and that the Catholic party promise to do all that is possible to convert the non-Catholic.

—The Catholic Encyclopedia, 1908

15

H ILDA HAD FEARED THIS, but she gasped. Immediately she was sorry she had let her feelings show. Mrs. Chudzik turned to her and began to speak passionately.

"She says," the sergeant translated after a moment, "that she is afraid the man who goes about killing innocent young girls has murdered Nelka. That is her real name, you understand. She says she thinks you believe that, too, or you would not be so frightened. She pleads that you will do something to find her daughter. I'm going to tell her who I am and that the police will start looking."

Hilda could grasp much of the exchange that followed even though she understood not a word. Mrs. Chudzik was frightened that a policeman was in her house, and protested that she had done nothing. She looked to Hilda for protection, and Hilda tried to reassure her. Gradually the woman became calmer, as Sergeant Lefkowicz spoke quietly and patted her shoulder. Finally she collapsed onto a threadbare sofa and began to sob.

Hilda sat down next to her and took her hand. "Will you tell her, please, that I will do my best to learn what has happened to her daughter? And that I am very, very sorry?"

They sat in that small, bare, painfully clean room and waited for Nelka's mother to compose herself. When the sobs diminished to an occasional sniffle, Sergeant Lefkowicz began gently to question the woman. Slowly, with tears often choking back her words, Mrs. Chudzik answered him. Hilda could guess at the kind of information he was seeking, and itched to ask a few things herself, but the policeman would get on faster if he didn't have to translate as he went. Hilda waited as patiently as she could.

Finally he turned back to Hilda. "Mrs. Chudzik last saw her daughter on Wednesday of last week."

"But that is the day after—"

"Yes. That is one reason she is so worried. It seems that Nelka was assigned to the late shift at the hotel on the day before, the Tuesday, so didn't have to report for work until three-thirty in the afternoon. She was in a particularly good mood that morning, her mother says, smiling and laughing and helping with the housework. Mrs. Chudzik tried to get her to rest, knowing she would have hard work to do later at the hotel, but Nelka was happy to help. They are very poor, Miss Johansson—Mr. Chudzik died years ago and there is little income—but they are proud and like to keep things as nice as they can."

"I can see that." Hilda glanced at the crocheted doilies on the couch, at the hooked rug on the floor, at the curtains, so darned and mended that there was little of the original fabric left. She looked back at Mrs. Chudzik's gnarled and swollen hands and understood what pain had gone into the desperate attempt at respectability.

"So Nelka came home Tuesday night, and on Wednesday, her day off, she helped around the house again. But Wednesday afternoon she said she had to go out. She seemed excited about something, and she told her mother not to worry if she was late getting back. That is the last Mrs. Chudzik has seen of her."

"Did you ask her about the man at the hotel, the one who left without paying? Did Nellie—Nelka say anything about him?"

"I did ask her. She said that Nelka had talked about a rich man who gave her a big tip, but she said nothing more about him. It was not yet generally known that he had disappeared, you understand, the last time Nelka talked to her mother."

"And Mrs. Chudzik has heard nothing from Nelka in all that time?"

"She says not. I had the feeling she might not be telling me the truth there, but she insisted. It is certainly true that she is worried and afraid. She is also in desperate need of money for food and other things."

"Would not the people at her church help her? It would be your church, too, would it not?"

"I have never seen her there. There are two Polish churches. I go to Saint Hedwige's. I will ask her." The sergeant spoke again to Mrs. Chudzik. His face grew sad as he listened to her reply.

"She says that she and Nelka attend Saint Stanislaus, and they go always to the earliest Mass, where there are few other people, because they are ashamed of their poor clothes. Yesterday she did not go at all, because she has no shoes that will keep out the snow. Nelka had promised to give her enough money to have them repaired when she was paid on Friday."

Hilda's detective instincts were swamped by pity. She thought for a moment, and then said, "Ask her if Mr. Chudzik, when he was alive, if he worked at Studebaker's."

The woman's answer did not have to be translated, or not entirely. She nodded emphatically, said, *"Tak"* several times, and added some comments.

Sergeant Lefkowicz said, "Well, you heard. Her husband did work there, and times were good then, she said. They lived in a better house and had enough money. Nelka was only a baby when he died. He was killed when a stack of lumber fell on him at the factory, and ever since, things have been very bad."

"Does she not get a pension?"

"I asked her. She said she did for a few months. It was only a small amount, but it helped. But then it stopped."

"She used to live in a better house?"

"Yes—oh. You think that when she moved, the company could not find her?"

"I am almost sure of it. When a man dies working at Studebaker's, they give his widow a small pension, I think forever. I will go to Colonel George and find out, but do not tell her, in case I am wrong. Do tell her I will bring her some food and some better shoes. And I may need to talk to her some more."

Sergeant Lefkowicz volunteered to see Hilda home, but she refused. It was still quite light outside and she had many things to do.

"It is not safe, Miss Johansson," he said earnestly. "We do not know who the killer is. He could be anyone, anywhere."

"I will not stay out late, I promise. And I will never be far from home."

"Neither was Miss Jacobs. And Nelka—what has become of her?"

"I think you must go to the police station and tell them what you know. But please, do not tell them I was with you. They will tease, and besides, I do not want the newspapers to tell about me. My family would not like it, and neither would Patrick's."

The sergeant broke into a smile. "Miss Johansson, I have not yet heard the news formally, but may I offer you my congratulations and best wishes? I hope you will both be very happy."

Hilda, blushing, thanked him and went on her way with lighter feet. He, at least, did not see anything impossible about a Swedish Lutheran marrying an Irish Catholic. Maybe things would work out somehow.

How? asked a pessimistic voice inside her.

She ignored it.

Her first problem was to get some immediate help for Mrs. Chudzik. The poor woman needed someone to look after her while her daughter was away. *And maybe forever,* said that same nasty voice. Hilda refused to concede that possibility. They would find Nelka. They had to. Meanwhile she would have to go to the church, St. Stanislaus. But not directly. The priest might not speak English.

Hilda wasn't happy having anything to do with Catholic churches, but she did happen to know the priest at St. Patrick's. He was a nice man who had helped Hilda in a previous investigation. Hilda was comfortable talking to him. She would go to St. Patrick's rectory and see what could be done.

The priest, Father Faherty, was in. His housekeeper, who did not approve of Hilda, was a trifle starchy in her attitude, but

Hilda took no notice. She had learned that a pleasant smile often infuriated people who did not like her, so she smiled very pleasantly indeed and sat down, without being asked, in the best chair in the visitors' parlor.

Father Faherty came in almost at once, beaming his broad Irish smile. "It's a pleasure to see you again, my dear. Mrs. Riley, bring us some tea, if you will be so good." He eased himself into a chair close to the fire. "Ahh! That does feel good. I've been in the church, and it's cold enough to freeze the Old Nick himself, I do believe."

"I think he is not so easily dealt with," Hilda said primly.

"To be sure, to be sure! But it froze *me*, right enough, and it's glad I'll be of that good hot tea. Now, my dear, forgive an old man for his curiosity, but is it wedding plans you'd be wantin' to discuss with me?"

Hilda's heart skipped a beat. It had never entered her head that this kindly old man, at Patrick's own church, would almost certainly be the one who would marry them. At his altar, in his church, amongst all the idolatrous statues, in an ancient language she didn't know...

For a moment fear paralyzed her and she couldn't speak.

"I'm sorry," said the priest gently. "I've disturbed you. Forgive me, child. I forgot for a moment that you might be a bit apprehensive about your marriage. I should not have said anything."

"No—it is all right," she said faintly. "I am only—we have not yet begun to plan—oh, I do not know what we are to do!"

And she astonished herself by bursting into tears.

When she had cried herself out, the priest smiled gently. "Would you like to wash your face, my dear?"

Hilda was completely demoralized. She allowed herself to be led away by the grim housekeeper to a small bathroom, where she washed her face in cold water and tried to arrange her hair back into some order. When she returned, she felt a little better.

"I did not mean to do that, sir. I do not know why I—"

"I think I know why," Father Faherty said quietly. "Ah, thank you, Mrs. Riley. I'll pour out. You needn't stay."

The housekeeper left an almost visible aura of disapproval behind her. The priest ignored it. He poured the tea, added three lumps of sugar and a dollop of milk to Hilda's, and handed it to her with a cookie on the saucer.

"Now then. Drink that while it's hot. You need the warmth and the sugar. You're tired, I think, and upset. Have you become embroiled in this latest tragedy in our community?"

"Yes. I was asked to talk to people. Mr. Barrett thinks that the police suspect him and are not doing enough to find the real killer. He came to me for help. I did not want to do it, but he is a nice man, and he is old. And now I have discovered that there is another girl missing, and—oh! I came to you to see if you could find help for her mother!"

"We'll talk about that in a little while. For now, I want to know about your plans to marry Patrick Cavanaugh. I think you're frightened at the idea of marrying a Catholic, more frightened than you need be. May we talk about it?"

Hilda suddenly felt she could trust this man, even though he represented an alien faith. It all came out: her reluctance to step inside a Catholic church, her fears about what her family would say and do, her dread of being required to abandon her own faith. All the ignorant superstitions she had ever heard came to the fore.

Father Faherty sat and listened and nodded from time to time. When Hilda had poured out all her doubts and worries, he sat back in his chair. "Now, my dear, I must tell you that the Church is not in favor of a marriage between a Catholic and a Protestant."

"I know that!"

"Yes, but I am required to tell you. Nor is your church in favor of such a marriage. No—" He held up his hand as she began an angry protest. "Let me finish. It is my duty to point out to you the obstacles to such a marriage, but from what you have told me today, I know that you are aware of the problems. I have known you for some time, and so I also believe that you and Patrick will go ahead with this marriage, no matter what I or anyone else says."

He looked at her steadily. She held his gaze. "Yes, sir. We have decided."

"And in that case, the Church would far rather you be married according to its laws than in some entirely civil ceremony, or by your own pastor."

Again Hilda opened her mouth to speak; again he silenced her. "Now, then. I know that you are a Christian. I assume that you have been baptized?"

"Of course!"

"Then I can participate in your wedding. The rule is that you must be married by Patrick's parish priest—by me, in other words—in front of at least two witnesses." He stopped.

Hilda blinked. "Are those the only rules?" She had expected a much longer list.

The priest nodded. "Almost the only rules. You cannot be married in a Nuptial Mass, of course, since that involves partaking of communion. And you must promise to allow Patrick to continue to go to Mass, and to bring up your children in the Catholic faith. Patrick must promise to do his best to convert you to the Church."

Hilda frowned. The priest sighed. "Yes, well, he is stubborn, too. We only ask that he do his best."

"And I do not have to go to your church for the wedding? And I do not have to become a Catholic?"

"No. In fact, if you would care to be married in Patrick's home, that would be a solution to one problem, would it not?"

"It is too small for his family, but I do not know if they would want to come, anyway. Many of them do not like me. I do not even know if my own family will come. They do not all like Patrick."

"Those, of course, are some of the problems you will face, my dear."

"I had thought," she said hesitantly, "if, perhaps, after you married us, I might ask my own—"

"My dear child," said Father Faherty in a hurry, "if you are about to ask me if your own pastor may also conduct a marriage service for you and Patrick, please don't. For I would be obliged to tell you that such a thing is not permitted. But of course, if I know nothing about it, there is nothing I can do, is there?"

Hilda smiled, dabbed once more at her cheeks with her soggy handkerchief, and sat up straighter. "I understand, sir. I will tell you nothing that you do not want to know. It is not so bad as I feared. I think we can do those things, and my family will not be so angry, nor Patrick's family, neither. I thank you, sir."

He smiled. "Good. Of course I'll want to talk with you and Patrick together, but I think we've dealt with most of the issues. Now, you mentioned earlier that you needed help for someone?"

"Oh! I am ashamed, sir. I have talked about myself, and I came to ask you for help for Mrs. Chudzik."

She detailed the circumstances in the Chudzik family. Father Faherty shook his head sadly. "There are all too many cases of such poverty in South Bend. I cannot believe that her priest, Father Marciniak, knows of this. The parish is not wealthy, but I know that the parishioners will do what they can to help this poor woman."

"I did not go to him, sir, because I do not know if he speaks English, and I do not speak Polish."

"He speaks some English, but don't disturb yourself, child. I'll see that he hears about this. What can have happened to the daughter? You don't think she has become a victim of the same man who attacked Miss Jacobs!" He made the sign of the cross.

Hilda shook her head wearily. "I do not know what to think. I fear very much for her, but if she were dead, her body would have been found, I think. It has been a week, nearly."

"There is—I hesitate to say such a dreadful thing, but there is the river."

"Yes." There was nothing more to say. Hilda rose. "Please tell Father Marciniak that I will take some food to Mrs. Chudzik, and some better shoes. Mrs. Studebaker will agree to that, I think. And I will try to get her pension back, but I cannot promise that. And then I will try to learn more about who is doing these terrible things."

"Take time to rest a little now and then, my dear. You're working very hard for other people, but you must also look after yourself. There is Mr. Cavanaugh to think about, remember, and he'll be in a fine taking if you work and worry yourself to a frazzle."

"I will not become a frazzle," Hilda assured him. "And thank you, sir. You have been very good to me."

She curtseyed to him, and the housekeeper, sour-faced, let her out. Hilda returned a cold look. She would show respect to the priest, for he was old and a parson, and he had treated her well. But she would defer to no housekeeper!

The early winter twilight had fallen when Hilda left the rectory. The back drive of Tippecanoe Place was only two blocks away, but she had met danger in that short distance once before. She walked as fast as she dared on the brick sidewalk, frozen and treacherous again now that the sun had set, and tried to look ahead and behind at the same time in the thickening gloom. Tall spruces and firs in front yards cast even darker shadows, tossed furiously in the icy wind that had sprung up.

Her heart stopped when a hand gripped her arm.

*…the finger of unjust suspicion
pointed toward honest and
upright men…*

—South Bend *Tribune*
February 5, 1904

S HE SCREAMED. IT WAS only a small scream, for her breath had left her.

The hand immediately loosed its hold. "I'm so sorry, Hilda. That was very foolish of me. I should have realized that I would frighten you. I did call out, but the wind is so strong, you must not have heard me. I took your arm because I was afraid you would fall. Please forgive me."

Hilda recognized the soft voice of Mr. Barrett. She struggled to control her voice. "No, sir. I did not hear you. You should not be out, sir, in this weather. You are not well, and you will get pneumonia like Mr. Williams if you are not more careful."

"I've been out only a moment, my dear. I was visiting a friend nearby. May I see you home?"

Hilda's hesitation was only momentary. "You should not take the trouble, sir."

"No trouble. I wanted to talk to you, in any case. Shall we?"

He offered his arm and she took it. There was certainly no reason to be afraid of this gentle man. He had taken her arm only as a courtesy. He was lame, and ill. He would do her no harm. Certainly not.

His grip on her arm had been strong.

She could scream now, if she had to. Her breath had come back. Moving slowly, adapting her usual brisk pace to his halting one, she allowed Mr. Barrett to guide her down the street. But when he would have moved past the back drive, she demurred.

"It is quicker to go this way, sir, and with your leg, you should not walk farther than you need."

She led him to the porte-cochere entrance and let him in. The doors were not yet locked, and although she was always supposed to use the basement door, she felt that an exception could be made in this case.

Her sigh as she stepped inside was not a sigh of relief. Or if it was, it was only because she was glad to be in a warm place. She had not been frightened. Her heart was beating fast only because of the cold and the wind. That was all.

She led him to the library. "I will tell Colonel Studebaker that you are here, sir. And I will go down and get you something warm to drink. A cup of coffee? Or tea? Or perhaps cocoa?"

"Thank you, my dear. A cup of nice, hot tea would be most welcome."

He sat down slowly, carefully, in one of the luxuriously padded leather armchairs. The chandelier overhead glowed with the soft warmth of gaslight. The fire burned brightly.

Hilda looked at the comfortable room and the weary old man in the chair and chided herself. What harm could there be in such a frail old gentleman? She went to Colonel George's office to inform him he had a caller, and then on down to the kitchen to make some tea.

When she came back to the library a few minutes later, Colonel George was deep in conversation with Mr. Barrett, and Hilda was faced with a dilemma. Mr. Barrett had called, he said, to talk to her. She received callers in the servants' room downstairs. Clearly she could not take a gentleman, a friend of the Studebakers, down there. Nor could she intrude on a private conversation. With a tray in her hands, she was in the role of servant. She had put three cups on the tray, but could she sit down and drink the hot tea she badly wanted, with Colonel George in the room?

Her status was changing. Soon she would not be a servant, though Colonel George didn't know that yet. The rules would have to be bent. She sailed into the room, set the tray on the table, and poured out three cups.

"May I sit down, sir? Mr. Barrett said he wished to talk to me."

"Yes, certainly. He was just telling me he startled you a few minutes ago."

"Yes, sir, but he did not mean to." She handed the two men their tea and then sat primly on the edge of a chair, her own cup on the table beside her. "I did not hear him. How may I help you, Mr. Barrett?"

"It's early days, I know, but have you anything to report to me? My wife grows more and more anxious."

"Well, sir, I have learned much today, but I do not know if any of it will be a help, yet." She took a deep breath. The day seemed to have lasted for weeks, so much had happened.

Her tea had grown cold by the time she finished relating all she had found out. The stories about Miss Jacobs and her fears, Miss Lewis and her illness. She could not quite bring herself to mention the suspicions about Miss Lewis's absence, but from the hints she supplied, she thought perhaps the gentlemen understood. Then there was the mysterious man who left the Oliver Hotel in such an unorthodox manner, and most sinister of all, the disappearance of Nelka Chudzik. "And sir, her mother is in dire poverty," she finished, turning to Colonel George. "Nelka's wages were nearly all they had to live on, and now that she is gone, there is nothing. Do you think Mrs. George would allow me to take her some food, and perhaps some shoes? Hers have such holes in them that she cannot walk outside in the snow, and so cannot go to church." The last remark was almost sure to open Colonel George's heart and hand. The family were devout churchgoers.

"Of course, of course. Take what you need from the kitchen, and here." He pulled some money from his pocket and handed it to her. "Buy the poor woman some shoes. But you say the husband worked at Studebaker's?"

"Yes, sir. He was killed when some lumber fell on him."

"Then she should have a pension."

"Yes, sir, she did have one, but it has stopped. I think it might have been when they had to move to a different house."

"Ah, yes, and the company didn't know the new address. If

the checks came back, they'd have stopped sending them. Well, I'll look into that for you, Hilda. What's the woman's address now?"

"I will leave a note for you in your office, sir. Thank you. She will be very grateful."

"You've a kind heart, Hilda," said Mr. Barrett gently. "When did you say this unfortunate young woman disappeared?"

"It was the afternoon of the day Miss Jacobs's body was discovered, sir."

Mr. Barrett sighed. "And I was alone for much of that day."

With no alibi. He didn't say it, but he didn't need to. "You came here, sir," said Hilda. "I remember. It was in the morning."

"Yes. And the young woman vanished in the afternoon." His voice was heavy.

Colonel George snorted. "Stuff and nonsense, Robert. No one in his right mind would suspect you for a moment. You're not the sort who goes around abducting young servant girls."

Mr. Barrett's face grew even longer. "I wish I could believe that the police will be convinced of that. George, this is killing my wife. There's never been a breath of scandal about our family before, but now her friends are snubbing her. Why, they walked right past her at church yesterday morning, pretended they didn't see her."

"That is not fair, sir!" said Hilda hotly, and then put a hand to her mouth. "Oh, I am sorry, sir. I should not have spoken."

"It's all right, my dear. You're my partner in this, aren't you? Oh, and that reminds me." He, too, reached into his pocket and pulled out some cash. "You may have some expenses. This should be enough to cover them for now. And will you buy the young woman's mother some warm clothing, please? Only don't tell her it comes from me. I wouldn't want anyone to think..."

His voice trailed off.

Hilda rose, collected the tea things, and picked up the tray. "Thank you, sirs. I can do no more today, since it is dark. I will go down and do some of my regular work, Colonel George."

"I'll speak to my wife about that," he replied. "You look tired to death, and the house seems to be running smoothly. Why don't you just get some rest?"

Two people, now, had told her to rest. Two men who knew nothing of backstairs jealousies.

"Thank you, sir," she said, and went downstairs to help with preparations for dinner.

She was tired, she admitted as she helped set the table, stir the fire, fetch and carry and do the bidding of a temporary butler and an irritated cook. Elsa chattered volubly whenever they worked together, but Hilda replied in monosyllables. Her mind was fixed on the things Father Faherty had said and on her investigations. How would Patrick react to the idea of two weddings? And where was Nelka Chudzik? Who killed Miss Jacobs? Who and where was the man from the Oliver Hotel? What kind of wedding gown would she have? Would they be married in the summer?

"Hilda! I've told you three times to dish up the soup! If you're going to dream, don't do it in my kitchen!"

Hilda came back from a world of white satin and rosebuds and drearily ladled soup into the tureen.

She had no chance to sit down until after the family dinner had been served and cleaned up and the servants could at last have their meal. She buttered a piece of bread and then let it drop to the plate, too tired to eat.

"Are you too good for my soup now, girl?" Mrs. Sullivan was still in a temper. "My best cream of chicken, Mrs. Clem's favorite, and you let it sit and get cold."

Hilda was also too tired to argue. She dipped her spoon into the soup, tasted it, and suddenly found herself ravenous.

When she had eaten her fill of Mrs. Sullivan's excellent meal, she sneaked a look at the evening papers. With no butler to take them upstairs, they were still sitting untouched on a table near the back door. There was nothing of real interest in them except a notice of Miss Jacobs's funeral, to be held on Wednesday in Elkhart.

Well, she needed to think of a way to go to that, but not now.

Now she wanted nothing more than to go upstairs and fall into bed, but her Swedish good sense kept her in the kitchen, helping put away the china used by the family, teaching Elsa some of the finer points of her duties.

She finally remembered to ask the cook about Mr. Williams.

"Huh! Took you long enough to ask. He's no better. Delirious an' all. Mrs. George went to see him today, but she couldn't get no sense out of him. The doctor says the crisis will come tonight."

"The—crisis?" Hilda's face turned even paler than usual. She steadied herself with a hand on the kitchen table.

The cook took a good look at her for the first time all evening, and took pity. "Here, girl, sit down before you fall down. You're wore out, I reckon, gallivantin' here an' there all day. The doctor meant he'll take a turn for the better or for the worse tonight. If his fever breaks, he'll be on the mend. We're all prayin' to the blessed saints it'll be that way." Mrs. Sullivan cocked her head and eyed Hilda, whose views on praying to saints were well known.

For once Hilda didn't take the bait. "I, too, will pray," was all she said.

Mrs. Sullivan was alarmed. When Hilda lost her will to argue, she was unwell. "Child, go to bed. Your sister's gettin' along just fine, and we can do without you for a spell. Go on up. We can't have you gettin' sick, too."

Hilda obediently went, and she never knew when Elsa came up and crept into bed.

17

WHEN SHE WOKE, her sister was trying to dress quietly in the dark. The alarm had not sounded, but the hands of the clock still glowed faintly. Hilda stretched a little to see; it was just past five-thirty. "It is all right," she said. "You can light the gas."

Elsa gave a little shriek. "I thought you were asleep!"

"I was, but I am not now. We must speak quietly, but you may have a light."

"I'm scared to. Suppose it exploded in my face."

Making a sound of annoyance, Hilda slipped out of bed, felt for the matches, and lit the gas lamp hanging on the wall. "If you light the match first, and then turn up the gas slowly, there is no chance that it will explode." She reached for her undergarments.

"So you say. Why are you getting up?"

"I am awake. I may as well get up and work."

"I don't need any help."

"Perhaps you do not, but if I want to help, you will allow me, will you not?"

"I guess so. Say, Hilda, have you found out who killed Erik's teacher yet?"

"No." Hilda stepped into her petticoat and buttoned it at the waist. "I have learned some things, but not enough. Elsa, are you happy working here?"

Elsa blinked at the change of subject. "It's all right. I told you yesterday."

"I am glad, because it is safe for you here. You should not be out on the streets at night. Another girl has disappeared."

Elsa sat down on the bed. "No! Tell me!"

"Yes, but finish dressing, and keep your voice down. We must not wake Mrs. Sullivan. She does not rise for another half hour."

Hilda told Elsa about the man at the hotel, and then about Nelka Chudzik. The story lasted all the way down to the main floor. "I do not know what has happened to her, but I am very afraid. There is much I must do today, but I worry about Mama and our sisters. I do not think the police are doing enough to keep them safe."

"Then you must hurry up and find out who the killer is." Elsa stopped at the cleaning closet and got out supplies. She handed Hilda a brush. "And I think you'd better talk to Sven about seeing Mama and the others home. He has friends who would do it."

"That does not protect all the other working girls in town," said Hilda with a sigh.

There was no news at servants' breakfast about Mr. Williams. Everyone ate quietly, not daring to express their hopes or fears. Hilda decided to take a side trip to the hospital as she went about her chores this morning. The first errand, though, was to Mrs. Chudzik with the food Mrs. Sullivan had supplied.

Hilda hadn't thought it necessary to take along an interpreter. Mr. Lefkowicz had told the woman that Hilda would bring some food. Surely she would understand. And surely Hilda could convey by sign language that shoes and other clothing would follow.

As it happened, she was in luck. When she knocked on the door of the pathetic little house, it was opened by a man in a black cassock. Hilda didn't need to ask.

"Good morning. You will be Father Marciniak. I am Hilda Johansson. Do you speak English?"

"A little." He bowed politely to her curtsey. "I take your basket, yes?"

"Yes. It is food for Mrs. Chudzik, from Mrs. Studebaker." She was glad to hand over the basket, heavy with half a ham, eggs, some bacon, flour, butter, sugar, and a few other groceries.

"Oh, is good of you."

"Of Mrs. Studebaker," said Hilda firmly. "She gave the food. I brought it only."

"Yes, yes," said the priest, smiling happily. "I give to Mrs. Chudzik." He gestured Hilda inside and called out in Polish. Immediately Mrs. Chudzik appeared, dressed in what was plainly her best to receive the priest.

She unleashed a torrent of Polish, and then turned anxiously to Father Marciniak.

"She says thank you," he translated.

Hilda smiled. Mrs. Chudzik had said a great deal more than that. "Can you tell her I will bring her some new shoes and some warm clothing later?"

"Please?"

"Shoes." Hilda lifted a foot. "Clothing. A coat." She gestured toward herself. "I will bring soon. From Mr. Studebaker."

"You give shoes?"

Hilda gave it up. "Yes. And a coat. And—do you know what a pension is?"

The priest shook his head helplessly.

"Never mind." She turned to go, and then remembered something Mr. Lefkowicz had said. "Father, has Mrs. Chudzik heard from Nelka? A letter, perhaps?"

But the priest shook his head firmly at that. "No letter. Mrs. Chudzik not read."

"She cannot read? Not even Polish?"

"Not read," he repeated.

There was no point in pursuing it further. The priest either did not understand or was not willing to tell her anything. Hilda wished she knew which.

The January thaw was in full flow today, the air soft, the sun warm. Winter would not give in as easily as this. After so many years in South Bend Hilda knew there were storms to come. But the respite was pleasant—except for the mud.

Now where? She needed to talk to Erik, but first she would call on Mr. Lefkowicz. She wished she knew whether he was at home or at the police station. Probably at the police station. It was unlikely he would have two days off in a row.

He was at the station and came out to see her immediately, quelling his jeering colleagues. "I am sorry, Miss Johansson," he said in an undertone. "They are not bad fellows, but they are rough. And I must go out on patrol soon."

"It does not matter. I cannot stay, either. I want you to tell Mrs. Chudzik, when you have time, that her husband's pension will be coming to her again. Colonel George will see to it. And he gave me money to buy her shoes and clothing. I told the priest that, just now, but I do not know if he understood."

The sergeant beamed at her. "She thinks you are an angel."

"She does not know my temper," said Hilda briskly. "There is one other thing. You said you thought maybe she lied about a message from Nelka?"

"It seemed to me that she hid something from me."

Hilda nodded. "I asked the priest. He said—I think he said—that she could not read, not even Polish. But I am not sure, and I thought maybe he would lie to me, too, if she told him to. Can you try to find out?"

The sergeant stood up a little straighter. "Miss Johansson, I hope one day to be a detective. I will do what I can."

He held out a hand and she shook it, to more derisive cries from his fellows.

The next stop was the hospital. It was several blocks away, but her boots were still dry, though terribly muddy. She wiped them carefully before going in the front door of the imposing brick building.

She had never been in a hospital, and the atmosphere frightened her. It was as hushed as a church but for the busy steps of nurses bustling across the large entrance hallway. They wore veils that reminded her of nuns. But this was a Methodist hospital. Surely there were no nuns here.

Hilda shivered a little. The building was cold, and she had no idea where to go to ask about Mr. Williams.

"May I help you, miss?" The voice came from a sort of booth off to one side of the big room. A woman, not in nurse's uniform, was seated behind an open window.

"Oh! *Ja.* Yes. I want to see Mr. Williams."

"First name?"

Hilda realized that she had no idea. In all the years she had worked under him, it had never occurred to her that the butler had a first name. "I do not know. He is butler at Tippecanoe Place, and he is very ill. I am a maid there, and I worry."

"Oh, yes." The woman consulted a large book that looked like a ledger. "I'm afraid you can't see him."

"Oh—but—can you tell me if he is better?"

"I'm sorry. We can discuss patients only with their families."

Hilda was upset and her temper was rising. She had not walked all this way to be turned out without any information. "I wish to speak to his doctor, then."

"He's busy, and he'll only tell you the same thing. We can't—"

"Why, Hilda! Have you come to ask about Williams?"

It was Mrs. George, clad in furs and wearing a corsage of violets. She looked very feminine in these stark surroundings, and very rich. The rules would surely not apply to such as her.

"Oh, madam, they will not tell me about him! Do you know? Is he—?"

She could not continue. Mrs. George laid a hand on her arm. "I've been up to see him. He's very weak, of course, but his fever has broken and the doctors think he's on the mend."

"Oh, madam—" And then she was in tears, and never afterwards could she have told anyone why she cried.

18

I T WASN'T EVEN MIDMORNING YET when Hilda and Mrs.
Studebaker parted at the hospital, Mrs. Studebaker climbing into her carriage and Hilda walking down Main Street
back toward the center of town. The next thing was to get
a report from Erik, if she could find him.

As it turned out, there was no trouble about that. Her path
took her right past the Oliver Hotel and on impulse she went inside. Andy was in the lobby idling against a pillar. He snapped to
attention when he saw Hilda, and beckoned to her.

"Me an' Erik and the boys've found out some stuff," he whispered, mindful of the hotel traffic bustling about them in the lobby. "I can't talk about it now, though. I'm on duty."

"Where can I find Erik?"

Andy looked vastly disappointed. "I wanted to tell you myself."

Hilda liked boys. She smiled. "I will let Erik tell me his part,
and then I will come back and you can tell me your part. When
are you relieved from duty?"

"I get a half hour off for lunch most days, around twelve."

She made a quick decision. Mrs. Sullivan was probably not expecting her back at any particular time for lunch, and she had
money, lots of money, in her pocket. "I will come at twelve and
we will eat lunch together, if you would like that. I will treat you,
anywhere you like." It could, she thought, almost count as a legit-
imate expense. Andy was one of her sources of information. "But
do you know where Erik might be?"

"I think he was going to the fire station. He reckoned he could get in some extra time with the horses, even if there wasn't any real work for him."

Hilda nodded. "I think he loves those horses more than his family."

Andy grinned. "He says they try to nip him sometimes, but they never try to boss him."

Hilda laughed. "Twelve o'clock. And if you are not ready I will wait."

The prospect of a visit to the fire house was pleasing. Of course, Patrick might not be there. But then again, he might. She quickened her steps.

She was glad, when she got to the stables, to sit down on a bale of hay. She had covered a lot of territory already that morning, and her feet were beginning to protest. The horses whinnied softly as she entered, and Erik's head popped up over the side of a stall.

"Ooh! I hoped you'd come. I've got a lot to tell you. Me and Andy—"

"I have already seen Andy," she said hastily, "and I promised to let *him* tell me the things he learned. And if you will tell me what you learned, I will know everything."

"But that's not fair." Erik came out of the stall and pulled up his favorite bucket for a seat. "He found out a lot more than I did, 'cause he had all the bellboys workin' for him. Anyway we agreed that we would—what did he call it—would pool our information, so everybody'd know everything."

Hilda laughed. She found it easy to laugh this morning, or cry. Something in her had been set free, somehow. "Very well, tell me everything."

"Well—you know Andy was talkin' to all the other boys about where Mr. Perkins went while he was in town?"

"Yes. And did they know?"

"They knew a lot. See, it's like you always say about bein' a maid, how nobody even notices you're there, and they say all kinds of things?"

"Yes. Servants are invisible."

"Well, it's the same with bellboys, only worse 'cause they're kids, and nobody thinks they know nothin'."

"Anything," Hilda corrected. "Hah! Your English is not so wonderful today, is it?"

Erik grinned, but plowed ahead with his story. "Well, so one of the boys—I think it was Dickie, or maybe Joe—"

"Never mind which. Go ahead."

"It was Joe. I remember now. He got off the same time the man left the hotel, and he followed him."

"What day was this?"

"On the Monday, the first day he was there, the man, I mean. So anyway, Joe didn't exackly follow him. He was just going the same direction the man was walking, because that's where he lives, Joe, I mean."

Hilda sighed. Erik's narrative style lacked a certain zest. "Yes, I understand. Go *on*."

"Well, I can't if you keep interrupting me! So he's going down the street, Washington Street, and Joe thinks maybe he's goin' to visit some of the swells as lives that way. 'Cause he's dressed fancy and Joe thinks he's rich, see? So after a few blocks Joe starts followin' him for real."

Hilda frowned. "It would have been dark, if the man only got to the hotel at dinner time."

"It was, Joe said, and cold fit to freeze a person solid. And Joe was hungry, too. But he got to thinkin' it was funny, see, this rich fellow walkin' all that ways when he could have hired a cab easy. And it was still on the way to Joe's house, so he just kept up with him. The man was walkin' fast, he said, but Joe wanted to go fast anyway, bein' so cold and hungry. But then pretty soon he'd passed the Studebaker place, and then even the Oliver place, and he turned right on LaPorte, goin' over toward Colfax. And Joe, he lives near Sven, so he shoulda turned left. But he was real curious by this time, 'cause the man was stoppin' every little while to look behind him, like he thought he was bein' followed."

"He was," Hilda pointed out logically.

"Yeah, but Joe doesn't think he knew that, 'cause Joe, he's good at sneakin' along real quiet, and it was dark. Not blind-dark, see, 'cause there was a moon and snow, but you know what it's like in moonlight. You think you can see pretty good, but things look funny and it's hard to tell what they are. Joe figgered if he just held real still he'd look like a shadow. And it musta worked, too, 'cause the man just kept on goin'. And Hilda, you'll never guess where he ended up!"

Erik's story had caught Hilda's imagination. She forgot to be impatient, but leaned forward eagerly on her bale of hay. "Where?" she whispered.

"At Mrs. Schmidt's roomin' house! And that's where—"

"Where Miss Jacobs lived! What was he doing there?"

"That's the most excitin' part! Joe says the man didn't do nothin'—"

"Anything," Hilda said automatically.

"—didn't do anything except stand outside in the bushes and watch the house. Didn't try to go in, didn't do noth—anything but hide and watch."

Hilda shivered. The stable wasn't very cold, but the image of that man waiting in the dark, watching—for what? A chance to kill? "How long did he stay there?" she breathed. "All night?"

Erik shrugged. "Joe don't—doesn't know. He was just about dead of cold, and starvin' too, and he had to go on home."

"Did he follow the man the next day?"

"He was off the next day."

Hilda made an irritated noise. "That is bad luck. I don't suppose he told any of the other boys what he'd seen."

"Not then. He had to do chores for his ma all day and didn't see none of his pals."

"Erik! Didn't see any of his friends."

Erik shrugged. "He told them when he came back to work on the Wednesday and they was all talkin'—"

"Were all talking."

"—were all talkin' about how the fella'd done a bunk."

Hilda opened her mouth to reprove him about his speech once more, but thought better of it. "And what did they have to say to Joe's story? The other boys, I mean?"

"Thought it was funny, like. But none of 'em'd seen him on the Tuesday. 'Course, we ain't talked to everybody yet, all the boys on all the different shifts."

Hilda stood up. She was getting cold. "Well, it is very interesting, what you have told me. I must try to find out why the man did what he did. That may be a way to find out who he is. You have done well, little—my brother. But Erik, you must try not to use so much slang and bad English. You do not want to be a stable boy all your life."

"Sure, 'n' what's wrong with bein' a stable boy?" Patrick entered by the side door, from the fire station. "Honest work, an' no backtalk from them as you're workin' with. Bein' as they can't talk. How are ye, darlin' girl?"

"I am well," she said primly, but she gave Patrick a dazzling smile.

"I'm off this afternoon, me girl. I saw you out here and I thought to myself, thought I, why don't I treat my girl to lunch?"

"Oh, Patrick! I would like that, but I cannot. I promised to have lunch with Erik's friend Andy. He is a bellboy at the Oliver, you know, and he may have some information for me."

"Can I come?" said Erik instantly.

"No, you don't, me lad. You're needed here. It's glad we were you came by today, with two of our other lads down sick, but you can't just up and leave when you please. I'll tell you what I'll do. I'm off all day tomorrow, too. The men who've been sick have come back to work, and as I've been doin' their shifts, I've some extra time comin' to me. So suppose I take the both of you out tomorrow, and you can eat all you want, Erik." He clapped the boy on the shoulder. Erik grinned.

"Yes, Patrick, that will be very nice, but it must be early. I must go to Elkhart tomorrow afternoon for Miss Jacobs's funeral. It is at three o'clock, and I must take the one-thirty train."

"We'll make it noon sharp, and I'll see you to the station.

I'd go with you, only I didn't know you were goin' and I promised me mother I'd paint the kitchen floor for her. Now, if you're ready, darlin', I'll walk you to the hotel." He held out his arm.

The moment they were out the door, Hilda said, "Patrick, I must tell you," at the same moment that Patrick said, "I've news, me girl." They laughed. Hilda said, "You first, Patrick."

"I've given me month's notice to the fire department! Uncle Dan's goin' to put me to work as soon as I'm free here, and teach me in the meanwhile. There's an awful lot to learn about the dry goods business, Hilda."

"You are smart," she said, squeezing his arm. "You will learn."

"I won't have a lot of time to see you," he said a little anxiously. "When I'm not at the station I'll mostly be at the store."

"It is all right, Patrick. We will see each other when we can. I will be busy, too."

Patrick stopped. Hilda, holding his arm, had to stop, too. "I wish I could spend more time with you. You know I worry about you gettin' into this murder business. If I could be with you—"

"But you cannot." She tugged him gently into a walk again. "Patrick, I will say what I have never said before. I, too, wish you could be with me. I know there is danger. But I am a sensible person. I will be very careful. Especially because—oh, Patrick, I must tell you! I talked yesterday with Father Faherty."

She told him of their conversation. "And it was very silly of me to cry, because now it will all be much easier. It might even be fun," she added, sounding surprised.

"Darlin', of course it'll be fun! We'll have a wonderful time at our weddin's! Have you given your notice yet?"

"No." She sobered. "That will not be easy. And Patrick, there is other news. Mr. Williams is better!"

"And it's glad I am to hear it! He's an old buzzard, but he's mostly been decent to you. When's he comin' home?"

"I do not know. He made the turn for the better only last night. It will not be soon, I think."

"No." Patrick was silent for a few steps, guiding Hilda over the slushy, slippery sidewalk. "I'm thinkin' of a good date for the weddin's. Do we want them on the same day, or different?"

"The same, of course, Patrick. Until my mother thinks we are properly married, she would never let me—I mean, I could not—that is, we could not—" She stopped, blushing.

Patrick, too, was blushing to the roots of his hair. "Yes, well, so we get married twice on the same day, in the early afternoon, say. Next month, maybe?"

"Oh, Patrick, how foolish you are! It takes much time to prepare for a wedding. I must have new clothes, and Mama and I must plan the food, and I must make linens for the house. I am not very good at embroidery, but I will try, and Mama will help me. It will take a long time."

"How long? Two months?"

"Six, at least."

He stopped once more and took her by the shoulders. "Look here, darlin' girl. I've waited years for you to agree to marry me. If you're tellin' me I've got to wait six more months for you to make a lot of fancy-work napkins, I'm tellin' you we'll buy them. You're forgettin' we'll have enough money to do that."

Hilda frowned doubtfully. "But it is a tradition in Sweden. Brides always make their household linens."

"We're not in Sweden, nor yet in Ireland. We're in America. And you say you're not so good at it, and I'm bettin' you don't like doin' it, neither."

Hilda laughed. They resumed their walk. "I hate it, if you have to know. I hate all sewing."

"Well, then. We'll buy the things, and we'll be married in February."

"That is too soon. There are still clothes, and it is nearly the end of January. March."

"We can't be married in Lent! April?"

"April." Hilda considered. "The weather will be better then, and we can have flowers. Daffodils, anyway, maybe tulips if it is late April. Do you know the date of Easter this year?"

"No, but I'll find out. And we'll be married directly after Easter. Never mind about flowers. I keep tellin' you, we'll have enough money. We can *buy* flowers if we have to. So we have the weddin's, and then we have the party. Where?"

"That is a trouble," said Hilda. "Your mother's house is small. My mother's house is tiny, and my brother's is not much better. I do not think both our families could fit into any of them, even if your family would come to my family's house, or mine to yours. And then there are our friends. I do not know where we can go."

"We-ell," Patrick said, and paused, apparently thinking. Then he couldn't restrain himself any longer. "What do you say, darlin' girl, we do it all at our own house?"

"Our own—Patrick, what do you mean?"

"I mean, Uncle Dan's givin' us a house for a weddin' present! Now what do you think of that?"

"Oh. Oh!" Hilda stopped. There was a bench nearby. She tugged her arm free of Patrick's and sat, heedless of the dirty snow here and there on the seat.

She looked up at Patrick. "It is—I cannot tell you. It is wonderful, but I cannot quite believe it. A *house!* Where? What is it like? A house of our own." There was a lump in her throat. She turned away quickly and got out her handkerchief, touching it to her eyes.

"Why are you crying?" asked Patrick, bewildered.

"Because I am happy," she said with a sniffle. "And you did not answer my questions."

Patrick shook his head and raised his eyes to heaven.

"Women cry when they are happy," said Hilda. "You must learn that. You are going to marry one."

"Lots I'll have to learn, I expect," he said with a grin. "And you, too. Did you think Uncle Dan would just up and buy a house without us havin' a say in it? He and Aunt Molly want us to come to tea on Sunday to talk about it."

Hilda rose and tucked her arm inside Patrick's again, and they went on their way. Hilda had little to say. She was thinking about the new hat she must somehow obtain between now and Sunday, and about a house, and about her wedding clothes, and about the strange land of America, where a servant to one of the wealthiest families in town was invited to tea in another wealthy household. With a fireman.

*...a young man who was calling on
her had made himself objectionable....*

—South Bend *Tribune*
January 23, 1904

19

S o, ANDY, WHAT HAVE you to tell me?"
They were seated at a table in the Philadelphia, the
elegant candy and ice cream shop. Andy had partaken
of a huge lunch and was now blissfully polishing off a
chocolate ice cream sundae with nuts on top. Hilda, too full of
happiness to be hungry, had toyed with some bread and butter
and a cup of tea, and had refused to let Andy talk while he was
eating.

"Well!" He put down his spoon and licked his lips. He raised
his arm to wipe his mouth on his sleeve and Hilda quickly handed him a napkin. "What's that for?"

She explained. Shamefaced, he used the napkin. "Thanks," he
muttered. "Workin' at a high-class place like the Oliver, I got to
know stuff like that."

"Yes. Now go on."

"Well, like I was goin' to say, one of the boys follered Mr.
Perkins home on the Monday night, and it was int'resting." He
proceeded to relate the same story Erik had told, with embellish-
ments about Joe's caution and bravery. Hilda listened politely,
pretended she hadn't heard it before, and showed astonishment
in the right places.

"And did any of the other boys know anything?"

"Not about that. None of 'em saw him on the Tuesday, and
then by Wednesday he'd gone. They was all mad at Joe for not
tellin' 'em nothin' about his prowlin' around that night, 'cause if
they'd'a known, they'd'a been on the lookout for 'im."

146 〜

"It is a pity," Hilda agreed, "but it cannot be helped. What you have told me may help us to discover something about him."

"Kurt, he found out Perkins left town by the first train on Wednesday morning. The seven-forty-three, it was, to Indianapolis."

"Then probably he really does live there, not in Fort Wayne. But that is interesting, Andy, because that is before Nellie disappeared. I do not understand that at all."

"And there's more," said Andy with a broad grin. "I told you none of the other boys found out nothin'. I didn't tell you what I found out myself, just this mornin'."

Hilda's attention now was more than polite.

"See, I was at the front when it came in, or I'd never've known."

"When *what* came in?"

"The money. He paid for his room, after all this time!"

"He walked in and paid?"

"No! I'd've told you first thing if I'd seen him! No, the way it was, see, the mailman comes around ten, ten-thirty—just after you was there this mornin'. He puts all the mail on the front desk, and takes away all the hotel mail. So this mornin' I was right there, not busy, when the mail comes in, and there's such a lot of it, Mr. Brady—he's the day desk clerk—he says for me to help sort it. So I'm puttin' the mail for the hotel guests in one pile and for the hotel in another, and I sees this envelope for Mr. James that says Perkins on the outside."

"You mean it was from Mr. Perkins?"

"That's what it said. Now, I thinks to myself, if it's the same fella, there ain't no such person. So what's he doin' sendin' letters? I'm curious, see? So I takes it in to Mr. James myself. Which I had no business doin', but Mr. Brady, he was sortin' the guest mail and he didn't notice."

"Did Mr. James open it while you were there?"

"He didn't want to. He was real snippy. 'Put it down there, boy,' he says, and points to a pile of stuff on his desk. Well, I wanted to watch him open it, so I says, 'It's from that Mr. Perkins and it feels like there's a lot in it. Do you reckon it's another one of them messages with no writin'?' I figgered that'd make him mad, see? And it did. He snatches up the letter from my hand and tears open the envelope, and all this money falls out. And he says, 'I'll be da—' I mean, miss, he says bad words. And he says the ba—the fella paid after all. And he counted it real careful, and there was fifteen dollars. That's *three dollars* more than he owed, miss! So Mr. James, he's not mad anymore, and he reaches in his pocket and gives me fifty cents, and he says that's for pester-in' him until he opened the letter. Fifty cents, miss!" Andy patted his pocket and grinned. "It's me should be takin' you to lunch, miss!"

Hilda matched his grin. "You are rich, Andy. Do not waste it on food. Save it for something you really want."

"You bet! Ellsworth's has some ice skates for sixty-seven cents, and with this, I have enough. If Ma doesn't need the money, I'm going to buy me a pair."

Hilda smiled at him fondly and then returned to business. "That is fine, Andy. Now, can you tell me anything else about the letter? Was there a return address on the envelope?"

"Nope, nothin' except the name, Harold Perkins, like I said. I looked special."

"What about the postmark?"

"It was all smudged. Couldn't make out nothin'. But there was a note inside, besides the money."

"A note! What did it say?"

"Well, I didn't read it. Mr. James just sort of looked at it and threw it on the desk, and I couldn't see without him noticin'. But he said somethin' about 'rotten memory,' so I reckon the fella said he forgot to pay."

"Hmm. Well, I can ask Mr. James. I think perhaps I will ask Patrick to go with me if he can. Mr. James is not a gentleman."

"No, miss," said Andy solemnly. "But he can be nice some-times." He reached into his pocket, brought out his shiny silver half dollar, and studied it lovingly.

Hilda was thoughtful as she parted with Andy. She wanted to

call on Mrs. Schmidt, with whom Miss Jacobs had roomed, but as she walked through the wintry sunshine she mulled over Andy's information. It was, she supposed, good news in a way. At least the Oliver Hotel had its money back. But why did the man—Perkins or whatever his name really was—act so oddly the night he came to town? And why did he leave in such a hurry? And what, if anything, did he have to do with Nellie's disappearance?

On the whole, Hilda was dissatisfied. Because the man could no longer be called a thief, the police would undoubtedly forget about him, and Hilda thought that a very bad idea. Thief or not, he remained a Mysterious Stranger, a character beloved in the annals of Sherlock Holmes (which Hilda read when she had a chance). His behavior needed explaining. She would talk to Patrick about it.

The thought of Patrick drowned every other, and she walked the rest of the way unconscious of her increasingly damp feet and the muddy hem of her skirt.

The very young maid who answered the door of the rooming house said that Mrs. Schmidt was at home. Hilda had hoped she would be, in the middle of the afternoon. When the woman thumped into the front parlor to see what Hilda wanted, she decided not to curtsey. She, Hilda, was not going to be a servant very much longer. She would be a lady with her own home. She might look like nothing on earth today, with her short, muddy skirt and her old cloak, but one day soon she would be several rungs up the social ladder from a landlady. She nodded pleasantly and held out her hand.

"Good day, Mrs. Schmidt. I am Hilda Johansson, and I am here to ask you some questions about Miss Jacobs."

Mrs. Schmidt looked at her sharply. "You're never with the police!"

"No, I am not. I am acting for a gentleman. May I sit down?"

The woman nodded a little unwillingly, and gestured to a straight wooden chair. Hilda took the plush one next to it.

"I've got it! You must be one of those Pinkertons. I hear tell they've got some women working for them. Don't know what the world's coming to. Time was, women knew their place."

"I am not with the Pinkertons, Mrs. Schmidt."

"I don't suppose you'd tell me if you were. Well, what do you want to know? I haven't got all day."

"I know you must be a busy woman. I have only a few questions. I have read in the newspaper that Miss Jacobs was afraid of something, the last few days of her life. Do you have any idea what was frightening her?"

"As if the police hadn't asked me that over and over again! And I always tell them the same thing: I don't know. She didn't confide in me, the way some of my roomers do. A little stand-offish, she was. I tell the young ladies, I say they must treat me just as they would a mother, seeing as how their own mothers ain't here to keep an eye on them. And I must say I treat them like I would my own girls, if I had any, which I don't, of course, being an unmarried lady."

Hilda nodded. She was familiar with the custom of calling older women "Mrs." whether or not they had ever had a husband. Mrs. Sullivan, for instance, was a spinster.

"Well, so Miss Jacobs was always polite and all, but she never opened up to me. It hurt me, here." She put a hand on her ample bosom. "We're all just one happy family here, but she never quite fit in."

"But her fears…" said Hilda, trying to get the conversation back on track.

"Well, now, there was a young man she didn't like much, I can tell you that. I allow my young ladies to have gentleman callers in the parlor, as long as they leave by a decent hour and behave themselves. I stay with them, of course, unless there are other people in the room. I only have refined young ladies staying here, but human nature being what it is, I'm always very careful. There has never been any scandal about this house and there never will be, as long as I'm alive!"

"I am sure of it, Mrs. Schmidt. You were saying there was a young man Miss Jacobs did not like?"

"He came to call more than once, and usually she made some excuse not to come down. She had a headache, or she was tired, or she had some of the children's work to mark. I can tell you I got sick and tired of running up and down stairs with messages for Her Majesty. I'm not as young as I was, nor as slim as I was, and I told her so. Well, one day, just about a week before she died, I told her plain out that she could come down and tell him herself that she didn't want to see him. So she did, and he wasn't at all happy about it. Such a lot of shouting there was, and I finally had to tell them both to quiet down. They were disturbing everyone in the house."

"You were in the room?"

"Just outside. I told you, I'm a careful woman."

"But did she act afraid of him?"

"Not afraid, exactly. More like put out. As if he'd said something she didn't like."

"Didn't you hear what they said?"

"I hope, miss, you don't think I'd eavesdrop on a private conversation! I make it a point not to listen."

"You said they were shouting."

"That was later. I couldn't help but hear then. He was saying she was treating him bad, and how could she be so cruel, and she was saying she never wanted to see him again, and crying. I didn't understand why she was acting that way. He was a very presentable young man, and hadn't said anything wrong, not that I heard."

And you heard all of it, or tried to, thought Hilda, but she kept the thought to herself. "Do you know who he was?"

"He gave me his name, but there's so many of them. The police asked me that, but I couldn't remember. He was young, and nice-looking, well dressed, and very gentlemanly to me."

"Have you seen him again?"

"No."

Hilda found that short answer interesting. She filed it away. "I have only one other matter I wish to ask about. It is the night when—"

"When I came home and she heard me on the porch and acted scared. I've told the police and the Pinkertons and I'll tell you,
whoever you really are. I think that friend of hers, who said that
to the police, I think she made up the whole thing, just trying to
make herself important. Miss Jacobs was never scared of anything that she told me about, or told any of the other young
ladies about, either, and if you don't mind, miss, I have work to
do."

She stood and walked toward the front door and Hilda had
little choice but to follow. She was tired, in any case. Wondering
what would happen if she returned home to take her usual afternoon rest, she turned up the sidewalk. She was headed for Tippecanoe Place when she was startled by a small figure hurtling
across her path. Hilda's feet slipped in the muddy slush and she
would have fallen without a helpful extended hand.

"Oh, I'm sorry, miss! I didn't mean to trip you up!"

"You did not. I was surprised and lost my balance. You are
Mrs. Schmidt's maid, are you not?"

"Yes, miss, and I wanted to talk to you, only can we go around
the corner, because I'm supposed to be on me way to the bakery,
on account of they forgot the rolls when they delivered, and
Cook'll have me hide if she sees me lollygaggin', 'cause she needs
them for dinner."

By the time the child had finished her breathless explanation,
Hilda had whisked them around the next house, out of sight of
any impatient cooks. "Now we can walk more slowly, because it
is not safe to run with the sidewalks in the state they are. What
bakery?"

"Teuscher's."

"But that is on Monroe! It is a long way for you to go. There
are closer bakeries."

"I know, and better ones, too, but the rolls are a penny cheaper
at Teuscher's. She's a real skinflint, Mrs. Schmidt."

"*Is* she?" That was interesting.

"Yes, miss, and I wanted to tell you, it's a lot of lies she told
you. I know who you are, even if she didn't, and you're goin' to

marry me next-door-neighbor's third cousin, so I listened outside the door, and I didn't want you lied to!"

Hilda smiled. "That is nice of you. I could tell you were Irish from the way you spoke. What is your name?"

"Eileen O'Hara, miss."

"And you know that I am Hilda Johansson. You must call me Hilda."

"Oh, no, miss. That wouldn't be right. I'm only a maid."

"So am I," said Hilda. "And I will be a kind of cousin soon. Now, Eileen, what was it that Mrs. Schmidt did not tell the truth about?"

"Well, for one, she never run up and down stairs with messages for Miss Jacobs, nor for any of the other young ladies, neither. It's me does the runnin'. And she lied about not hearin' what them two was sayin' that night, too. She was right outside, listenin' for all she was worth."

"You saw her? Did you, also, hear what they said?"

"No." Eileen made a face. "I was just passin' through the hall, and the minute she saw me, she shooed me out of there, so I never heard a word. I could tell they was talkin', but they was real quiet."

"Are you quite sure Mrs. Schmidt heard?"

"Yes, 'cause I could see her face. I watched for a minute from behind the door after I left the hall, holdin' it open a crack, see. And I could see her gettin' madder and madder at whatever she was hearin'."

"Hmm. I do not understand that. If the gentleman was saying things that made Miss Jacobs upset, I would have thought Mrs. Schmidt would tell him to leave."

"Not much, she wouldn't! Not him. 'Cause that was the other thing she lied about, sayin' she didn't know him. She knows him all right. He's her own sister's son."

...there are still several clews out of which a path may be found that will lead to the murderer...

—South Bend *Tribune*
February 6, 1904

20

ER NEPHEW? Are you sure?"

Eileen nodded vigorously. "He's been comin' round ever since I started working there. And haven't I heard them talkin', and him callin' her Aunt, an' all? She didn't like it when she saw me listenin', but she doesn't like hardly anything I do. She only give me the job 'cause I come cheap. She's a penny-pincher, like I said."

"This must be your first job, Eileen. How old are you?"

"Twelve. That's why she can get by with payin' me almost nothin'."

Hilda sighed. The child looked thin and pinched, and much younger than twelve. She herself had been sixteen, and just arrived from Sweden, when she was hired at Tippecanoe Place. She had been used to hard work. Tending the family farm, after her father had died, had meant backbreaking work for everyone in the family. Even little Erik, only six when Hilda had come to America, had helped feed and water the animals. But twelve— "You should be in school still."

"I never been to school. Ma could never afford for us not to work. I worked at the shirt factory before. This is better, I guess. I get me meals regular, anyway—such as they are."

"Can you read, Miss O'Hara?"

"A little. I've taught meself a few words. Don't have no time for readin', anyway."

"No, I suppose not. Well, this is where I must go in, and you must go on to the bakery. Cook will be waiting for the rolls."

"Here, miss? You live *here*?"

154 ～

With the leaves off the shade trees, Tippecanoe Place looked even larger and grander than in summer. Hilda was used to it, and so was Eileen, probably, passing it from time to time on her errands. But from the look of awe on the child's face, Eileen had never imagined she would know someone who lived there.

"I work here, Eileen. It is a live-in position. My room is at the top of the house, very small and not grand at all. I am just a maid, like you, and my name is Hilda."

"And a detective, too. I've heard the family talkin'." She stopped abruptly.

Hilda could guess what else Eileen had heard in the family discussions—how terrible it was that Patrick Cavanaugh had got himself mixed up with that Swedish girl, not only a Protestant but meddling about in crime. Variations on that theme, no doubt, repeated endlessly. "I am not a detective, Eileen. I have helped to solve some crimes, because I am good at talking to people. And I thank you for talking to me, and I will not tell anyone what you said. Here." She thrust her mittened hand into her pocket. There was still quite a lot of money inside. She pulled out some coins and handed them to Eileen. "Buy a bun for yourself at the bakery. It is a long time until supper."

It had also been a long time since breakfast, Hilda thought as she trudged up the back drive to the great house. She doubted that little Eileen had gotten much lunch, if Mrs. Schmidt was a "skinflint." It was appalling that a child her age was forced to work full-time. Was there anything she, Hilda, could do about it?

Still pondering the question, Hilda walked down the back steps and into the basement. The house was very quiet, settled into the afternoon lethargy, except for some giggles coming from the servants' room. The dailies, Hilda thought. Elsa, who was technically their supervisor, was upstairs napping, and plainly the temporary butler wasn't keeping them up to the mark. Mr. Williams had always taken his rest in his big chair downstairs, where his presence, even if drowsy, kept the dailies from frivoling away their time. The new man couldn't be there or anywhere in the basement, or he'd have heard the maids.

Hilda thought for a moment about scolding them, and then shrugged. She was on leave. It was not her problem. She would find the butler and inform him, and then take a rest herself. She took off her filthy rubbers and brushed the mud from her skirts, but gave up on her shoes. They would need a thorough cleaning before she could wear them in the house. She slipped them off, and carrying them in one hand, went up the back stairs.

She started on the top floor, knocking on the closed door of the butler's bedroom. He was staying in Mr. Williams's room, a fact that, if Mr. Williams learned of it, would make him very angry. When there was no answer to Hilda's tap, she turned the knob and looked in. The room was empty. She left her shoes outside her own room and went down to the next floor.

There was no one in any of the family's sleeping rooms, or so Hilda judged by her quick, discreet tour, nor in any of the public rooms on the first floor. Apparently all the Studebakers were out. Well, why not? It was a nice day, for January.

So where on earth was the butler? Mr.—Mr. Barnes, that was the man's name. It was just possible that Colonel George had sent him on an errand, though Anton, the footman, was usually the errand boy. Just to make sure, she climbed the five steps up to Colonel George's home office. If he was there, she would ask him.

She lifted her hand to knock on the open door and then stopped, rooted to the spot.

Opposite the door was the fireplace, with a large mirror hanging over it. Hilda saw, reflected in the mirror, the striped trousers and coat tails of the butler. He was bending over, intent on his task.

He was trying to open the safe.

Hilda stood paralyzed for a moment, unable to think or move. He had not heard her approach. Her stockinged feet had climbed the carpeted steps silently.

After the first shock her brain began to work again. He must not see her there. As silently as she had come, she backed down the steps, slowly, carefully. She made for the back stairs and climbed them, her heart pounding in her chest.

What must she do? She could not take on the butler herself. He was a burly man, strong from years of carrying heavy trays. None of the family was at home. She thought fleetingly of John Bolton and then dismissed the idea. He would be out with one of the carriages, taking someone somewhere or waiting for the return trip.

The police, of course! She would send for the police....

No. The telephone was in the office. Besides, she didn't know how to use it.

Send one of the dailies! That was the solution, if there was one whose discretion she could trust. Anton, that was it. Anton had been there for years. He was loyal and trustworthy and would fetch the police quickly while she, Hilda, stood guard to make sure the butler didn't get away with anything he stole.

She headed back down the stairs to the basement and the servants' room.

The giggling was louder now. Hilda stepped into the room and looked around with dismay.

The three maids, Janecska, Sarah, and Anna, were lolling about the room, their caps and shoes discarded. Sarah sat in Mr. Williams's chair, a magazine in her lap. The other two sat at the table playing checkers.

Anton was not there.

"You are a disgrace, all of you!" said Hilda furiously. "And where is Anton?"

"Huh!" said Anna. "You're not our boss anymore. And that fine sister of yours is asleep and Mr. Barnes is busy somewhere, and who's going to know? There's nothing to do, anyway."

Hilda scarcely heard them. *"Where is Anton?"* she repeated, her voice rising to near-hysteria.

"Out," said Janecska, looking at Hilda curiously. "He had to drive Colonel George someplace or other, 'cause John's taken the ladies out in the brougham. And what's the matter with you, anyway?"

Hilda bit her lip, trying to think. Anton had recently been allowed to drive the lighter carriages occasionally, when expediency demanded. He might be out for hours if Colonel George needed him to wait.

"What's the matter?" Janecska asked again.

Hilda didn't dare tell them. "It does not matter. I needed him to run an errand, but I will do it myself. Now get yourselves to work or I will tell Mr. Barnes." She gave them a look intended to scare away any speculation that might have arisen in their minds, and whisked out the door.

There was no help for it. Despairingly Hilda ran up the back stairs, fetched her shoes, and ran back down, keeping as quiet as she could when she neared the first floor. Stopping only to tie her shoes and throw on a cloak, she headed downtown, hoping she would encounter a policeman on the way.

There is never a policeman around when you want one. Hilda half slid, half ran the seven blocks and burst, out of breath, into the station. "I need help immediately!" she said, panting. "Someone is breaking into Colonel Studebaker's safe!"

Hilda Johansson, acting in her private capacity, might have received short shrift, but the magic name of Studebaker commanded immediate attention. Three large armed men climbed into a wagon, pulled Hilda aboard with scant ceremony, and urged the horses to a gallop.

On the way they asked Hilda what she had seen. Some instinct kept her from speaking the name of the temporary butler. She said, several times, that she had seen the back of a man, working at the safe. She acted terrified—not much of an act, after all, for she was still badly frightened. Finally they left off questioning her and she had time for second thoughts. Was this wise? Would the Studebakers appreciate policemen trampling all over their house? What if Mr. Barnes had already opened the safe, taken what he wished, and left? There would be only Hilda's word for what had happened. Would she be suspected of theft herself?

The wagon rattled up the front drive and pulled up beneath the porte-cochere before Hilda could convince the driver of the need for quiet. The porte-cochere door was the closest one to the office. Shaking her head, Hilda opened the door and they all trooped inside.

Mr. Barnes was standing in the small entrance hall, looking down his nose. "And what, may I ask, is the meaning of this intrusion?"

"The young woman here said someone was breaking into the safe," said the largest policeman before Hilda could get a word in. "We'll need to take a look. Where is this safe?"

"It is in Colonel Studebaker's office, but I have no authority to admit you. I assure you that there are no strangers in the house and nothing has been touched."

They searched the office anyway, the butler expostulating all the way. They badgered Hilda for a description of the man she said she had seen, to which she steadfastly replied that she had seen only his back and could tell them no more. They went on and searched the whole house, much to the distress of the live-in servants, awakened from their rest, and the entertainment of the dailies. Hilda could feel the butler's cold eye on her at every step.

When the policemen had left, grumbling about false alarms, Mr. Barnes let them out the basement door. Then he turned from the door, folded his arms, and fixed his basilisk gaze on Hilda. "Now, young woman, suppose you tell me what this is all about."

Because...a new clew has developed,
the special board of inquiry has been
ordered to reconvene today.

— South Bend *Tribune*
February 12, 1904

21

S HE HAD SPENT THE TIME while the police were trampling over the house making up a story. Now, trem-
blingly, she produced it. "Sir, I heard—well, I thought I
heard a noise in Colonel George's office."

"It is not your place to refer to your employer by his first
name."

"But we all do that! It is because there were once two men in
this house, Mr. Clement Studebaker and his son Colonel George
Studebaker. We used their first names to make it clear which—"

"It doesn't matter what you did in the past. There is now only
one man, and his name is Colonel Studebaker. I would have
thought your butler would have insisted on it. But it is of little
importance at the moment. What do you mean, you heard a
noise? You told the police you saw someone."

"Well, I—I was afraid, because the house felt so empty. I
knew Colonel Geo—Colonel Studebaker was not at home, and
I saw—well, I thought I saw a shadow in his office that might
be a man, and—oh, I know I have been foolish!" She burst into
tears that were not entirely spurious. Her nerves were over-
wrought.

"A shadow! A noise! For that you brought the police into this
house?"

"Oh, Mr. Barnes! You will not tell Colonel George, will you?
Colonel Studebaker, I mean. I have been working very hard, and
I am upset. I promise I will never do such a t'ing again." She gave
an artistic sob or two and waited for what would surely come.

The butler dragged it out with a lecture on the proper be-

havior of servants in a gentleman's house, and followed with a
long lament about the additional work he would have to do,
placating the other servants, but in the end he said what she had
known he must. "Very well, Hilda, I will let it go this time. You
have, after all, served in this household for quite a long
time, though I do wonder about the standards set by your Mr.
Williams. You have my word that I will say nothing to Colonel
Studebaker, and I will instruct the other servants to keep their
mouths shut. You may go, Hilda. You have taken up far too
much of my time with this nonsense."

She waited until he was out of sight and then slipped out the
door and up the stairs to the drive. She shot across to the carriage
house, went in, and stood in the shadowy gloom of the stables,
listening to the small noises of the horses and the mice and letting
her heart slow down to normal.

She had but one ally in this house, and his allegiance was dubious. He was, however, large and strong, and Hilda had an idea he
didn't much care for the temporary butler, either.

She pulled a stool into a dark corner and settled down,
wrapped in a horse blanket, to wait until John Bolton came
home.

Her teeth were chattering and shadows were growing long by
the time the brougham with its two horses clopped up the drive.
She waited to show herself until John had assisted the ladies out
of the carriage and had driven around to unhitch the horses.
Then she stepped into the light.

John saw her and whistled. "Waiting for me, are you? Got
tired of Paddy already, eh?"

"John, this is serious. Leave the horses for a moment and come
in here. I must talk to you."

"Can't leave them long. They need wiping down, and they're
hungry."

"Five minutes, no more. They can stand that long. It is not
very cold today."

Grumbling, John stepped into the stable. "So what's so all-
fired important?"

"Mr. Barnes is a thief," she said baldly. "I saw him trying to get into Colonel George's safe."

"I knew it!" He smacked his knee. "Something about that fellow got my goat the minute he showed his face around here. But why are you telling me? You need to telephone the police!"

"I went for them." Quickly Hilda sketched out what had happened, and her pretense to Mr. Barnes. "I had to make him think I knew nothing. But, John, someone must tell Colonel George. Only I am afraid. If Mr. Barnes is discharged, he will know it is I who told, and I do not know what he might do."

John whistled and scratched his head. "Tell you what. You'd best get back to the house while I take care of the horses and the carriage. When the other servants ask, you can tell them the same taradiddle you told Barnes—you were mistaken, you exaggerated, you're very sorry. Then I'll come in and find you, and we can work out what you can do."

Hilda nodded. "Thank you, John. But you will think while you deal with the horses?"

"That I will. Now off you go."

She slipped into the house without anyone noticing. The work of the household had begun again. If voices seemed pitched a little higher, a little faster, it was the only sign of the disruption of routine.

She had to find Elsa. Mr. Barnes would have told the others her careful lies. She didn't care if they believed him, but Elsa should know the truth. The afternoon was half gone. Elsa should, at this time of day, be cleaning the dining rooms and making sure all was in order for dinner. Hilda quickly reviewed in her mind the duties of the other servants and decided she had a good chance of catching Elsa alone.

Her luck held. Elsa was at the far end of the state dining room, carefully cleaning the tooled leather wall-covering with a soft, long-handled dust mop. She had not turned on the gas, and the day had darkened enough that the room was shadowy. Hilda tapped on the door, held a finger to her mouth as Elsa turned around, and went to her quickly.

"Say nothing, my sister. I do not want anyone to find us. I lied to Mr. Barnes. What he told you was not true. I did see someone."

Elsa uttered a little squeak of fear or excitement, Hilda couldn't tell which. "You are in no danger, I think, so long as you do your work and stay where you belong. You will say nothing to show Mr. Barnes you do not believe him. And do *not* tell any of the other servants what I have told you. It is better that they believe Mr. Barnes, but I did not want you to think me such a fool. Now I must go, but I will see you later tonight and tell you more."

She gave her sister a hard hug and stole out of the room to wait for John near the back door.

She was far too near the kitchen door for comfort. Mrs. Sullivan was humming as she worked, in a good mood for once. She was baking a pie for dinner. The rich smell of cinnamon and apples drifted out to Hilda's corner and made her mouth water. Breakfast was only a memory and lunch had been nearly nonexistent, but Hilda had no wish to enter the kitchen. Mrs. Sullivan's good mood might not last, and Hilda wasn't sure how much lying she was prepared to do. Once Elsie, the scullery maid, came out of the kitchen with a tray full of crockery for the servants' supper table and passed by Hilda, nearly close enough to touch. Hilda shrank back, but Elsie was too worried about breaking something to notice.

Elsie, Elsa. For the first time Hilda thought about the confusion of two maids in the house with such similar names. Then she dismissed it. The two worked in entirely different spheres, and if anyone found the similarity a problem, one of the names would simply be changed. It happened to servants all the time. The convenience of the masters outweighed any feelings servants might have about—

The back door opened and John stepped through.

"I am here," said Hilda in a whisper. "We should go out."

John nodded and drew her outside. "Come back to the carriage house with me. Don't worry. I'm on my good behavior, for once. Your virtue is safe. For now."

Hilda went with him. This was John at his best, helpful and

kind. She wouldn't stay long, though. His kindness could change to something else in the blink of an eye, as she had good reason to know.

"Now, listen," he said, when he had her settled on a chair in his room over the stables. "I've thought about this. You've got to get away. I'll tell Colonel George. He has to know, so he can see if anything is missing. Then he'll have to decide whether to sack the fellow. But even if he doesn't, you're for it. Barnes knows he was really in there, and he doesn't know how much you really saw. You're not safe to have around, and there's no telling what a crook like Barnes might do."

"But once Colonel George knows, he will tell the police."

"Yes, and what will they do? You've already told them a lie— or less than the truth, anyway, when you didn't tell them it was Barnes you saw."

"I was afraid!"

"Understandable, but it isn't going to make them very anxious to arrest Barnes."

"Colonel George—"

"Colonel George is an important man, and they'll listen to him, but unless Barnes actually got into the safe and took something, there won't be much they can do. And he probably didn't get in. That safe is the best they make, not a baby's toy to be broken into by a tuppenny-ha'penny thief. No, Barnes will likely stay out of jail and out of this house, and he'll be a danger to you. That's why you have to go someplace for a while."

"Not to my family. Mama would have a bed for me, with Elsa here, but it would be the first place Mr. Barnes would look. And there is no room at Sven's."

"Hmm." John scratched his chin. "Tell you what. How about that uncle of Paddy's? He's rich as Croesus, and from what I hear, he pretty much thinks you're queen of the world."

"That is a very good idea!" said Hilda. "I do not know why I did not think of it. Yes, I think they will give me a place to stay until it is safe to come back here. I will go at once!" She gave John a dazzling smile.

"Am I a clever fellow?" said John smugly. "Going to give me a nice kiss, then?" He reached for Hilda, but she ducked under his arm and disappeared down the stairs.

She wasn't dressed for a call on her wealthy soon-to-be relations, but she was afraid to take the time to change. She did take a quick tour of the basement, but Elsa had gone on to other duties. That was a pity. Hilda had hoped to tell her sister not to worry, but there was no time. She slipped into her cloak and muddy rubbers, clapped her old hat on her head, and tiptoed out the back door.

22

*The city is somewhat disgusted with
the status of the case.*

—South Bend *Tribune*
February 24, 1904

D ANIEL MALLOY'S HOUSE was not far away. Hilda
hurried through the deepening gloom. The clear
skies of the day had given way to thick, sullen
clouds. It looked very much as if it might rain,
which would take away the snow but would turn the streets into
rivers and the river into a raging flood. In fact, a fine mist hung in
the air even now, damp and unpleasant.

She very much hoped she would find Mrs. Malloy at home.
Mr. Malloy was not likely to be there, not during a working day,
and the butler didn't much care for Hilda. It seemed to her,
reflecting a little as she rushed to safety, that there had been many
butlers in her life, and only one who had even tolerated her. She
thought about Mr. Williams with something approaching affec-
tion. If only he hadn't become ill! The annoyances she had
endured every day under his rule were as nothing compared to
the danger she faced from Barnes, the thief. For thief he was in
Hilda's mind, whether or not he had actually managed to steal
anything.

The butler answered the door of the Malloy mansion. He surveyed her with an absolutely blank expression, and Hilda knew
he was tallying up her sartorial sins.

"Mr. Riggs," she said with a smile and her most appealing
manner, "I am in a dilemma and need, please, to speak to Mrs.
Malloy, if she is at home. You remember me, perhaps? Hilda
Johansson?"

She knew perfectly well that he remembered her, and that he
also knew she was about to become a member of the family. That

was undoubtedly why his expression was frozen, instead of openly disapproving.

"Yes, Miss Johansson. I will tell Mrs. Malloy that you are here." His glance fell to her muddy rubbers.

"Thank you," she said, smiling again. "If you do not mind, I will wait here in the hall. And is there perhaps a cloth I might use to clean my shoes after I take off my rubbers? It is very muddy on the streets."

That earned her a silent bow, but he fetched a rag from a closet and gave it to her before he went to his mistress. Her manners, his demeanor indicated, had improved, but she was still a servant and he was not about to clean her footwear.

Hilda sat on a chair and took a deep breath. There were still many troubles ahead, but this house, solid and comfortable, was a refuge. She very much hoped Mrs. Malloy would allow her to stay. She had nothing with her but the clothes on her back, plain and grimy as they were. Would she, in fact, be welcome in a lady's fine house?

She had time to work up a fine case of nerves before Mrs. Malloy came into the hall, black silk skirts rustling, and held out both hands.

"My dear! It is so good to see you. I had not looked for this pleasure until Sunday. Now, come into the parlor and warm yourself. This hall is freezing."

"I am wet, Mrs. Malloy, and my skirts are muddy. I did not want to soil your furniture."

"Pooh! Furniture will clean. I don't want you catching your death of cold, child. And you must call me Aunt Molly. Now come along."

So, wet and bedraggled as she was, she followed the tiny woman into her exquisite parlor, where a fire roared and the draperies were tightly closed against the gloom and the weather.

Mrs. Malloy pulled a bell rope before she sat down, and when Riggs responded, she said, "Tea, please, Riggs. And would you ask Mrs. Hall for some of those delightful little cakes we had yesterday, if there are any left, and a few sandwiches, please."

Riggs bowed and departed, and Mrs. Malloy, seated on a thronelike chair with a needlepoint stool at her feet, said, "Now, child, tell me what your trouble is and how I may help you."

"I am ashamed to ask, Mrs.—Aunt Molly, but you have been very kind to me and my family, and I cannot think of any other place to go."

"Is it money you need? You're more than welcome—"

"No, no, please. I am sorry to interrupt, but I would not ask you for money. I know I look—well, I am not properly dressed, but that is because I have been out walking nearly all day, and I had no time to change my clothes. I do not have troubles about money. What I need is a place to stay for—I do not know how long. A few days, perhaps a little longer. You see, I do not dare to go back to Tippecanoe Place."

"And why might that be?" asked Mrs. Malloy in some astonishment.

"There is someone there who wishes to do me harm, and I do not know how bad it might be."

"Tell me all about it," said Mrs. Malloy crisply.

So Hilda launched into her tale, stopping abruptly when Riggs brought in the tea. When he had left, Mrs. Malloy got up and checked to make sure the door was firmly latched, and then sat down again. "Now, Hilda—for you won't mind me being as informal as I've asked you to be—you must be half-starved. Drink your tea and get some of that food into you, and then tell me the rest."

Hilda did as she was bidden. With all the details, it took her through three cups of tea and nearly all of the food in front of her.

"Well, child, you do get into some predicaments, don't you? You bought yourself a load of trouble when you went for the police!"

"Yes, but what else could I do? There was no man in the house at the time, not even Anton. And I could not use the telephone, and I could not just let him steal whatever he wanted!"

"Actually that might have been best. Then he would not have been put on the alert, and you could have told Colonel Studebaker when he came home. But that's hindsight, and hindsight is always perfect. The question is what to do now. Because if the man did get into the safe, he'll probably have had the sense by now to put back anything he took. That leaves Colonel Studebaker in a dilemma, too."

"I know." Hilda was disconsolate. "He will not know whether to believe me or the butler."

"Oh, I expect he'll believe you. You've worked there for years, after all, and he knows you're trustworthy. But he's a just man, and he may not want to dismiss a servant on the basis of an unproven story."

"If he does dismiss him, I think I am in danger. Mr. Barnes knows I saw him. He will know it is I who told Colonel Studebaker, and he might…" Hilda didn't want to think about what Barnes might do. "But even if Mr. Barnes is allowed to stay on, he will be angry with me because I spoiled his robbery attempt."

"Well, it's an unpleasant situation, but you're quite safe here, my dear. When Mr. Malloy comes home, we'll put our heads together and see if we can figure out something you can do for the long term. You don't want to be a prisoner in this house for the rest of your life."

Hilda looked around her and smiled a little. "It is a very fine prison, but no, I do not want to be a burden to you."

"Now that's enough of that kind of talk! And how would you be a burden? You're to stay here as long as you like, but the trouble is, you won't be able to go out alone. And you'll not like that, I'm thinking."

"No, I have much to do, and I must be free to go out."

"Yes, well, we'll work on that later, with Mr. Malloy. Now, child, we need to get you out of those wet, filthy clothes and into a hot bath. And then you'll come down and we'll talk of other things."

She rang a bell and when the butler answered said, "Riggs, please have Agnes show Miss Johansson to the rose bedroom. She will be staying with us for a few days. And tell Mrs. Hall the cakes and sandwiches were delicious."

"Yes, madam. Thank you, madam." Disapproval written in every line of his face, every movement, he went away to do his mistress's bidding.

When Hilda had finished her luxurious bath she slipped into the robe that Agnes had hung on a hook in the bathroom. It was of heavy silk in a beautiful floral print, and was made in a loose, flowing style that Hilda was later to hear called a kimono. Now she knew only that she had never worn a garment that was at once so beautiful and so comfortable. It was also at least six inches too short for her. Mrs. Malloy was a very small woman.

Some clothes had been laid out for her on the bed. Hilda examined them, wondering whose they were. Not Mrs. Malloy's, for they were big enough for Hilda. Nor could they be Agnes's. They were simple, a blue skirt trimmed only with braid, and a white waist with tucks and a single row of lace, but the skirt was perfectly cut from a soft lightweight wool, and the waist was of fine silk. Hilda looked at herself in the mirror as she brushed her hair and did up her coronet braids. She would, she decided, have to find a more fashionable hair style soon. The neat golden braids, traditional to her Swedish heritage, looked fine with a maid's uniform, but with the modish clothes of a well-to-do lady she needed a more American look.

She had not put on a corset that morning and she feared the clothes would be tight around the waist, but they fit quite well. Once she had put them on, she felt she looked very nice, hairdo notwithstanding. She went down to meet Mrs. Malloy—no, Aunt Molly, she had to remember—well pleased with herself.

The lady was waiting for her in the front parlor. "Charming, my dear. They fit well enough?"

"Very well, thank you, Mrs.—Aunt Molly. But they are not yours, and I wondered—"

"They belong to one of my nieces. She and her parents, my sister and her husband, live in Ohio, but she visited here last summer and left some things behind. They're not suitable for winter, really, and she's coming back in June, so I kept them here for her. Are you sure you find them warm enough?"

"Yes, thank you."

An awkward little silence fell, broken when both women started to speak at once.

"Aunt Molly, you—"

"Hilda, my dear—"

They broke off. Hilda said, "I am sorry. Please go ahead."

"No, I interrupted you."

"It is just that I want to tell you—want to thank you for all you are doing for me—for us. You take me in and are kind to me, you give me clothing to wear and treat me like one of the family, you give me tea as if I were a lady. Patrick says Mr. Malloy will give us a house for a wedding present. A house! Never have I imagined owing a house of my own, and now…"

She paused and then went on, slowly. "It is hard for me to—to adjust to this. I am a maid, but you treat me like a daughter. Patrick is your nephew, but he is now almost like your son. I— I do not know quite how to act, how to behave. The rules I have known are changing. If I say something stupid or do something wrong, I hope you will forgive me. You have been so kind."

Mrs. Malloy looked down for a moment and then smiled gently. "That is a little of what I wanted to talk to you about. I was going to say, a moment ago, that I want you to know something. Patrick may have already told you, but if not, I must. When I first realized that you two cared for each other, two years ago during that dreadful trouble for Mr. Malloy, I was deeply distressed."

Hilda's face lost all its animation. "But I thought you liked me!"

"I do, Hilda. I am very fond of you indeed, and I was even then. I liked you for yourself, and of course this family owes you a debt we can never repay. You saved Mr. Malloy's life and we will never forget that. No, my objections had nothing to do with you personally, but I saw many problems ahead for you and Patrick. You are of different nationalities, different classes, and most troubling of all, different religions. I knew that your family would not approve of your marriage to Patrick, and that most of

Patrick's family would not approve of his marriage to you. I spoke to Patrick about it."

"He did not tell me!"

"No, I can see that he did not. Even at the time I didn't think he would. Though I was as persuasive as I knew how to be, he didn't listen to more than one word in ten. It was during the time that you were missing, and he was nearly demented with worry.

"Since then I have observed you, my dear. You may think me a prying old woman, but Patrick is very dear to me and Mr. Malloy, and it was clear that he was becoming more and more dear to you. So I watched and I listened, and I liked what I learned. You are brave and determined. You will need both qualities to survive the prejudice you will encounter as Patrick's wife. You have considerable intelligence and a fierce loyalty. You are stubborn, of course, and sometimes foolhardy, but age will likely cure the latter, and surely life with Patrick will moderate the former."

Hilda listened, her cheeks going alternately red and white.

"So, Hilda, now you know. I was once determined to stop this marriage. I am now equally determined to do all I can to make it a success. It won't be easy, child. You've just said yourself, you have a great deal of adjusting to do. You'll leave Tippecanoe Place a servant and walk into your own house a well-to-do young bride. Your life will change completely, and you won't like all of it. But at least money won't be a worry to you, and I'll try to help you through the rest."

"And there will be Patrick," said Hilda, very quietly.

"What's that, dear? I don't hear as well as I used to."

"I said, there will be Patrick to help me, also. He is the bridge between my old life and my new one. He has moved in your world for many years, as well as in his own and in mine. It will be strange sometimes, but I am not afraid. I will have him."

"By the saints, girl, you'll do!" Mrs. Malloy slapped the arm of her chair. "We'll have a little something to celebrate your engagement. Just ring for Riggs, will you?"

And Hilda, for the first time in her life, pulled a bell rope and thought again about America, where a servant, one to be summoned at her master's will, was now the summoner.

Riggs brought sherry at his mistress's order. He set the tray, with a decanter and two glasses, on the table by Mrs. Malloy's chair. He tried hard to keep his face under control, but he failed.

"Mr. Riggs does not like me," said Hilda after he had left the room.

"Riggs, dear. He isn't your superior. And he will get used to you. Riggs doesn't like change, but you're a member of the family now. Take no notice of him, if you can manage that. If you can't, then let fly with that temper of yours. He respects authority. Now, will you take a glass of wine with me?"

*That lawlessness has existed in South
Bend for a long time...that bawdy
houses are seldom molested...is
of common knowledge.*

—South Bend *Tribune*
February 10, 1904

23

ILDA HAD NEVER tasted wine in her life, save for the tiny sip in church on Communion Sundays. She eyed the decanter dubiously. "I do not know, Mrs.—Aunt Molly. I think maybe I should not. It is not allowed at Tippecanoe Place, and our family has never had money to spend on drink. Also, our church does not approve of drinking."

"Well, I don't want you to violate your conscience, but if you're marrying into an Irish family, girl, you need to learn to drink—in moderation, of course."

Hilda thought about that. "I do not know that I mind," she said slowly. "If we drink it in church, and the *Herre Gud* told us to, it cannot be wicked. I will try a little."

"Splendid. Just a bit at first, as you say, and sip it slowly."

The wine was sweet and heady. Hilda downed her meager half glass in a few sips, feeling deliciously wicked. "I like it," she said in surprise. "It is not so different from what we have in church."

"Well, as to that, I can't say, since only the priest drinks the wine in our church. But this is lovely stuff, in moderation, as I say. Drink too much and you'll be wishing yourself dead in the morning."

"The Irish do—I am sorry, Aunt Molly, but it is said that the Irish do drink too much."

"Sure, and they do, some of them. It's a tragic habit. See you never get into it yourself. But I'm pleased to say that Patrick is a temperate man. You'll never need to worry about him, no more than I ever have about Mr. Malloy."

She said nothing about her son, Clancy. Hilda knew that drink was one of Clancy's many problems, but Clancy was never likely to come home from New York, so he would never become a problem for Hilda.

"Aunt Molly, I know much about the proper way to do things in a gentleman's house. I have been helping to do them for many years. But Tippecanoe Place is teetotal, so I do not know anything about serving drink. Is it always served in these tiny glasses?"

"Gracious, no, child! Those are for sherry. Other kinds of wine are served in glasses something like these, with stems, but larger, because the wine is not so strong. Beer is served in mugs, and whiskey —"

"Oh, I would never drink whiskey!"

"Of course you won't, because you are a lady, and ladies drink only wine. But your servants need to know how to serve whiskey to the gentlemen, and you must teach them."

Mrs. Malloy was well launched on the beginning of Hilda's social education when Mr. Malloy came home. An array of glasses was set out on the tea table, and Hilda was studying them intently.

"Is it an orgy we're having, then, Mrs. Malloy?" he said as he walked into the room. "Good day to you, Miss Johansson."

"It's Hilda to us now, Mr. Malloy. She's part of the family. Hilda, ring and ask Riggs to take the glasses away and bring Mr. Malloy some tea."

Perhaps it was the sherry, though she had drunk it more than an hour before. Perhaps it was Mrs. Malloy's instruction. At any rate, when the butler came into the room, Hilda smiled at him pleasantly. "Please take these things away and bring a pot of tea for Mr. Malloy, Riggs. Thank you."

He did as he was told, and Hilda breathed a sigh of relief. One hurdle crossed.

"Now, Mr. Malloy, Hilda has come to us with a very serious

problem. We aren't sure what we had best do, and we need your advice. Tell him, Hilda."

So she related the whole story once more. "I was maybe a fool to do what I did, sir, but I could think of nothing else."

"Couldn't tackle the fellow, not without help. Might better have let it wait until later, but what's done is done. The fellow's on the alert now. You're staying here with us, of course?"

"Yes, sir. Aunt—that is, Mrs. Malloy—"

"I've told her she's to call us Aunt and Uncle, Mr. Malloy. And of course she's staying here until it's safe for her to return."

"Hmph. Don't see any need for her to go back there at all, unless Mrs. Studebaker is shorthanded. How's that butler of yours doing, Hilda? Williams, I mean, not the sly fellow."

"He is better. The doctors think he will recover, but it will take time. And if Colonel Studebaker lets Mr.—lets Barnes go, the household will be in trouble. I think I must go back to work when it is safe, but I do not know when that might be."

"Don't like the idea of my niece slaving in somebody else's house. I'll tell you what. After dinner I'll go over there myself and see what's what. The fellow ought to be in jail."

"Oh, if you do that, sir, would you please have someone tell my sister where I am? She will be very worried. I told her I was coming back and she will not know what to think."

"Right you are. Now, Mrs. Malloy, what's for dinner? I could eat a horse."

"Roast beef will have to do, I'm afraid, Mr. Malloy."

Hilda watched them as they ate their meal, watched the looks they exchanged, listened to their gentle joking. *Why, they are still in love, after all those years of marriage, and all their trouble with their children,* she thought, and her heart warmed at the sight. *Maybe Patrick and I, years from now...* But the thought was too private even to think in company.

Immediately after they finished the meal, Mr. Malloy ordered the carriage. Hilda sat with Mrs. Malloy in the parlor and talked, but her mind was not on the conversation. She started every time she heard hoofbeats, and when at last the front door opened, she sprang to her feet, waiting anxiously while Mr. Malloy shed his outer garments in the hall.

"Well, Hilda, I saw your sister and set her mind at rest. She's a bit confused, but not worried. For the rest, it's not the best news, I'm afraid," he said, when he came into the parlor. "The fellow's gone. Didn't wait to be sacked, didn't pack his clothes or anything, just took French leave. And took some documents with him, it seems."

"Documents?" said Hilda with a frown. "I thought he was looking for money. I do not know what Colonel Studebaker keeps in the safe, but I thought there would be lots of money."

"Some. Not a great deal, according to what he told me. Most of his money's in the bank, of course. He keeps a little cash in the house, not more than a few hundred, and he says it all seems to be there."

A few hundred! Dear heaven, to Hilda that was a fortune. It had taken her and her family years to save four hundred dollars to bring the rest of the family here from Sweden, and when the money was stolen from them it was a major catastrophe. Now here was her new uncle talking as if hundreds of dollars was pocket change. Truly it was a new world she was about to enter.

Mr. Malloy had gone on talking. "Mostly he keeps important documents in there. Business ledgers, legal papers, his will, deed to the house, that sort of thing. Said his father kept almost all the Studebaker company records in that safe, and he, the colonel, hasn't cleaned them all out yet. But there were some other papers there, important ones, and they're all gone."

"But what were they?" Hilda had to know.

Mr. Malloy cleared his throat. "Something he was looking into, he and some other men in town. An investigation, I suppose you'd call it. He'd put all his notes in the safe and now he's lost them. Mrs. Malloy, I'd like a drink. Dry work, going through papers."

Mrs. Malloy rang for the butler and then turned to her husband. "Mr. Malloy, for pity's sake tell us what the papers were, unless Colonel Studebaker bound you to secrecy."

"No." He cleared his throat again. "Fact is, not a suitable topic for ladies."

"But I am not yet a lady, sir. Uncle Dan. And I would like to know."

"As would I, Mr. Malloy." The tiny woman pulled herself up to her full height. Her voice was quiet, but her husband capitulated at once.

"Oh, very well. You'll not like it, mind. Might as well all sit down. This'll take a little time."

They settled. Riggs brought his whiskey and he took a sip from his glass and thought for a moment, then began to speak.

"It's this way. You'll know—that is, Hilda, do you read the papers?"

"Yes. I am not supposed to, but I do, when I can."

"Then you'll know that the *Tribune* keeps going on and on about how corrupt this town is, how bad the police are, how the mayor ought to do something."

"Yes," said Hilda warmly, "and I think it is a terrible thing, those cartoons they put on the front page making fun of Mayor Fogarty and the Irish."

"It makes me blood boil, and that's a fact," said Mr. Malloy, "but the only way to fight it is with the truth. So some of us on the County Council have been lookin' into the matter, to see just how much there is to it, and it's sad to say, but we've found a lot of shady business goin' on."

He sipped a little more of his drink. "Of course, the Republicans have done their lookin' too, and they've come up with more than we Democrats have. Could be they've made up a little bit here and there, but maybe not. They say there's vice everywhere. Illegal liquor sales, gamblin' dens—and houses that are not as respectable as they ought to be."

Mrs. Malloy looked at Hilda. "You do understand what he's talking about, don't you?"

"Yes, Aunt Molly." Hilda blushed. "I am a housemaid. I am in the room, often, or in the hall outside, when men talk about such things. They forget that I am there, but I hear, and I know."

Mr. Malloy looked relieved. "Then I don't have to spell it out. Well, it seems that Colonel Studebaker is one of the Republicans investigating the corruption, and the particular area he's lookin' into is these—er—irregular establishments."

"You might as well call them bawdy houses, Mr. Malloy," said his wife gently. "We all know about them, and it would save you trouble."

"Hmph! Don't know what the world's comin' to when decent women know of such things. However, the point is that Colonel Studebaker had quite a file of information about the bawdy houses in South Bend, including reports from an investigator he'd hired. He wasn't eager to tell me about it. We're on opposite sides of the political fence, of course, but he's an honorable man, and so am I, I hope. So in the end he did tell me. And believe it or not, it was that file that the butler fellow stole."

"But—" said Hilda and Mrs. Malloy. The older woman continued. "I don't understand, Mr. Malloy. What use would a butler have for such information?"

"That's what we can't figure out. It can't have been just that he wanted to—er—patronize one of the establishments. He could find one easily enough just by asking around, more's the pity. He wouldn't take the risk of stealing. We talked about it, the colonel and I, and the only thing we could think was that Barnes wanted to sell the information somewhere."

"That does not make sense, sir—Uncle Dan. He might be able to get a little money from someone who did not want the information made public, but he could have got much more money, I think, just by stealing it from the safe. Why try to get it in such a complicated way?"

"There's somethin' here we don't understand," Mr. Malloy admitted. "We'll have to hope the police catch that feller right away, so we can get some answers."

"Meanwhile, Mr. Malloy, Hilda is staying right here with us, where she'll be safe."

"But that is not so good! I am sorry, Aunt Molly. I am grateful to you. But I cannot yoost—*just* sit here and be safe. Tomorrow is

Miss Jacobs's funeral, and I must go to Elkhart and talk with her family."

"The police have been doing that, child, and I'm sure some of them will go to the funeral."

"Yes, but they have not found the killer yet. And I am sorry to have to say it, Uncle Dan, since you are in the government, but I do not think the police are very good. Some of them are good men, but they are maybe not so smart. And Mr. Barrett has asked me to talk to people. I must go!"

"Yes," said Mrs. Malloy with a sigh, "I see that you must. Mr. Malloy, will it be possible for you to be away from the store tomorrow?"

"Don't see why not. Not much business in January anyway, once the white sales are over. I've a bit higher opinion of the police than you do, Hilda, but I admit they don't seem to have got very far with this murder. It's making the girls in the store nervous, my clerks and my customers both. They don't like walkin' around alone, even in the daytime, and I'm tellin' you, by late afternoon you could fire a shotgun through the store and not hurt a livin' soul. I'm as eager as you to get this thing behind us. I'll take you to the funeral, Hilda, and good luck to you."

24

Treat your servants always with kindness.

—Richard A. Wells, A.M.
Manners Culture and Dress, 1891

HILDA SLEPT, IN THE strange bed, the sleep of the emotionally spent. It was by far the best bed she'd ever known, in the prettiest room, though she went to sleep too soon to appreciate it much. She woke early, yawned and stretched, and wondered what time it was. There was a clock by her bed, but the room was pitch dark. The electric street lamps on Colfax were only on the corners; their light didn't reach the Malloy house in the middle of the block.

The house, entirely modern and up-to-date, was wired for electricity. There was an electrolier in the room that she could turn on from a switch on the wall, but the room was chilly and her bed was warm. She was just about to drift off to sleep again when she heard soft footsteps pattering down the hall outside her door, and in a moment a tap on a door and the rattle of china.

Agnes bringing early-morning tea or coffee to her master and mistress, Hilda surmised. It couldn't be all that early. She'd better be up and dressed.

Then the tap sounded at her own door. It opened a crack, letting in light from the hall. "Are you awake, miss?"

"Yes, Agnes. I am getting up."

"Please, miss, Mrs. Malloy said as I was to ask you if you'd like some coffee or tea. It'll warm you before you have to get out of bed, miss. And she said to tell you there's no need for you to get up until you please."

"Thank you, Agnes. I would like some tea. And would you leave the door open a little, please, so I can see my way?" She badly wanted coffee, but she had learned that the Irish idea of coffee and the Swedish idea were two very different matters. Good tea was infinitely preferable to bad coffee.

"I'll light the gas for you, miss, shall I? It's a kinder light for the morning, to my way of thinking. Softer. The electric glares so."

So Agnes lit one of the wall sconces and turned it to a low level. Hilda lay in bed watching her. Agnes had improved in the two years since Hilda had first met her. The raw girl had turned into an accomplished maid.

When she left, Hilda spent a little time looking around her room. It was nothing like the guest rooms at Tippecanoe Place, of course. It was much smaller, for one thing. The rug on the floor was not Persian, but a good, thick, American-made Axminster. The fireplace was pretty, but not elaborately paneled and tiled like the ones in nearly every room of the Studebaker home. The curtains, the wallpaper, the furniture all spoke of solid comfort rather than vast wealth.

In her own house, Hilda decided, she would have a room very much like this one. She was just deciding on the colors and patterns she wanted when Agnes came back with her tea.

"I'll just light your fire, miss."

Hilda lay sipping her tea and watching someone else work. It made her feel peculiar. She wasn't entirely sure she liked it. And when Agnes spilled a little coal on the hearth, she could stand it no longer. She sprang out of bed, picked up the coal, and placed it neatly in the grate.

"Miss, you didn't ought to do that!"

"I am used to doing it, and I can show you an easier way. Here, if you hold the scuttle *so*..." She demonstrated, while Agnes knelt watching, open-mouthed.

"Agnes, do you like working here?" Hilda asked abruptly.

The maid turned to her, startled. "Yes, miss." She stood, dusted off her skirt where she had knelt on the floor, and started for the door.

"No, I mean, do you really? Or are you just being polite? Because I am a maid myself, you know. Soon I will not be one, but

for many years I have done the kind of work you are doing. I
want to know. Is this a good place to work?"

"Well, it is and it isn't, if you know what I mean, miss. I don't
like Mr. Riggs. He's got a temper."

"I think all butlers do," said Hilda.

"But Mr. and Mrs. Malloy are good people, and Mrs. Malloy is
very kind."

"I know," said Hilda feelingly. "She has been kind to me,
more than once."

"Yes, miss, I know what you did for the family."

"What I did was not all good."

"About Mr. Clancy, you mean? Yes, but Mrs. Malloy doesn't
hold a grudge about that. She says to Mr. Malloy, she says Clancy
was headin' for a bad end, and havin' to go away might be the
makin' of him. She says if you hadn't found out all you did, he
might've got into worse trouble. And she's right about that. He
went with a real fast crowd, he did, when he was here, and he got
to be an idler and a masher, just like them. It's better he's gone.
Mrs. Malloy, she's sad about him, but she doesn't blame you,
miss."

"I am glad. I have worried. Agnes, does it seem strange to you,
a maid like me marrying and coming into a family with money?"

"No, miss. You're real smart and real pretty, and I reckon you
could do most anything you wanted to. I got to go now, miss.
There's breakfast to see to."

"Thank you, Agnes." The room was still chilly. Hilda crept
back under the covers and lay in bed for another few minutes,
basking in the luxury of getting up when she chose, and to a
warm room. The clock beside the bed ticked more quietly than
the busy alarm clock beside her own bed, the clock that forced
her out of bed at five-thirty every morning, but at last it drew
Hilda's attention.

Nearly seven! At Tippecanoe Place she would have a solid
hour's work done by now. She threw back the covers, washed
hastily, and dressed in yesterday's borrowed clothes. She also put
Patrick's ring on her finger. No need for secrecy here.

Before she went downstairs she made her bed. The force of habit is strong.

Mr. and Mrs. Malloy were not yet downstairs, but Riggs was. All Hilda's trepidation returned. She greeted him with a nervous smile. He bowed stiffly.

"Good morning, Miss Johansson. Mrs. Malloy instructed me to serve you with breakfast whenever you came down, madam. What would you care for?"

His deference, though plainly unwilling, was correct. Hilda swallowed. "Thank you, Riggs. Are there any boiled eggs?"

"Whatever you like, madam."

She licked her dry lips. "Two boiled eggs, please, and toast."

"That is all, madam?" He managed to make it sound ridiculously meager.

"And some bacon, please. Thank you."

She didn't want the bacon. She didn't want anything except to get rid of Riggs. And perhaps some good coffee, but she dared not go to the kitchen to show the cook how to make it. She was afraid of the butler, afraid of the cook, afraid of being a lady.

At home, at Tippecanoe Place, the servants would be sitting down to a large meal about now. Mrs. Sullivan had learned from Hilda how to make coffee. There would be porridge, eggs, ham, toast made from Mrs. Sullivan's own delicious bread, perhaps griddle cakes with maple syrup, rich butter....

There would be conversation. All the live-in servants would talk about the family, about their own concerns, about the work of the day to come, about Mr. Williams's health. They would joke and complain, make a good meal, and clean it up quickly so that they could attend to the family's breakfasts and the other chores of a huge house.

Hilda sat alone in the Malloy dining room and crumbled her toast.

She jumped when Mrs. Malloy came into the room.

"Why, child, you haven't touched your food! Did the wine upset your stomach, then?"

"Oh. No. I had forgotten the wine. No, I am—I am not

hungry. We had a large dinner last night." Her voice wobbled despite her best efforts.

"Hilda, my dear, what is it?"

"I am—I do not know. Lonely, and—oh, already I miss my old life!" A tear rolled down her cheek, and then another. She felt for a handkerchief. There was none in her pocket.

"Oh, is that all it is?" Mrs. Malloy was brisk. "Use your napkin, child. You're homesick, that's what you are. What do you miss most?"

"Coffee," said Hilda before she thought.

"Then we'll get you some coffee." She reached for the bell.

"No! No, I—" She'd done it now. She would have to explain. "I like Swedish coffee. It is different from the coffee in America."

"Better?"

"I think much better."

"Good. Then come to the kitchen with me right this minute, and teach me how to make Swedish coffee. I can't abide the stuff, myself, but maybe I've never had it made properly."

So Hilda found herself in the kitchen teaching Mrs. Malloy and her cook how to make coffee the Swedish way. The cook was none too pleased, but Mrs. Malloy was delighted. Not only was the coffee delicious, quite unlike the pallid brew Mrs. Malloy had tasted and rejected years ago, but Hilda was animated and voluble, her brief fit of panic forgotten.

It returned, however, when she went back to the dining room. Riggs was there and had cleared the table.

"Oh, Riggs, we hadn't finished eating. Bring us some more bacon and eggs and toast, and Mr. Malloy will be wanting porridge soon."

"Yes, madam. I am sorry, madam. You had left the room and I assumed—"

"Yes, yes, quite natural. We had stepped into the kitchen for a moment."

"Yes, madam."

He left and Hilda sighed. "Never will I be able to do that."

"Do what, dear?"

"Give orders to a butler. He frightens me. This morning I got out of bed and helped Agnes with the fire, and then, just now, I made coffee in the kitchen. That is where I belong. That is where I am comfortable. I do not know how to be a lady!"

"Of course you don't, but you'll learn, and the first thing to learn is never to let a servant intimidate you. You are in charge, not they."

"But I am accustomed to taking orders, not giving them."

"Are you? Have you not given Patrick orders for years? And the under-housemaids? And I daresay the Studebakers, as well, though with them you had to be a little more subtle. From what I know of your character, I'd say that you usually got your own way, somehow. Why is it so different now?"

Hilda had not thought about it quite like that.

"You see, it's all a matter of attitude. If you expect a butler to be rude to you, he probably will be. If you are polite to him, but firm in what you want, he'll respect that—and if he does not, you sack him and find someone who will obey you. Of course one never takes advantage of a servant. That is not only unkind and unchristian, it is also stupid, for servants talk to one another—as you know—and one must not get a reputation for injustice, or no good servants will ever enter the house again. Kind but firm, that's the rule. You'll have no problem with that, I'm sure."

Riggs returned with their breakfasts. Hilda wondered if he had been listening outside the door. Never mind if he had. She inspected her plate, with two fried eggs staring up at her. "I prefer my eggs boiled, Riggs," she said pleasantly.

"Yes, madam." He reached for her plate.

"No, I will eat the bacon, but please bring the boiled eggs."

She picked up her knife and fork. Riggs bowed and retreated.

Mrs. Malloy winked at Hilda, and then they both burst into laughter. They were still laughing when Mr. Malloy came into the room

"Well, well, you're both cheerful this morning. It's a morning that needs some cheer, for certain. Those clouds are going to burst soon, or I'm a Chinaman. Porridge, Riggs, good and hot, and some eggs and sausage and toast."

"Yes, sir," said the butler, who had materialized with Hilda's boiled eggs. "Tea, sir?"

"You should try the coffee this morning, Mr. Malloy," said his wife. "Hilda taught Mrs. Hall how to make it properly, and it tastes like a little bit of heaven."

Mr. Malloy couldn't understand why both women were convulsed by the scandalized expression on Riggs's face.

...a disposition that helped to make her one of the most popular girls in town.

—South Bend *Tribune*
January 23, 1904

25

Now, Hilda," said Mrs. Malloy when they had finished eating, "what we must do this morning is find you a few clothes. Have you anything to wear to a funeral?"

"Only my uniform. I could go home and get that. I do not look like a maid if I do not wear the apron, and I have a black hat."

Mrs. Malloy herself was still in mourning for her son Sean, but she had reached the stage of wearing touches of white at her neck and wrists, and white petticoats. With her graying hair, the clothing was becoming.

She considered Hilda's suggestion. "Well, it's possible, I suppose, but you're going to need proper blacks anyway. There's no time to have anything made up. What do you have in the store, Mr. Malloy, that would do?"

"A very nice line in ready-to-wear mourning, if I do say so meself. Some lovely black hats, as well. Why don't you spend the morning shopping, and I'll take you to lunch before we catch the train."

"Oh, I cannot, Uncle Dan." The name was beginning to come more easily to her lips. "Patrick is taking me and Erik to lunch."

"Well, then, the two of them can join us."

"No, Mr. Malloy," said his wife firmly. "They will not want us sharing their lunch. I'll come home after we find what we need, and Hilda can go to the store after lunch and change into her blacks. They'll likely have needed alterations, so she can just leave them on after the final fitting. Then we'll pick her up there and go to the station."

Hilda submitted meekly to the plan, asking only that someone get a message to Patrick that he would find her at Malloy's Dry Goods at lunch time.

So began the most dizzying morning of Hilda's life. They got to the store shortly after it opened and began choosing new clothes. The mourning dress and hat were the first order of business. Mrs. Malloy insisted on the full outfit: black wool skirt and matching jacket, black waist with a bit of white at the throat, black petticoat, black-edged handkerchiefs, black gloves, jet earrings, black umbrella, and an elaborate black hat. "For you're not close to the deceased on this occasion, but there will be other funerals, and you might not have enough notice to get a proper outfit made."

The suit and waist did, in fact, have to be altered slightly, so while that was being done they looked for less somber clothing. "You'll need lots of clothes, but we don't want to buy them all at once. For now, what you want is a ready-made wool skirt, one or two nice waists, and a good warm coat. And of course, underthings. Then we can look at some nice woolens and some patterns for other things."

They bought Hilda a new corset. She protested that she had just purchased one, but since it was at the Studebaker house and she needed one now, her protests were overridden. Nightgowns and a silk kimono like Mrs. Malloy's. Petticoats, underdrawers, chemises. Stockings and a pair of enchanting new shoes, black patent leather with grosgrain bows.

Hilda suddenly remembered about Mrs. Chudzik and the things she needed. Estimating sizes, Hilda shopped for appropriate clothing. Of course, the money she had been given was in her own pocket, not in the borrowed skirt, but it didn't matter. Everything was put down to the Malloy account, and Mrs. Malloy said Hilda could settle up later.

By the end of the morning Hilda was exhausted, but happy.

"It is so kind of you to do this for me," she said again and again. "I do not know why you are so good to me."

"Nonsense, girl," said Mrs. Malloy in high good humor. "It's like having a daughter again. I haven't had such a good time since my Mary was a bride, and her with two little girls of her own now. Now, I'll have everything except your blacks sent to our house, and we can sort them out tomorrow. And as it's nearly time for that rascally nephew of mine to come and fetch you, you'd better scoot off to the dressing room and see if your blacks are ready now. You'll like to impress Patrick with them, I expect. Then as soon as he comes for you I'll go home and put my feet up. We can meet you at the station."

When Patrick arrived at the store, he tipped his hat politely to the beautifully dressed young widow who was standing at the door. Then he blinked and looked more closely.

"Glory be to God, what've ye done to yerself?"

Hilda giggled. "Aunt Molly made a wager with me that you would not know me. I shall have to pay her. Am I not fine?" She revolved slowly to give him the full effect.

"You're—you're gorgeous," said Patrick, recovering his American accent. "But who died?"

"Miss Jacobs, of course. Aunt Molly said I might as well get full mourning while I was doing it, so I'd have a set if I needed it later."

"And who's Aunt Molly?" Patrick asked with a grin.

"She said I was to call her that. And oh, Patrick, she and Uncle Dan have been so generous to me! I have much to tell you while we eat lunch." She looked around. "Where is Erik?"

"Meetin' us at the hotel. I thought I'd splurge and take you to the Oliver. It's a good thing I didn't plan to go to an ordinary sort of place, and you lookin' like that!"

"It is a good thing," she said, giggling again, "that I did not wear my ordinary clothes, and you takin' me to the Oliver."

"Begorrah, it's the Irish colleen you're soundin' like, me girl!"

A good many people on the busy streets of South Bend that morning wondered, somewhat disapprovingly, at the high spirits of the attractive young widow and her escort, who was not dressed in mourning at all. If her gloves had not covered her diamond ring, tongues would have wagged even faster.

On the way to the Oliver, Hilda told Patrick most of what had transpired since she had seen him the day before. It was a long story, and Patrick didn't much care for the end of it.

"So the scalawag's got away, has he? And with a grudge against you. That fine colonel of yours'd done better to clap him in jail."

"Yes, but Mr. Barnes left before Colonel George got home. It was I who did the stupid thing, letting him know I had seen him."

"Well, that's water under the bridge now. What're they doin' to find him?"

"I don't know. You see, I have thought about this. If Colonel George tells the police what Mr. Barnes stole, they will not like it, because they will think the police, too, are being accused of corruption. If he does not tell, there is no reason to arrest Mr. Barnes."

"Hmph. Seems to me we're in a tricky spot, and you especially, seein' as how—"

"Shh! Here is the hotel, and there is Erik. We will not talk about that part of it while he is with us."

Patrick nodded. Discussions of rampant vice were seldom appropriate table conversation, and never in front of a thirteen-year-old boy.

When Erik spied his sister, he was for once in his life speechless. This vision of elegance was so unlike the girl who had told him bedtime stories that he was quite shy with her for a good two minutes. He, too, was dressed in his best, but beside Hilda he looked very much the country cousin.

"So," Hilda said, when they were seated and had ordered. "Have you spoken to Andy?"

"Not today." His sister's voice, her same normal voice, reassured him. He knew the person under that finery, after all. "I couldn't find him when I got to the hotel. One of the other boys told me he had to take up a lot of stuff for some customer."

"He told me something interesting yesterday."

So they talked about the Perkins bill that had been paid, and speculated endlessly without coming to any conclusion.

Hilda had no dessert. Her new corset wouldn't allow it, and she was afraid of being late for the train. She hurried Patrick along.

"You didn't tell Erik when we're gettin' married."

"Boys don't care about wedding plans, and I must tell Mama first."

Patrick sighed. "How's she going to take it?"

"Badly, I imagine. I will do it soon, so she will have time before April to stop being angry. Just as soon as I can go freely around the town again."

"Whenever that might be," said Patrick darkly. "I've a good mind to find him myself."

Hilda sighed and said nothing. She was not minded to argue, and Patrick would do as he wanted in any case.

He waited with her at the station until the Malloys arrived. When he had greeted them and hugged his aunt, he tipped his hat to all of them. "I'll be off, then. Have to see a man about a dog."

"Wonder what he meant by that?" said Mr. Malloy, staring open-mouthed as Patrick strode off.

"I am afraid I know," said Hilda, but she said it so quietly that no one heard.

The train ride to Elkhart was uneventful, except that it began to rain slightly. Hilda was glad she had not worn her beautiful new shoes. The train made good time, and they got to the church a half hour before the service was to start.

"Now, my dear, what is it you want to do here?" Mrs. Malloy spoke softly, but she couldn't keep the doubt out of her voice. She thought this was a fruitless errand.

"I want only to watch, for now. I want to see which people, besides her family, are most upset. They are the ones I will want to speak to afterwards."

"Sensible idea," said Mr. Malloy, trying not to sound surprised.

So Mrs. Malloy chose a pew in a side balcony from which they could see nearly everyone, while Mr. Malloy and Hilda lingered at the back of the church to watch people as they came in.

"Those women, see?" Hilda whispered to him. "Three of them. They are all about the same age as Miss Jacobs, and they are all crying. They are not sisters, or they would come in with the family. They must be friends. Oh, and look at that man! He is also young, and his eyes are red. Gentleman caller, maybe?"

"Mmm," said Mr. Malloy. His eyes were scanning the incoming crowd for a different sort of man, someone who looked like a butler. If that scoundrel Barnes had somehow got wind of Hilda's movements today, he might be in the crowd. Mr. Malloy's fingers were itching to get hold of the fellow.

The church was packed. This murder was the biggest sensation to hit Elkhart in years. Everyone who had ever known Miss Sophie Jacobs in any capacity was there, from her kindergarten teacher on, and quite a few who had not. Representatives of the press were there in force, some bearing cameras. They were made to wait outside, where the drizzle dampened their equipment and their spirits. The police, also there in force, were allowed to enter the church, but told they must stand at the back. That seemed to suit them. They were there to observe and to prevent trouble, not to mourn.

At last the family entered, the women swathed in veils, with the coffin following. Hilda and Mr. Malloy edged to their seats, and Hilda settled down to watch. This was when people would start to cry in earnest.

She paid scant attention to the service, but her sharp eyes missed nothing that went on in the congregation. The family, she decided, was truly devastated. She would make no attempt to talk to them. It would be cruel.

The man and three women she had spotted seemed deeply affected. The man sat next to the family and frequently exchanged glances with them. Definitely a gentleman friend, thought Hilda. She watched and sorted and categorized. People who had known the girl well, people who had some slight connection, people who had come out of curiosity.

She knew she was making some mistakes. People varied in their reaction to death. Some who would weep over the death of a kitten would remain dry-eyed at the funeral of a cousin. Some would cry bitterly at the funeral of a stranger. But she was especially interested in two men at the back of the church. They showed no emotion at all, nor did they look as though they were keeping emotion in check. They watched, just as Hilda was watching. Fortunately they seldom looked up to Hilda's balcony, but when one of them turned his head her way, she was able to drop her head and lift a handkerchief to her cheek before their eyes met.

She touched Mr. Malloy's arm. "Look at those two men," she whispered. "The ones in the center of the back row who do not look sad at all."

"Shh!" said a woman behind them.

Mr. Malloy turned his head, spotted the men, then discreetly took a fountain pen and pad out of his breast pocket. *What about them?* he wrote, and passed the pad and pen to Hilda.

I think they know something. Watch them. She showed the note to Mr. Malloy and then buried the pad under a fold of her skirt.

The service was long. Not only the minister but several other people spoke of Miss Jacobs's devotion to her church, of her volunteer work with young people, of her piety and sweet nature. When the proceedings finally ended, Hilda stood with the rest of the congregation as the coffin was borne out of the church on the shoulders of six men. When it was proper to speak, she turned to Mr. Malloy. "I want you to watch those men. I must go and speak to the three friends."

"No," said Mrs. Malloy. "Hilda, you go nowhere by yourself."

"Mr. Barnes is not here. I looked."

"No matter. You will stay with Mr. Malloy." Her tone made it clear that there would be no argument.

Hilda knew a stone wall when she saw one. "Yes, Aunt Molly. Perhaps you, then, would watch those men while I—*Herre Gud!* What was that?"

A muffled explosion, a blinding light. Women screamed, men shouted.

"Only one of those cursed reporters, taking a photograph with flash powder. The stuff is dangerous, shouldn't be allowed—" Mr. Malloy broke off and suddenly bellowed, "Stop that man! He tried to shoot me!"

"The state of Indiana in this case is not in earnest. It does not want to know who killed this girl."

—Judge J. N. Palmer, quoted in
South Bend *Tribune*
May 27, 1904

26

STOP HIM! POLICE! He's got a gun!"

"Daniel! Are you hurt? Where did he hit you?" Mrs. Malloy was pale.

"There, that's done it. They're after him. I'm sorry if I scared you, Molly, me dear, but don't worry. Nobody tried to shoot anybody. That man running away is one of the ones Hilda was watching. He's been acting peculiar. I think he's up to something."

"But you said—"

"And do you think anybody'd have paid any attention if I'd shouted, 'He's a suspicious character,' eh?"

Hilda had been frightened, too. She tried to rescue her composure. "But, sir—Uncle Dan, do you think he might have run away because he was frightened? It took everyone by surprise."

"It took you by surprise because you didn't see that blasted man with the camera raise his arm. I've seen flash pictures taken before, so I knew what he was about. Bad manners, but then what can you expect from a reporter? The point is, I saw him, so I knew what was coming. And *so did the man who ran*. He ran *because* photographs were being taken."

"Oh." Hilda digested that. "Oh! Then he did not want his picture in the newspaper! And that must mean…"

"It means he's up to something shady, or I'm a Rooshian."

"But where is the other man, the one who was with him?"

"Don't know. Sorry, me girl. Lost him in all the confusion. And it looks like the police lost the fellow I set them on, too." For several policemen were walking back to the church, shaking their heads.

"It cannot be helped." She was discouraged, and furious with the lout whose flash powder had cost her the best opportunity she'd seen yet to learn something useful. Slowly she made her way with the Malloys out of the church. The crowd was dispersing, climbing into the carriages that were waiting in line.

Hilda surveyed them. "I think perhaps everyone is going to the cemetery now. I had not planned to go, but I want to talk to Miss Jacobs's friends."

"But how would we get there?" asked Mrs. Malloy gently. "We know no one here, and we have no carriage, remember?"

"A cab?" said Hilda doubtfully.

"My dear." Mrs. Malloy gestured. The few cabs available had been snapped up almost immediately and were now filled to capacity and waiting in line with the other carriages. The hearse began to move off, plumed horses snorting and dancing a little in the cold, and the procession slowly followed. The bystanders were hurrying away. The rain began to come down in earnest.

Hilda and the Malloys opened their black umbrellas and began to walk to the train station.

It was after five when they arrived back in South Bend, and raining harder than ever. Fortunately there was a telephone at the train station. Mr. Malloy called home, and soon his coachman arrived with a closed carriage. Hilda, whose teeth had begun to chatter, huddled gratefully under the fur rug. "Hot tea, the minute we get home," said Mrs. Malloy, looking at Hilda with concern.

The rain was beginning to freeze by the time they reached the Malloy home. They hurried inside, took off their wet coats, and made for the roaring fire in the front parlor.

And there, sitting comfortably with a cup of tea in his hand, was Patrick.

He rose hastily as the women came into the room. "Aunt Molly, I hope you don't mind. I came with news, but you weren't home, so Riggs let me come in and get warm. I've only been here half an hour or so."

"My dear boy, you're welcome any time, of course. Hilda, ring for more tea if you would. Patrick, dear, if you're warm enough let Hilda sit there in front of the fire. She's chilled through. What is your news?"

Patrick settled Hilda in the chair nearest the fire with a cushion at her back. He took one of Aunt Molly's shawls from a nearby chair and draped it across her shoulders. "Are you warm enough, darlin' girl?" he asked anxiously.

"I will be warm soon," she said impatiently. "Do not fuss. Tell us your news."

"Well, it's simple enough. I found Barnes."

"You mean you found where the scoundrel was hiding?"

Riggs entered with tea and cookies, unasked. There was a decanter on the tray as well.

"Thank you, Riggs." Mrs. Malloy smiled at him. "You read my mind."

"The weather is most inclement, madam. Would madam wish to put dinner back, since you are having tea now?"

"Half an hour, perhaps. And Mr. Patrick will be joining us." She poured out the tea, adding to Mr. Malloy's a dollop of whatever was in the decanter. "Now, Patrick, go on. You say you found Barnes hiding somewhere?"

"Not exactly. That is, I did find his hiding place. He didn't dare go back to his old roomin' house, of course, the one where he was stayin' before he got took on as a live-in, so he'd holed up in an empty house near the Studebaker warehouses. One of those they're gonna tear down to build the new automobile paint shop?"

Hilda nodded. She knew the area. "And you found him there? What did you do?"

"I found him, all right. And I walked straight back to the police station."

"But Patrick! We talked about that. There is nothing he can be arrested for unless Colonel George tells the police he stole the papers, and—"

"I didn't ask the police to arrest him. He didn't need to be arrested. He was dead."

Mrs. Malloy stood and poured some of the stuff in the decanter into Hilda's cup. "Get that right down, now."

Hilda took a healthy sip and choked. "What is it?"

"Brandy. It's good for shock. You were as white as that napkin. Go on, drink it."

She made a face. "Thank you, but—"

"It burns a bit, yes, and the taste is odd until you're used to it.
Drink it right down."

Shuddering, Hilda drank it. Mrs. Malloy studied her for a
moment and then sat back down. "That's better. I didn't want
you fainting on me, child. Now go on, Patrick. You found the
man dead. Since you went for the police I assume he did not die
of exposure."

"No." He hesitated, looking at Hilda for a moment, but the
color had come back to her face. "Someone killed him, with a
blow to the head. And I'm mighty glad that Hilda's been with
you folks, Aunt Molly, because the first thing the police wanted
to know was who he was and where he worked, and when I told
them, the first person they thought of was Hilda."

"Me! But I was afraid of him, not—"

"I know. But you know how the police are. And when the
words Tippecanoe Place and murder get together, you know
who's going to come to their minds."

"Well, that's not a question now," said Uncle Dan impatiently.
"Hilda hasn't been out of our sight since yesterday afternoon, and
the man was alive enough then. At least, I suppose he was. Do
they have an idea when he died?"

"Don't know. He was cold when I found him, but he'd have
cooled off fast in that old house with no heat."

"However did you find him in such an out-of-the-way place,
Patrick?" asked Aunt Molly. She wanted to move the conversation away from the condition of a dead body.

"Thought where I'd go if I was on the run," said Patrick.
"Knew he wouldn't go back to his roomin' house if he could help
it, and they might not have kept his room for him anyway. He
thought he'd be at Tippecanoe Place for weeks. He could've lit

out, caught a train for somewhere, but if he did there was nothin'
I could do about it. Anyway, if he was gone I didn't care. It was
what he might do to Hilda if he was still in town that sent me
after him. Besides, I was thinkin' he'd be wantin' to do somethin'
with the papers he stole, and that'd almost have to be in South
Bend. Maybe he took care of that yesterday when he first ran off,
but maybe not.

"So I thought to myself, if I was him and had to lie low for a
while, I'd have to have shelter somewhere. It's January. I
wouldn't go to my friends, or anywhere I'd be expected to be. So
then I thought of those old houses. Nobody lives close to them,
and the Studebaker shops are far enough away that nobody
much would be around. A man could break up some wood,
doorframes and floorboards and that, and make a fire if he got
too perishin' cold."

"Had he done that?" asked Hilda. "You said he was very cold.
And what about food?"

"No sign of a fire that I saw, but I didn't stop to take a tour of
the house. Don't know if there was any food. He'd have had to
steal it, if there was. Couldn't take the risk of goin' to a store, even
if he'd had money. Somebody might see him."

"I do not understand any of it," said Hilda flatly. "I do not understand why he took those papers. I do not understand why he
ran away. He could have put the papers back and said I was
lying. I do not understand why he was killed. Oh! I have thought
of something, Patrick. Did he still have the papers he stole?"

"If he did, they weren't on him. I went back with the police
and watched while they turned out his pockets. There was nothin' in them except a couple of handkerchiefs and a penknife. Not
even a billfold."

"Ahem." Riggs had entered the room on silent feet. "Dinner is
served, madam."

They dined well. Hilda wished she had removed her corset
and changed clothes, there was so much good food. She always
ate well, of course. Mrs. Sullivan was an excellent cook, and the
servants were never stinted in the Studebaker household. But

somehow food had a special savor when one could eat it at leisure, off expensive china in a luxurious room.

There was no conversation of murders and mysteries during the meal. Mrs. Malloy wouldn't have it, and Mrs. Malloy's word was law. But Hilda thought of little else. What had Mr. Barnes been doing, and why was he killed? Who was that man who ran away from the funeral? Who was the mysterious "Mr. Perkins"? Where was Nelka Chudzik? And above all, who killed Miss Jacobs?

After dinner they returned to the parlor. Hilda was restless. It had been a busy day in some ways, but she had spent a great deal of time sitting. She was accustomed to being on her feet all day. She couldn't seem to settle down.

Perhaps Mrs. Malloy noticed her fidgeting. At any rate, she smiled and said, "Now, Hilda. Patrick has told you we wanted you to come to see us on Sunday to discuss this matter of a house."

Hilda's restlessness turned instantly to excitement. Patrick, sitting in the next chair, reached over and took her hand.

"Since you're both here now, Mr. Malloy and I thought we could talk a little, and perhaps on Sunday we could look at one house he had in mind. It isn't new, but it's quite nice and very clean, and big enough for a family when they come along. Had you been thinking of what you wanted, either of you?"

So they talked about houses, the advantages of different locations, the ideal size, the modern conveniences a house should have, until Hilda's head spun. She had never considered these matters until the past few days. She didn't know what she wanted.

Then they talked about servants, and here Hilda had definite opinions. "I do not know how much money we will have, Aunt Molly, or how many servants we will need, but I want to pay our servants enough that they can live decently. And I do not want to have children working for me. Yesterday I met the maid at Mrs. Schmidt's house. She is a nice Irish girl named Eileen O'Hara, and I could see that she works very hard. She is twelve, and she has never been to school. It is not right!"

"No, it isn't," said Aunt Molly gently. "But consider this,

Hilda. If Eileen O'Hara were not working and bringing money home, her whole family would suffer. Everyone in your family works, and how old is your brother Erik?"

"Thirteen. But he works only after school. Mama will not let him take a day job, except in summer, until he has his education. And he *likes* his job."

"That is fortunate, and your mother's desire to educate her family is admirable. Your family can afford to do that, because everyone makes enough money. What would happen if your brother Sven were unable to work, or your mother?"

"But—but—oh, what you are saying is true, but children should not have to work, not so hard as some of them do!"

"There's harder work than bein' a maid, darlin'," said Patrick. "There's the mills in some towns, where the kids work mornin' to night. And the coal mines, where they get diseases and die when they're still little."

"And there are the houses we talked about earlier, Hilda," said Mr. Malloy. "Maybe you don't know that some of the girls there start very young."

Hilda was growing angry. "I *know* all that, and it is wrong, all of it. A father, or a mother if she is the only one left, ought to make enough money to support the family. When the children are grown, they should go to work, but until then they should go to school. There should be laws!"

"My dear," said Mrs. Malloy, "your feelings do you credit. You've wanted to change the world ever since I've known you, and probably before that, too, but you can't, you know. Not by yourself."

"If women could vote," Hilda began, rebellion in her voice.

"But they can't. What you can do, though, you and other women like you, is help those children. Hire a young maid, so her family gets the money they need so badly, and spend part of your time teaching her yourself. Treat her well, train her for a better position. Do what you can, seek others to assist you, and speak out! I have no doubt," she added dryly, "that you'll do a fine job of that last."

*After the Pinkertons came... it was
hard to tell whether reporters were following the Pinkertons or the Pinkertons were following the reporters.*

—Eli B. Stephenson
*Sarah Schaeffer Murder
Mystery,* date unknown

27

B
Y THE TIME PATRICK went home that night and the
Malloy household retired to bed, they had settled on
the kind of house Hilda and Patrick wanted, in broad
outline if not in detail. Small enough that Hilda could
look after it with a minimum of servants, big enough for a growing family, old enough to look seasoned but new enough to be
clean and equipped with electricity. "And not too fancy," Hilda
had insisted. "My family must feel good when they visit, as if they
belong there."

They set up a time on Sunday to go and look at the house Mr.
Malloy had seen, and Hilda went up to bed so exhausted she
could hardly climb the stairs. It had been a long and eventful day,
at least emotionally. She fell into the soft, comfortable bed and if
she had dreams they were forgotten by the time she woke.

Agnes brought her coffee in the morning. Mrs. Malloy must
have spoken to her. Hilda sipped it cautiously, but Mrs. Hall had
learned well. It was good.

"Agnes, how long have you worked as a maid?" she asked as
the girl made up the fire.

"Four years now, miss."

"And how old are you?"

"Eighteen, miss. 'Course, I weren't nothin' but a scullery maid
to start, but Mrs. Malloy, she told Mr. Riggs he was to teach me
the proper way to do, and she helped train me herself. Now I'm
teachin' the scullery maid and the girl as comes in twice a week to
help."

"Can you read?" It was a blunt question, but Hilda wanted to know.

" 'Course, miss! Mrs. Malloy, she wouldn't have no servant as couldn't read. She's taught me to do some figgerin', too."

Hilda thought she might have known. Aunt Molly was the kind to practice what she preached.

She dressed in some of her new clothes (minus the corset) and went down to breakfast early. Riggs was just finishing setting the table. She smiled at him. "Good morning. Porridge this morning, please, and toast and coffee. And Riggs, would you tell Mrs. Hall that the coffee is excellent?"

"Yes, Miss Hilda. Thank you." And he went away without a single disparaging look. Well!

The two Malloys came into the room together as Hilda was finishing her coffee. "Good morning, my dear. You're looking very pretty this morning."

"Thank you. Is there not a saying about fine feathers?"

"Hah! I'm thinkin' you're a handsome bird, no matter about the feathers," said Mr. Malloy, sitting down at the head of the table. "I'll try some of that coffee. Smells good."

Hilda cleared her throat. "Aunt Molly, Uncle Dan, I must leave this morning. I thank you for all you have done for me, and I would like to stay, but there is no longer any danger to me. Mr. Barnes is dead, and I have much work to do. Also, I think my family will not like it if I stay here very long. They will be jealous. Mama will think I am leaving them already, even before I marry. So it is best that I go."

Mr. Malloy started to protest, but Mrs. Malloy nodded her head. "Yes, that's sensible. I don't need to tell you you'd be more than welcome to stay here until the wedding, but you've responsibilities elsewhere. But child, come to me if you need me. For anything."

She held out her arms and Hilda stepped into the embrace, surprised to feel tears starting.

"I'll drive you back, me girl. It's on me way to the store, and the weather's turned right nasty. Solid ice on the sidewalks, would be my guess."

Mrs. Malloy said she would have Hilda's new clothes packed and sent to her, along with the clothes for Mrs. Chudzik, so she accepted the ride with gratitude. The heavens were producing every possible kind of disgusting weather. Snow, rain, and sleet fell together in a slushy mixture that made the going hard even for the horses, with their four legs. Hilda hated to think what she would have done on two.

But she asked her new uncle to set her down at the end of the back drive. "For I cannot be driven up in style. Here, I am still a servant, and it would not be proper. There would be jealousy."

Uncle Dan argued with her, but gave in eventually. "Patrick's got his work cut out for him, I'll say that. You're as stubborn as Mrs. Malloy, and she's the most determined woman I've ever known."

"Thank you," said Hilda demurely. "I am glad I am like her."

She left Uncle Dan roaring with laughter as she skated cautiously up the drive.

The servants were dispersed through the house when she arrived, getting ready for family breakfast, cleaning, scrubbing. Mrs. Sullivan, the only one in the kitchen, didn't see her come in, so she was able to slip up the back stairs and change into her uniform (and hide her ring) before anyone could comment on her appearance. Down in the basement again, she walked into the kitchen and cleared her throat. "Good morning, Mrs. Sullivan."

"Glory be to God, but you startled me! And where did you blow in from?"

"I came to help. It must be very hard for you, with no butler. How is Mr. Williams feeling?"

"Doin' well. I went to see him yesterday afternoon. He's as weak as a new kitten, but he's not coughin' near so bad. He'll be comin' home in a week or so, they say, though of course he'll have to have nursin' for quite a while after that. And as for us, we're doin' well enough. That sister of yours is a good worker. But oh, there's been hullabaloos around here while you were gone!"

Hilda picked up a knife and began slicing bread for toast. "Tell me about it." She knew the story from one angle, but it would be interesting to hear it from another.

The cook had little to add to what Hilda already knew, except for the reactions of the servants to the dramatic events. "Your sister was the only one who didn't have hysterics. She said you'd have the whole thing figgered out in a day or two. You doin' anything about it? Seein' as how it was you started the trouble in the first place?"

That was so patently unfair that Hilda had to defend herself. "I did not! It was Mr. Barnes who—"

"Yes, and if you'd kept your head instead of runnin' off for the police, we coulda kept the whole thing quiet, instead of it havin' it spread all over town that anybody who wants can get into Colonel George's safe! I shouldn't wonder if he doesn't have to get a new one now, and by rights it should come out of your wages!"

There was enough truth in that to make Hilda uncomfortable. She was not about to admit it in front of the cook, however. She stood and smoothed her apron. "If you do not need me to do anything in the kitchen, I have other work to do." Head high, she marched out of the kitchen and up the stairs to the first floor.

Once there, she assumed a more humble demeanor. It was not entirely pretense. She was genuinely embarrassed about her role in the Barnes debacle, and she owed Colonel George an apology. He would almost certainly be working in his home office on such an inclement day. Taking a deep breath, she climbed the five steps and tapped on the open door before stepping in.

Colonel George looked up from his desk. He frowned when he saw Hilda. "What is it? I'm very busy."

"I am sorry to bother you, sir. I came to apologize. I acted stupidly when I saw Mr. Barnes, and I have caused great trouble. I am very sorry."

"Yes, well, no help for it, is there? I daresay you did what you thought was right at the time. Would have been better if you'd used your head, but what's done is done."

His tone was dismissive, but Hilda wasn't quite finished with her speech. "If there is anything I can do, sir, to help recover the stolen documents—"

Colonel George barked a short laugh. "Precious little you can do there, girl. I'll just get in touch with Perkins and have him send me a copy."

"Perkins, sir? Who is he?"

The colonel raised his eyebrows. "If it's any business of yours, Hilda, Perkins is the Pinkerton's man who's investigating—"

"Oh, sir! Excuse me, sir, but does he have a mustache?"

"What on earth does that have to do with anything? Yes, he does, as a matter of fact. Full handlebar, sort of sandy colored. *Thank you*, Hilda." He turned back to his desk.

This time she dared not ignore the dismissal. She curtseyed to his back and fled from the office, thoughts whirling in her head.

Think. She had to think. Where could she be alone and undisturbed to get her thoughts in order?

Mr. Williams's room. With the household in some disarray, it was unlikely anyone would bother to clean a room that wasn't in use. She ran lightly up the back stairs to the top floor and crossed the ballroom to Mr. Williams's bedroom.

There was no fire, of course, but there was a scuttle of coal standing ready. Hilda laid the fire quickly and skillfully and lit it, and soon a gentle warmth began to spread through the room. She sat down at Mr. Williams's desk, found pen, ink, and paper, and began to put her thoughts in order.

PERKINS

That was the heading, in bold capitals. She paused a moment, shaking her head. If only Colonel George read the paper more carefully, he would have seen that a man named Perkins was missing, and might have put two and two together. As it was, valuable time had been wasted.

She didn't intend to waste any more. Rapidly she began setting down details:

Red mustache.

Pinkerton's man, working for Col. G.

Spying at Mrs. Schmidt's.

She paused at that last entry. She had assumed, when she had heard that story, that Perkins was the murderer, looking for prey. She had assumed that he was the man in the overcoat seen at the head of the alley where Miss Jacobs had been killed, and that he was probably her killer.

But suppose she had been looking at this from the wrong end altogether? Perkins wasn't a policeman, but he was a detective. Pinkerton's men had a good reputation for honesty and integrity.

If he wasn't lurking as a killer outside Mrs. Schmidt's house that night, what was he doing?

There was only one answer to that, and Hilda wrote it down: *He suspected that Mrs. Schmidt operated a bawdy house.*

Hilda shivered. She had been inside that house. Little Eileen O'Hara worked there. Did she live there? Was she—surely not! Twelve years old!

Miss Jacobs had lived there, too. Erik's teacher, whom he loved. The girl who had been so active in her church, who had loved to sing to the accompaniment of a mandolin, who was cheerful and friendly, but didn't go out much and didn't have much money.

Was it possible that such a girl had also been a prostitute?

Hilda remembered something Colonel George had said in passing, when Mr. Barrett had first asked her to help with the investigation. "There's some doubt about how good she was." Something like that.

Hilda didn't want to believe it, but there was some further evidence. Miss Jacobs had been a close friend of Miss Lewis, and Miss Lewis, if rumor was to be believed, was or had been with child. And Kathleen, the maid at the boarding house, hadn't thought she had any particular men friends. It was more than possible, it began to seem likely, that the man responsible for Miss Lewis's baby was not a friend at all, but a—Hilda didn't know what to call him. Customer?

If there was a baby. If all of this weren't the merest speculation. Hilda wished she had just one solid fact, one thing she could
say for certain that she knew. She held her head in her hands. A
headache was coming on, she thought.

She reached in her pocket to see if she had a packet of the
headache powder that sometimes helped. Her fingers met folded
paper. Money! The money Mr. Barrett and Colonel George had
given her for Mrs. Chudzik. She would have to take her the
clothes and shoes soon, but they wouldn't be delivered by the
Malloys' coachman today. The weather was—

She became very still, her thoughts backtracking. There *was*
one thing she knew for certain. Nelka Chudzik was missing.
And Nelka worked at the Oliver Hotel, and was there the day
before Perkins disappeared.

It was slender, but it was fact. Hilda didn't know why Perkins
had fled. She didn't know why he had failed to pay his bill, and
then had sent the money. She didn't know why he had given a
false name and address, though she knew that Pinkerton's men
often did work in disguise. She didn't know what the blank message for him meant. But she meant to know those things as soon
as she could.

Her headache forgotten, she ran downstairs and approached
Colonel George once more.

"Sir, I am sorry to trouble you, but I must know how I can
speak to Mr. Perkins. It is very important. I believe he might help
to discover who killed Miss Jacobs."

28

S HE HAD CAUGHT HIM in the middle of a complicated calculation. He put down his pen. "Hilda, I am very busy today. I don't have time for this sort of thing. How could Perkins possibly be connected with the Jacobs affair?"

"It would take a long time to explain, sir, but if you can tell me how I can find him and talk to him, I believe I might learn some important things."

His expression changed. He sighed wearily. "Well, I hope you're right and you're really onto something. I saw Robert Barrett yesterday and he's not a well man. If you don't find out something soon... Well. The Perkins fellow gave me an address where a telegram would always reach him. I meant to wire him today anyway about those reports. Why don't you send that, and ask him whatever you want in the same wire? I know that address is around here somewhere...."

He produced it eventually, after scrabbling around in several drawers, and Hilda took it with a murmur of thanks. She had never sent a telegram in her life. She didn't even know where the Western Union office was, but Anton would know. He was the one who was always dispatched with messages, unless Colonel George phoned the telegraph office himself. Hilda didn't know how to do that either, but she was on the scent now, and nothing would keep her from sending that wire.

She trudged upstairs for the third time in an hour. Really, there were a great many stairs. She would not miss *them* when she left this house.

She paused on the second floor and moved out onto the landing of the main part of the house. It was shadowy on this dark winter day, but some of the architectural details were visible. The graceful curve of the stair railing. The carving on window and door frames. The well-fitted louvered shutters, folded now into the recesses on either side of the many windows. The rich carpets on the floor. The elegant chandelier hanging from the ceiling, not lit now, but ready to cast its warm gas glow when evening came. The plants on their delicate stands.

It was beautiful, and familiar, and yes, Hilda admired it. But she knew just how much work it took to keep everything in shining, spotless order, the dusting and scrubbing and polishing that had to be done day in and day out by the five resident servants and the many dailies. Then there were the laundress, and the gardener, and the secretary who came in sometimes to help in the office, and the waiters and waitresses who came in for big parties.

This house had been the center of her life for seven years. Things were about to change. Perhaps she would never see the inside of this house again.

And then she laughed. Of course she would! She and Patrick would, with any luck at all, soon be very well-to-do indeed. She, Hilda Johansson Cavanaugh, would sit on committees with the likes of the Mrs. Studebakers and the Oliver ladies, and she and Patrick would be invited to parties at this house. Then and there Hilda resolved to keep an eye on the housekeeping standards of Tippecanoe Place when she was a fine lady visitor, and have a word with Mr. Williams if they were not acceptable.

It was such an agreeable thought that she ran up the remaining flight of stairs as if on wings. How good life was! How fortunate she was! But it was not all good fortune. If she, Hilda Johansson, had not had a good brain, if she had not solved the Malloys' problem for them, none of these wonderful things would have happened. And before she could settle into her new life, there was another problem looming before her to be solved, a big one. She'd best stop mooning about and get to work.

Sitting in Mr. Williams's room, she gave careful thought to the wording of the telegram she needed to send. Telegrams were not very private, not like letters. She didn't know who might see it on its way to Mr. Perkins.

After many attempts and crossings-out (and the waste of a good deal of Mr. Williams's paper), she sat back to look at what she had written (in capital letters, like a proper telegram):

YOUR REPORTS TO G STUDEBAKER STOLEN STOP SEND COPIES
IMMEDIATELY STOP ALSO ARRANGE TO MEET AS SOON AS
POSSIBLE STOP URGENT SIGNED H JOHANSSON FOR
G STUDEBAKER

It was going to be a ruinously expensive wire to send, but Hilda would pay for it herself. She still had plenty of expense money from Mr. Barrett, and she felt at least partly responsible for the loss of the reports.

She looked out of the window. The weather was worse than ever. A stiff wind was driving the mix of rain and snow horizontally, and it was freezing as it hit the ground. She could see almost no one on the streets, not even in carriages. The roads were too bad to risk driving horses that might easily break a leg on the ice. Sighing, she went to her own room to don her warmest and most waterproof garments.

She found Anton in one of the cellars, stoking the furnace. He looked like a guttersnipe, his face and shirt black with soot.

"Have you been rolling in the coal?" asked Hilda pleasantly.

Anton grinned. "It blew back on me when I opened the door. I'm not real good at the furnace yet, but I'm learning."

"Be careful you do not burn yourself to a crisp before you do learn. Now, Anton, I must take a telegram to Western Union."

"In this weather? I'll take it, Hilda. Leastways, as soon as I get cleaned up I will."

"Thank you, but this one I prefer to take myself. Where is the Western Union office?"

"Main Street, next door to the Oliver. Well, it's in the Oliver, actually, in the building, I mean. But it's no weather for a lady to be out in. Better let me."

She smiled at that. "I am not a lady. Not yet. Not quite. I will be careful, Anton."

Main Street was four blocks away. Hilda was chilled to the bone before she had reached the end of the driveway. The wind, coming straight from the north, blew rain against her cheek with the force of hail and penetrated every seam of her clothing. She could barely keep her footing. She was numb with cold and nearly blinded from the ice on her eyelashes when she reached the Washington Street side of the Oliver. That was the main entrance, and she could step in and get warm and cut through the lobby to the other side.

"Be careful, miss!" A bellboy caught her arm as she slipped on the wet marble floor of the entry. "You didn't ought to be out in that there ice storm, miss. Was you wanting a room?"

She fumbled in a pocket for a handkerchief and wiped her eyes. "No, I only want to warm myself for a little. If I go out that door over there, how far is it to the telegraph office?"

"No need to go out, miss. There's an entrance right here in the hotel. If you was wanting to send a telegram, I can do it for you, miss."

His voice was eager. Business had not been very good this morning, Hilda surmised. She reached in her pocket for the message she had composed so carefully.

The paper was wet. Unfolding it, she found that the ink had run a little. "Will they be able to read this, do you think?" She handed the note to the boy.

He read it, and his face changed. "Say, miss, if you're writin' to that Perkins fellow, you need to know there ain't no such person. Well, there is, if you know what I mean, only that ain't his name. And whatever his name is, I could get your message to him quicker if I just took it myself. 'Cause, on account of he's here in the hotel right this minute!"

Hilda blinked away the water that had dripped from her sodden hat into her eyes. "How do you know? Is your name Joe, perhaps?"

"That it is, miss, and—oh! You'd be Miss Johansson! I didn't reckernize you, but you talk kind of funny, like a Swede. Beggin' yer pardon, miss."

"It does not matter. Joe, if you will go up to Mr. Perkins's room and ask him to come down here, I will give you twenty-five cents. If he comes back with you, I will give you another twenty-five cents. Tell him it is about Colonel Studebaker's business and I am a messenger for him. And is there a place where I can dry my face and tidy myself a little?"

"You bet, miss! The ladies' retiring room has towels, and mirrors, and there's a maid there to help you. And when you're done you can come back out to the lounge, and I'll bring Mr. Perkins-or-whoever-he-is to you in a jiffy!"

Hilda gravely handed him a quarter and went in the direction he pointed out to effect repairs.

When she came out, as dry and neat as possible in the circumstances, she looked around for Joe. He was just coming out of the elevator with a man, and Hilda uttered a regrettable Swedish expression under her breath. The man was not well dressed—not shabby, exactly, but not the natty dresser Andy had described—and he was clean shaven. Plainly this was some other Mr. Perkins, and she had wasted time while the telegram to the real detective could have been on its way.

Joe bowed the man to a seat and came to get Hilda.

"Joe, that is not—" she began in an undertone.

"Yes, it is, miss. He looks different, but he's the same man. I follered him all one night. He can change his name, and he can change his clothes and shave off his mustache, but he can't change his voice nor the way he walks. That's the man as was callin' hisself Perkins the last time he stayed here."

"You are sure?"

"Sure as I'm standin' here, miss."

"Very well." She handed over the other quarter and allowed herself to be escorted to the bored-looking man in the armchair by the potted palm.

"This here's Miss Johansson, sir, as was asking for Mr.

Perkins." And without waiting for the man's reaction, Joe melted away, leaving Hilda to cope as best she could.

The man had risen, of course. Now he bowed slightly. "I'm afraid there's some mistake. My name is not Perkins."

"No," said Hilda very quietly. "I do not imagine that it is. But you are a detective hired by Colonel George Studebaker to investigate a problem in this city. My first duty is to tell you that your reports to him have been stolen, and he needs you to give him copies. But I am investigating a problem, too, that I begin to think may be connected. We should go somewhere more private to talk, should we not?"

"Here," said the man in a near whisper, "are you a Pinkerton, too?"

"Then it is true that they have hired some women? No, I am not, but I am an investigator, and we must talk."

"There's always my room," he said dubiously.

"No." Hilda blushed and was furious with herself. "I am an unmarried woman. That would not do at all. But there is a writing room, and I do not believe anyone is in it now."

He gestured acquiescence and Hilda led the way.

"Now, how the dickens did you figure out who I am?" he said, when they had reached the quiet sanctuary of the writing room.

"I still do not know who you are, only *what* you are."

"My name's Frank Lowell, if you must know. But how—"

"I work for the Studebakers. Colonel Studebaker told me your name—the name of Perkins, I mean—and I put that together with some other things. But there are questions I need answered, and quickly. A man is wrongly accused of murder, and he is very ill."

"I see." Mr. Lowell looked at her sharply. "All right. There's apt to be things I can't tell you, but ask away. I'll tell you what I can."

Hilda had tidied her thoughts while she tidied her face and hair. "The first matter is, where is Nelka Chudzik?"

"And what makes you think I know?"

"Mr. Lowell, if you ask me a question every time I ask you one, I will never learn anything. Let us not waste time. Do you know where she is, or not?"

"You're a businesslike young woman, aren't you? All right, all right." He held up his hand. "No more questions. Yes, I do know where she is. And no, I'm not going to tell you. I sent her off as much for her own good as for mine. She'd found out just a little more about me than was quite safe. I arranged with a cousin of mine, a respectable maiden lady, to meet her here at the hotel on the Wednesday afternoon and take her home. And as soon as I've finished with my work here, Miss Nellie'll come back safe and sound."

Hilda nodded, trying to conceal her relief. "I was not sure, but I thought it might be something like that. Does her mother know where she is?"

"Not where, but she knows the girl's okay. At least, I let Nellie send her a letter. I guess the old woman can't read, but if she got someone to read it to her, she shouldn't be worrying."

"The last time I saw her she was very worried indeed. I do not think she knew where Nelka was. I hope that by now someone has read her the letter. I will see to it. Now, Mr. Lowell, I must tell you that I know what you were investigating for Colonel Studebaker, and I know that you went on at least one night to the house where Miss Jacobs roomed."

"How—"

"A boy followed you," she said, noting with some satisfaction the man's embarrassment. "But that does not matter. Mr. Lowell, do you believe that Mrs. Schmidt's house is—er—irregular in any way?" It was one thing to use the term "bawdy house" in the bosom of her soon-to-be family, and quite another to use it to a stranger, and a man at that.

"Now, how the deuce—oh, sorry, sorry. Sorry for the language as well. I don't know how you know all these things, but the answer is yes. Mrs. Schmidt keeps a very irregular house indeed."

"And do you believe that the matter you are investigating had anything to do with Miss Jacobs's murder?"

"I'll be hanged if I don't, but I can't make the connection. When there are nasty goings-on in a house, and then one of the girls is murdered, it's more than I can believe that the one has nothing to do with the other. But I've followed all the leads I could, all the men I could find out about who patronized that house, and they've all led nowhere." He lifted his hands in a gesture of disgust.

"Mr. Lowell, forgive me, but I must ask you this. You were seen at the head of the alley where Miss Jacobs was killed, on the night that she was killed. Then the next morning you left South Bend so quickly you did not stop to pay your hotel bill. The police were looking for you for quite a while. They may still think you killed her." Hilda took a deep breath. "Did you?"

"By all that's holy, girl, you've got guts! You think I'm maybe a murderer and you come and track me down and sit for a nice polite conversation in a hotel! I tell you, Pinkerton's could use a girl like you."

"I have other plans, sir," said Hilda primly, but her heart warmed a little just the same. It is pleasant to hear praise, and Hilda wasn't always praised for her detective instincts. "But you have not answered my question."

"No, I didn't kill the girl. But when I found out she was dead, I skipped town as fast as I could. I reckoned I'd be a suspect, and in order to prove I wasn't I'd have to tell the police who I really was—and that didn't suit me at all. I hated to rook the hotel, but I thought the cops might be watching for me. I sent 'em the money later."

"Yes, I know. I also know about the message that was left for you."

"Message? I never got a message." He looked alarmed.

"When the boy took it up to your room he found you had left. Mr. Lowell, why would someone leave you an envelope full of blank paper?"

The man began to laugh. "Oh, is that what it was? That's easy enough to explain, though the police must have found it mighty suspicious."

"I believe they did. Please tell me what it means."

"It's a signal among the Pinkertons. If there's more than one man working in a town, we know about it, and we look out for each other. Now the police called us in the minute they found the body, am I right?"

"I believe so."

"Well, the men who came would have known about me, and they'd have known the situation might not be good for someone working undercover. So one of them sent me that message. It just means 'problem—get out.' But I'd already got out, so I never saw the message, and it just turned into one more misleading piece of evidence."

"I see," said Hilda. "But Mr. Lowell, there is still one thing I do not see. If you do not believe any of Mrs. Schmidt's—um—customers killed Miss Jacobs, then who did?"

The court of inquiry investigating the murder... began work today... on the theory that the murder had criminal assault for the motive.

—South Bend *Tribune*
January 27, 1904

29

THE PINKERTON'S MAN smacked the arm of his chair. "That's what I can't figure out. All I know is, I was in the alley that night, and it must have been right before she died. I'd followed her there, because there was something about her I didn't understand. Of course, I wasn't followin' her too close. It was a bright, moonlit night and she would've seen me."

Hilda nodded. "Others did see you."

"Well, so when she turned up the alley it took me a minute or two to catch up with her, and when I got there, she was just plain gone. Not a sign of her. I waited around a minute or two, but I was kind of conspicuous just standin' there, so I finally decided she must've stepped into some house without me seein'. It made me mad. I'm supposed to be pretty good at trailin' people."

Hilda tactfully said nothing to that.

"Anyway, it was mighty cold out, so I stepped into a doorway myself, to wait for her to come out of wherever she'd gone. And the doorway just happened to be a saloon, with a nice big window at the front. So I went in and sat at that front window for a solid hour, and never saw a thing."

"Perhaps you were too busy with what you were drinking," said Hilda, and there was just a little acid in her tone.

"Say, listen! I was drinkin' coffee, and you can ask the bartender. Pretty fed up about it, he was, but we're not allowed to drink on duty. Well, after I was tired of sittin', I went up the alley a little ways, but it was pretty dark—the moon had just about set— and perishin' cold. I tell you, that girl had just flat disappeared!

So next morning, when I heard the news she was missing, and I heard the cops had found a body just off that alley, I put two and two together, and I was off on the first train I could catch!"

Hilda thought he had shown less courage and more concern for himself than a Pinkerton's man should. Perhaps their reputation was overblown. In any case, she did not intend to tell him what she thought. She needed this man as an ally. "Mr. Lowell, have you told the police this? That Miss Jacobs disappeared in the alley at—at what time?"

"I got there right around seven, a few minutes one way or the other, and went back to the hotel around eight. And no, I haven't told the police anything. I told my friends, though, the Pinkertons investigating the murder, and they couldn't make anything of it."

"Do you think that, perhaps, one of the men who—er—had seen her at Mrs. Schmidt's house was hiding, lying in wait for her? And when he tried to—er—make her go with him, she resisted and their struggle ended in murder?"

"There's two things against that, Miss Johansson." He got her name right, which surprised Hilda. This man might be unpolished, but he was observant. "For one, if anyone had tried to grab her when she went into that alley, I'd have heard. She would have screamed. And there was no scream, and I'll swear to that. And for the second thing—do you read the newspapers, Miss Johansson?"

"Yes."

"Then you must have read that Miss Jacobs was—that she hadn't ever—hang it all, she'd never been with a man!" It was his turn to blush.

Hilda didn't. She was too busy feeling like a fool. "Of course! I did read that, but I forgot! Much has happened since then. But, oh, Mr. Lowell, I am so glad that you reminded me. I have been very worried. You see, Miss Jacobs was a teacher. You knew that. But you did not know that she was my little brother's teacher, and he loved her. I did not want to believe bad things about her, and now I do not have to. But Mr. Lowell, she must have screamed! She was dragged from that alley. She grasped hold of fence posts to try to keep her killer from taking her away. Oh, and I know she did! A woman heard her!" She looked at him with grave suspicion.

"All I can say is, she didn't while I was standing there looking for her. And the other Pinks in town haven't been able to find anyone who heard a scream, except one crazy old woman who's always hearing things. And that was hours later, near ten, and it turned out to be a kid next door who was being spanked."

"Oh. Are you sure?"

"Sure as I'm sittin' here."

"But that means she must have gone with someone of her own free will, someone she knew. But why, then, has no one come forward to say that they saw her, talked with her?"

"That's easy to see, isn't it? Because the person she went with willingly turned out to be not such a good friend after all. Because he killed her."

Hilda stood and paced the floor in frustration. "But why? How could a friendly meeting become a terrible quarrel, a quarrel *so* terrible that it ended in beating and murder?"

Lowell shook his head.

"She was afraid," Hilda murmured, almost to herself. "She was afraid of someone, so afraid that she trembled when a man came to her boarding house."

"When was that?" asked Lowell, alert.

"About a week before she was killed. But it could not have been that man who killed her, because she was afraid of him—or someone. She would not have gone with him."

"Well, whoever she was afraid of, it wasn't that man who came to Mrs. Gibbs's that day."

"And how do you know that?"

"Because if we're thinkin' of the same fellow, it was another of us. A Pinkerton's man. He was trying to get into the boarding house, because a lot of the girls who boarded there roomed at Mrs. Schmidt's, and we wanted mighty bad to talk to those girls. But he didn't have any luck there, and another case he was workin' on came up with a new development, so they pulled him off and sent me a few days later."

"It seems to me, Mr. Lowell, that there have been a great many detectives in this city who have done very little! I suppose it was your men who ran away from the funeral, afraid of being photographed."

"It was, and one of 'em near as near as anything got caught, thanks to some blankety-blank Irishman. Look, Miss Johansson, don't be so hard on us. Give us a little time. It's only been just over a week, and you know the Pinkerton's motto: We Never Sleep!"

Which was all very well, thought Hilda as she made her careful way back home, but Mr. Perkins/Lowell certainly seemed to have fallen asleep on this case.

However, she had learned some important things and answered some vexing questions, at least if she believed what Lowell had said. It was good to hear that Nelka Chudzik was safe. Hilda planned to go to Mrs. Chudzik, with Sergeant Lefkowicz to translate, and tell her the good news. But not today. The weather was too bad, and Hilda couldn't rid herself of a few lingering doubts about Mr. Frank Lowell.

Was it not just a little peculiar that he was at the very scene of the crime just a few minutes before Miss Jacobs was attacked? And that he was in the hotel when Nelka disappeared? And that he left town even before news of the murder hit the streets?

No, she would reserve her opinion of Mr. Lowell, and she would say nothing to Mrs. Chudzik until she was sure the man was to be trusted.

She wished, when she got back to Tippecanoe Place soaked and freezing, that she could slip into a hot bath as she had at the Malloys' house. For a moment she wondered if she dared. Both the ladies of the house were customarily busy downstairs at this hour of the morning. They would never know.

But the servants were in and out of the family bedrooms and bathrooms all day, working. Someone would see her, and would certainly tell. Even if she asked Elsa to stand guard—and she could not do that, could not encourage her to break the rules.

Hilda removed her shoes, soaked despite her rubbers, and squelched her way to her bedroom. Her clothing would all have to dry before she could wear it again, and wool dries slowly. Later she would take it down to the laundry, sponge and brush the mud from her skirt and petticoats, and hang it to dry. For now, she simply stripped, dried herself with a rough towel that brought some feeling back to her chilled skin, and dressed in her oldest, warmest clothes. She hadn't another clean uniform, and at any rate she intended to do no housework until she had cleared her mind.

Then she went back to Mr. Williams's room and took up her list.

The questions about "Perkins" had been answered. Were the answers true?

Suppose he was lying. Suppose he was both a Pinkerton's man *and* a murderer. He *was* investigating Mrs. Schmidt's house for Colonel George. But suppose he became enamored of Miss Jacobs, followed her, and tried to assault her. She protested, fought, tried to save herself, but he grew wild with anger and frustration and hit her too hard. She died and he fled town.

That hung together very well, too well for Hilda's comfort. She had sat talking with the man, after all, had revealed that she knew a great deal. If he was the murderer, she was in great danger.

And yet—she hadn't felt threatened. He hadn't struck her as a dangerous man, only as something of a coward and somewhat incompetent.

Of course, he was skilled at disguise and probably also at playing a role.

What if he was the man who had caused Miss Jacobs such distress at Mrs. Schmidt's? What if he had made an improper advance to her there? Mrs. Schmidt would have been angry that Miss Jacobs turned down a paying customer. That fit, too.

Except it didn't. The little maid, Eileen O'Hara, had said quite definitely that the man involved in that nasty little scene had been Mrs. Schmidt's nephew, seen around the house for some months.

So that was one offense of which Hilda could definitely exonerate Mr. Lowell, but the rest of his story was still open to question. She made some notes on her list and sat for a time chewing on the pen.

Take it from the other side. Suppose everything he said was true. Hilda was nearly certain that he was telling the truth about Mrs. Schmidt's establishment, so start from there. If that were true, Mrs. Schmidt had lied about everything she had told Hilda. Suppose the nephew had made the same suggestion Hilda had just attributed to Mr. Lowell, and Miss Jacobs had turned him down in horror.

That had been—when? Hilda couldn't remember for certain, but it had been not long before Miss Jacobs was killed.

Suppose the nephew—she really would have to find out his name—had become determined to try again. Suppose it was he who met her in the alley that night…no. She wouldn't have gone with him willingly. She would have screamed, or at least have protested, the moment he tried to take her arm.

Yes, but…suppose it was Mrs. Schmidt herself who met Miss Jacobs? That would have been perfectly natural. Miss Jacobs might not have liked Mrs. Schmidt very much, but she surely wasn't afraid of her, or she would have tried to find someplace else to live.

So Mrs. Schmidt met Miss Jacobs in the alley, pretending to walk home with her. At some point along the way the nephew showed up—Miss Jacobs tried to run away—the nephew caught her—and the rest of the tragic story unfolded.

Yes, it worked. It definitely all held together. It left out a few things. Hilda still didn't know what part Miss Lewis played in the sordid story, unless it was she who encouraged Miss Jacobs to live at Mrs. Schmidt's. Perhaps she, Miss Lewis, thought Miss Jacobs was a different sort of girl from what she really was. Perhaps she simply knew that Miss Jacobs had little money and thought she wouldn't mind how she made a little more. Hilda hoped that Miss Jacobs never knew what sort of place it was that she was living in.

And the "Mrs. Schmidt and nephew" explanation left out Mr. Barnes, too. Why did he steal those papers, and where were they now, and who killed him?

Hilda wanted those things explained. She was still sore over her rash actions in that little episode, and very much wanted to get to the bottom of the matter to redeem herself. But the Barnes affair was not her immediate problem. She was on the trail of Miss Jacobs's murderer now, she was sure of it. What she needed now was some solid evidence of the nephew's guilt. And in order to get it, she was going to have to go once more to Colonel George.

...*nothing to base the arrest of
anyone even on suspicion...*

—South Bend *Tribune*
January 27, 1904

30

ILDA LOOKED AT THE CLOCK in Mr. Williams's
bedroom. Nearly noon; time for the family to have
lunch. It would be politic for her to help serve and
clean up. Unfortunately, she had no uniform to
wear, but that would not matter so much in the kitchen. Carefully, she folded away her notes into her pocket, tidied up the desk,
and went to her room to put on cap and apron.

Mrs. Sullivan was too busy to be scandalized at her appearance, though she did make a caustic comment when Hilda
walked in. Then she handed her a tureen with orders to fill it
with soup, and the luncheon routine progressed.

After lunch had been taken care of and the servants had eaten
their own, Hilda changed her clothes yet again to something suitable for an interview with her employer. She was beginning to
feel like a butler, changing all day, and she was getting very tired
of it.

Colonel George, she knew, would be sitting in the library
enjoying a cigar. She would hate the smoke and he would hate
being interrupted. Never mind. This was important. She walked
in and curtseyed, trying not to cough.

"Sir, there is something important I must discuss with you. I
know this is not a good time, but I think I have learned who
killed Miss Jacobs, and I need your help."

He put down his cigar and stared at her in astonishment. Part
of his reaction may have been to the way she was dressed—he
had never seen her in anything but a uniform—but she took it as
encouragement to continue.

"I went out this morning to send the telegram to Mr. Perkins, but I did not need to send it. He is staying at the Oliver Hotel again, and his name is not Perkins, it is Lowell, and he has shaved off his mustache. Unless it was false. That does not matter. We talked, and he told me a great many things, and then I came home and thought about them, and I think I know what happened the night Miss Jacobs was killed."

She took a deep breath and recited her scenario. When she had finished she stood and waited.

"Well!" he said, and repeated it. "Er —sit down, Hilda, please. I am amazed. You do seem to have come up with something. But you said you needed my help."

"Yes, sir." She sat, obediently. "I must tell the police what I know, and what I think. But the weather is too bad to walk to the police station, and they would maybe not listen to me anyway. They did not believe me about the safe, and they mostly think I am only a dumb Swede. I thought, if you would telephone to them, they might believe you."

"Hmph. They believed you, all right, after that man Barnes went missing and I discovered what he had taken. I don't suppose you came up with any explanation about all that?"

"No, sir. I did ask Mr. Lowell—the Pinkerton's man, you know—to give you another copy of his reports."

"Yes, fine. But it sounds as though you know most of what was in them."

"Yes, sir. It is very bad, and I hope now they will close down Mrs. Schmidt's rooming house. But I think, first the police must arrest Mrs. Schmidt and her nephew, because murder is more important than—other things."

"Yes, indeed. Very well, Hilda. I'll phone the police right now. I'll also give Mr. Barrett a ring. He'll be glad to know things are cleared up. Er—consider yourself commended, Hilda." He looked her over again, head to toe. "Isn't there something different about you today?"

She was able, by strong force of will, to keep from rolling her eyes. "Yes, sir. I do not have a clean uniform. The one I wore this morning is still very wet, so I had to wear my street clothes."

"Ah, that's it. Very becoming, I must say. Thank you, Hilda." He stood and strode to his office. Hilda sat where she was for a moment, and then went off in search of her sister.

She found Elsa in their room, taking her afternoon rest. She was sound asleep and looked very young, her cheeks rosy, her golden braids in slight disarray. Hilda dropped down in the room's one chair and watched her as she slept.

She had been worried, when she thought about marriage with Patrick, about her family's strong prejudice against the Irish, and against Catholics. Now for the first time she wondered how they were all going to feel when she was rich and they were still poor. How would Elsa feel about slaving, day after day, in Hilda's old job, while Hilda lived the life of a prosperous matron? Hilda and Patrick could give gifts to her family, of course, but they couldn't support all seven of them.

Sven, as a highly skilled laborer, made good money, but most of the family did not. Hilda and Sven had been helping out the whole family for years now. Gudrun and Freya lived in Sven's house, and Sven helped pay the rent for Mama's house.

Things were changing, though. Freya was almost certainly going to marry Gunnar Borglund, who had moved up in the Oliver Plow Works and was now working as a bookkeeper in the office. Sven had his eye on a young woman, a secretary for Stude-baker's, who was Protestant, though not Swedish. Mama had protested slightly at the idea of Sven marrying an American, but she didn't mind, really. That left Gudrun, who didn't seem inter-ested in marriage, Birgit and Erik, who were much too young, and Mama. They could live together, Hilda supposed, though Mama and her eldest daughter had never got on very well. The four could fit into Sven's old house if he took his bride to a new one. They would have enough money to live on, but not much over. Would they be jealous of Hilda?

Elsa became aware of someone looking at her. She opened her eyes. "Hilda! Is something wrong?"

"No. I did not mean to wake you."

"But I want to hear everything! Everyone talks about you, but they all say different things, and I want to know."

"Well, I have solved the murder, or I think I have."

"Ooh!"

So Hilda had to think of a way to tell the painful story to one of Elsa's tender age and inexperience. She had to leave out a good many things, though she said to herself that one day she was going to have to sit Elsa down and have a talk about some of the dangers facing young girls. Now didn't seem to be the time.

"So as soon as Colonel George gets the police to act, I think my work will be done."

"So you'll come back here to work?" Elsa sounded anxious.

"Do you like it, working here?" asked Hilda. She sounded anxious, too.

"Oh, I do! This is a wonderful house, like a palace. The work isn't really hard, if only there weren't so many stairs. And I'm getting to know the other girls, and we have fun talking while we work. Even that Janecska is getting to be friendly. It's much better than the shirt factory. We couldn't talk at all there, and the bosses were always standing over us, getting us to work faster."

Hilda made up her mind then and there. "Elsa, I have something to tell you. Patrick and I plan to be married in April. And between now and then I think I will move to Mama's house. She can help me get ready for the wedding. And that will mean you can keep this job, if you want it and Mrs. George agrees."

"Oh, Hilda! It is so exciting!" Elsa bounced a little on the bed. "You're to be married, and rich, and I'm to have this job! I wasn't sure I liked America, but it really is as wonderful as you said!"

Hilda got up and gave her a hard hug. "It is you who are wonderful. Now listen. I have not yet given Mrs. George my notice, so say nothing until I tell you to. I must go now to hear what Colonel George has learned from the police."

The news was discouraging. "Hilda, I'm afraid it's no good. I'm no great friend of the current city administration, you know, and the lout who answers the phone at the police station wasn't impressed with what I had to say. He said he'd tell the superintendent when he came in, but I got the idea that might not be today. It's this confounded weather. Nobody much is working, it seems."

"No, sir. It is not a day to take out horses, even. The ice is much worse than snow. And perhaps it does not matter, but you said Mr. Barrett is ill, and I wish we could bring the matter to an end."

"No more than I do, I can assure you. I did phone him, but he sounded very low in his spirits, even with my news."

Hilda thought for a moment. "Sir, do you think it would help at all if I told my story to Mr. Malloy, and he called the police? He is not as important a man as you, of course, but he is a Democrat and a county councilman, and even the most stupid of policemen might think it best to listen to him."

"Hmm. Malloy's a decent man, for a Democrat. I'll phone him. Bound to be home in this weather, I'd think."

"He went to the store this morning, but he has maybe come home by now," said Hilda. "The weather, it would keep shoppers away, I think."

Hilda waited a little nervously while Colonel George picked up the telephone receiver, jiggled the hook to signal the operator, and spoke into it. She had dusted the shiny nickel-plated instrument every day. She had even answered it on the rare occasions when Colonel George was not in his office and Mr. Williams was not in the vicinity. She had never quite overcome her fear of it, but now Colonel George pushed the instrument to the corner of the desk and gestured her to a chair. "Here you are. Butler's getting Malloy now."

"Hello?" the instrument quacked in her ear.

"Hello, sir. Is this Mr. Malloy?" she said loudly.

"It is, and there's no need to shout. Who's this?"

"Hilda Johansson, sir." She simply could not call him Uncle Dan, not with Colonel George listening.

"Hilda! Something wrong?"

"No, sir. Not exactly. Colonel Studebaker is allowing me to

use the telephone because I need your help." She told him the story as briefly as she could. "So if you could telephone the police, please, and tell them they need to find Mrs. Schmidt's nephew, you would help me very much. They will not listen to me." She left out the detail that they hadn't listened to Colonel George, either. That didn't seem a tactful thing to say, with him right there.

"I'll do it now. Stay by the phone. I'll call back."

Gingerly Hilda put the receiver back on the hook. "He will call me when he has something to tell me. That is, I hope you do not mind, sir. I know it is not my place to receive telephone calls."

Colonel George waved that away. "This is an unusual circumstance. I'll ring for you when the call comes in."

"Thank you, sir."

Hilda left the room feeling unsettled. She was caught between two worlds, belonging to neither of them. On the one hand she was a servant, required to be deferential and obedient. On the other she was a young woman about to be married into a prosperous merchant's family. The Malloys were not quite of the same social standing as the Studebakers. but they were not far below them, and Hilda would soon take on that rank, close to the same rank as her present mistress. It was a little dizzying, and not at all comfortable.

Part of the trouble, she realized, was that she had not told Mrs. George. She was in a false position, and she needed to remedy that as soon as possible.

Putting Patrick's ring on her finger for courage, she went to seek an interview with her employer.

Mrs. George was in the family sitting room, reading. This was a smaller room than the drawing room or the library, thus warmer and less drafty on a windy winter day. She put down her book at Hilda's approach.

"You look very nice today, Hilda," she said in a questioning tone.

Hilda explained again about her wet uniform. "I am sorry to be improperly dressed, madam."

"It doesn't matter. You're not officially on duty in any case, are you? Have you made any progress in your investigations? The Barretts are very much upset by this whole thing, Hilda."

"I know they are, madam, and yes, I think I have made progress. I am waiting now to hear from the police." She didn't detail how she would hear. Mrs. George was a reasonable mistress, but she might well draw the line at telephone use.

"I'm glad to hear it. Thank you, Hilda." She picked up her book.

"It was not about the investigation that I wished to speak to you, madam."

Mrs. George put the book down again. "Oh?" On her face was a look of foreboding.

"Yes, madam." Hilda moistened her lips. "I wish to give you my month's notice, madam. I am to be married in April."

Her mistress sighed. "Sit down, Hilda. I think you'd better tell me all about it."

Hilda sat on the edge of a chair. "There is little to tell, madam. I have known Mr. Cavanaugh for some time. We thought we could not marry because we would not have enough money, but Mr. Malloy has taken him into the family business. There will be enough money, and I will no longer need to work. And I thought, madam, if you are willing, that I would prefer to forfeit my wages and leave as soon as possible. I would like to move to my mother's house until I am married. I have much to do to get ready, and if Elsa is a satisfactory substitute, you would not be too much bothered. If you needed me at any time, of course I would come to help."

She waited anxiously. At last Mrs. George spoke.

"Hilda, you have served us well and faithfully for many years now. I will be very sorry to see you go, but I understand that you have your own life to live. You've considered the difficulties of marrying someone not of your own faith, I presume."

"Yes, madam. It will not be easy, I know. Our two families will not be pleased. But the Malloys are fond of me—they are Mr.

Cavanaugh's aunt and uncle—and I like them. And my brother respects Mr. Cavanaugh. It is a start."

"Well, you seem to have thought things out. Very well. You may tell your sister that she will stay here in your place, and you may leave any time you choose. There is no hurry; you need not feel you must go immediately. This is your home until you wish to relinquish it. And Hilda?"

"Yes, madam?"

"Please allow us to give you your month's wages as a wedding present."

...detectives...say they never before found a crime that contained so many conflicting elements...

—South Bend *Tribune*
January 27, 1904.

31

WHEN HILDA HAD stammered her thanks and left the room, she fled to the servants' room. In this house, it was where she belonged. It was deserted at this hour, and she needed to be alone.

She had done it. She had broken the tie to her old life. Soon, tomorrow perhaps, she would go to Mama and explain her plans. Maybe in those two months of working together, making wedding preparations, the two of them could come to an understanding. There would be little money for those two months, but thanks to Mrs. George's generosity, they could get by. And then...

A bell rang. Hilda looked up at the indicator. Colonel George's office! She sped out of the room and up the stairs.

"Malloy is on the phone for you, Hilda. He has news. Sit down." The colonel pushed the instrument her way, and she took the receiver.

"Yes, sir?"

"Hilda, the police have tracked down the name and address of Mrs. Schmidt's nephew. Fred Hartz, he is, lives over on Division. But they're not willing to go out there in this weather. They say the man will stay put, since he's got no idea anyone's after him, and they're not going to risk breaking a horse's leg. I think they're just lazy, meself, though they have a point about the horses. You can tell Colonel Studebaker for me that I'm beginnin' to agree with him about the police force in this town."

"I, too. But the rain and sleet cannot keep up forever." She glanced out the window. "It looks like snow, only, now. I would be willing to walk on that. What is the address on Division?"

"Blessed saints, girl, you don't think you're goin' over there to talk to a murderer!"

"Not alone. I will ask Patrick to go with me, and Sven, perhaps, if he is not working. I wish only to talk to him. I will be careful. Mr. Barrett is very low in his mind, sir. We need to know."

"Tomorrow'll do well enough. The police are right about that much. Nobody's about to go anywhere they don't have to on a day like this. I'll keep the police up to snuff, make them go tomorrow first thing, if the weather's fit."

Hilda sighed, but she recognized an ultimatum. However—"I want to go with them."

"It's not safe, I tell you!"

"I want to go." Hilda's voice was becoming more and more firm. "This is my own idea, I thought of it myself, I deserve to see him caught. I will not interfere."

"Ah, for the love of Mike! Of all the stubborn, willful, pigheaded females I've ever met, you are the worst! Patrick's welcome to you!"

Hilda ignored that. Men seemed to feel obliged to try to tell her what to do. It never worked. "Will you pick me up, if the streets are safe for horses?"

"Mrs. Malloy will have my hide if I do."

"I will be waiting. Early."

She handed the phone to Colonel George, smiled her thanks, and left the room while he was talking to Mr. Malloy—about her, no doubt.

The waiting until tomorrow morning seemed long. She had little to do and could talk to no one. Elsa was busy, Norah and Patrick and her other sisters might as well have been in Peru. It would be nice, she thought, if everyone had telephones, even poor working people, so she could speak to her family and friends any time she wanted to. What a dream!

☙

Morning eventually came, as it does even for the most anxious. Hilda had slept only fitfully and was glad to climb out of bed with Elsa at five-thirty. She dressed quickly and helped Elsa with her morning chores, then went in to breakfast with her.

"Well, look at you, dressed up like a fashion plate," said Maggie unpleasantly. "Think yourself too good for the rest of us, do you? Where's your uniform?"

"Drying in the laundry. I had to go out in it yesterday, and it got very wet. But I will not need it anymore."

That got everyone's attention.

"I want to tell you all. I have given Mrs. George my notice. I am giving up my place to Elsa, and in April, just after Easter, I am going to be married to Mr. Cavanaugh."

The reaction was so loud and hearty and congratulatory that it nearly drowned out the bell. Mrs. Sullivan looked at the indicator. "Glory be, who's at the front door at this hour?"

"I think it will be for me, Mrs. Sullivan. I must go out. I will be back later." She stopped to collect her outdoor things and the key, and ran to the front door.

Mr. Malloy stood outside. "Early, you said," he growled. "The police are on their way. This is a damn-fool idea, girl."

She closed the door behind her and put her arm through his. "Thank you, Uncle Dan."

Snow had fallen thickly all night. The world would be very beautiful when the sun came up, for the snow had stuck to every branch, every twig, every fence post or railing. It was a world of white lace, just visible by the light of a setting moon.

A large sleigh waited outside the door, its two horses blowing and snorting. Mr. Malloy helped Hilda inside, and she was delighted to find Patrick there.

"Sent for him," said Mr. Malloy gruffly. "Need someone to keep an eye on you."

"Thank you, Uncle Dan," she said again, with a meekness that deceived no one. "Do you think we could go and get my brother Sven as well?"

"Oh, and why not? Make a party of it! The more the merrier! We're off to catch a murderer, hooray!"

"He lives on Prairie Avenue at Tutt Street," she said serenely, and Mr. Malloy gave the order to the coachman.

The world was very still. Few people were abroad so early, and those few went with silent footfalls in the deep snow. Hilda sat huddled under the carriage robe close to Patrick. She didn't talk to him. She had things to tell him, but in private, and she chose not to talk about their errand. Not yet. She would wait until Sven was with them and then spring on all of them what she planned.

For his part, Patrick didn't grumble. He had no objections at all to a nice sleigh ride with his beloved close by his side. He wasn't sure what she was up to, but between them he and Uncle Dan ought to be able to restrain one woman, no matter how determined.

Sven was just getting ready to leave for work when the sleigh pulled up to his house. Hilda's sisters, due at their jobs somewhat later than he, had not yet risen, so Hilda could use her persuasive powers on Sven without Gudrun's interference.

"For you see," she said, "I must be able to tell Erik that I have seen the man arrested, and that he is safely behind bars. And though I believe there is no danger, I feel better with the two bravest men I know, you and Patrick."

Put that way, Sven made no objections. "Except I must not be very late for work. We did not work at all yesterday, and there is much to be done. We will watch, only, and then leave, *ja?*"

Hilda didn't reply. She preferred not to lie to her brother unless it was absolutely necessary.

Once they were all back in the sleigh and on their way, Hilda began to explain. "You see, I would like to talk to him. Only when the police are there and it is very safe. I believe that his aunt is also concerned in the matter, and I think he will tell me, if I ask him the right way."

"Why not just get the police to talk to him?" said Patrick.

"Do you believe the police are skillful in getting people to talk?"

After that no one objected. They would be there, after all, with several policemen. There could be no possible danger.

They approached almost silently. Mr. Malloy had left the bells off the horses' harness, and the hoofbeats were mere dull thuds in the snow.

The police, three of them in a small buggy, had waited for their arrival. Now they jumped out and beat on the door. It was some time before a yawning, angry woman answered it. "And what do you think you're doing, waking up an honest woman at this hour?"

"We want to talk to Fred Hartz."

"Well, you'd better go to California, then, hadn't you?"

"California!" said the oldest of the policemen.

"If it's Fred Hartz you want, that's where you'll find him. Decided he hated this climate and moved there, lock, stock, and barrel. Got on the train two weeks ago—what's today?"

"Friday," said the policeman. "The twenty-ninth."

"Yep, two weeks ago today. The fifteenth. I know because it's my birthday, and he never even wished me a happy one, as good as I've been to him these three years!"

"The fifteenth. You're sure?"

"I just told you, didn't I? And since he's not here, you've no more business here!" The woman slammed the door in his face.

He and the other two policemen turned to look at Hilda. "The fifteenth," said the older man. "He left town on the fifteenth. Miss Jacobs was killed on the nineteenth. That was some fine theory of yours, miss. Getting us out in the snow at the crack of dawn, and the man's got a perfect alibi!"

Grumbling, they drove off, the buggy's wheels floundering through the sticky snow.

"But I am right! I know I am! She would not have gone with someone she did not know. It had to have been Mrs. Schmidt—oh!" Her hand flew to her mouth. "She is large and I think strong. But the torn underclothing—that could have been to pretend it was a man—but surely another woman would not—"

Mr. Malloy and Sven looked at Hilda in total confusion, but Patrick, who understood something of the way her mind worked, said gently, "What is it you're tryin' to think out, darlin'?"

"I cannot believe it—it is too terrible—but it must be." She thought furiously for another moment, and then said, "Uncle Dan, will you take me to Mrs. Schmidt's house?"

He looked at Sven, and then said carefully, "It is not a place I would like you to go, Hilda, my dear."

Sven looked confused. "Who is Mrs. Schmidt?"

Before either of the other men could speak, Hilda said, "It is the place where Miss Jacobs roomed. I wish to speak to her landlady." She looked sternly at Patrick and Mr. Malloy, daring them to speak. "Only for a moment. I think she can tell me something important, and then we can go home."

Patrick and Mr. Malloy looked at each other and then shrugged, in a motion so similar that they looked more like father and son than uncle and nephew. Sven looked dubious, but he certainly intended to accompany Hilda anywhere she went with two Irishmen.

The Schmidt house was beginning to stir when they arrived. Lamps were lit, smoke rose from the chimney. "Wait here," said Hilda as the sleigh pulled up at the front door. "I will not be long."

She went around to the side door and tapped gently. In a few minutes the door was opened, as Hilda had hoped, by young Eileen O'Hara.

"Miss? What're you doin' here so early in the mornin'?"

"May I come in, Eileen? I am cold."

The little maid let her in. "But miss—Hilda, I mean—nobody has time to talk to you now, if you was wantin' to ask about Miss Jacobs. They're all workin' girls, and they're gettin' ready to leave."

"It was Mrs. Schmidt I wanted to talk to. She would be finished with her breakfast chores now, would she not?"

"Yes, miss—Hilda. She's in her office. But nobody ever comes to call before ten."

"I know. I will not be long. The office is next to the parlor, is it not? I will find my way. You might be scolded for wasting time."

And indeed the cook's voice was raised in wrath. Eileen shrugged and pointed to the door that separated the backstairs region from the rest of the house, and Hilda opened it and went through.

Several girls, pretty girls all, were trudging up the stairs to make their final preparations for a day at their regular jobs. They looked curiously at Hilda and then passed out of sight. She found the office and knocked on the open door.

Mrs. Schmidt was not pleased to see her. "So it's you. I told you everything I knew last time you were here. And if you think this is a decent Christian time to come calling, you must have been brought up in a barn."

"I must talk with you, Mrs. Schmidt. Let us go out on the porch."

"Anything I have to say to you I can say right here, and it's go away. I'm busy."

"It is business that I want to talk about this time. I have an idea you might like to discuss. I am not rich, and—but I think you will not want others to hear or interrupt."

Mrs. Schmidt looked her over. "So it's that way, is it? Well, you're skinny, but we can talk. Outside, if you're shy about it. Just for a minute, though. It's cold out there."

She shrugged into a coat and opened the front door. The air was very still. The fir trees in front of the house, heavy with snow, stirred not at all.

"So you're wanting to come to work for me, are you?" said Mrs. Schmidt, smiling unpleasantly. "Well, there are worse jobs, no matter what you might think. Our gentlemen are very generous, and I don't take a big cut. When were you wanting to start?"

"That is not what I wanted to discuss, Mrs. Schmidt. I have another sort of business arrangement in mind." Hilda moved closer to the front steps. "You see, I saw you that night. I know what you did to Miss Jacobs. I think you would be wise to pay me not to tell what I saw."

She had planned to run to the sleigh, but Mrs. Schmidt was too fast for her. One powerful arm came around her throat, the other hand across her mouth. Hilda used the only weapon she possessed. Her teeth had always been excellent. It was Mrs. Schmidt who screamed first, and then both of them tumbled down the steps. It took all three of Hilda's knights-errant to separate them.

There was a rumor this morning that
a man prominent in...social circles
had confessed to knowing much about
the murder...

—South Bend *Tribune*
February 3, 1904

32

KNEW IT HAD TO BE Mrs. Schmidt. There was no one else. But there was no proof, so I had to make her attack me."

"If you'd only told us!" said Patrick. It was the next day, Saturday. They sat in the Malloy parlor over a lavish tea, with Mr. and Mrs. Malloy and Sven and Colonel George and Mr. Barrett. And Erik. He had insisted on being present, and since he, in a way, had started the whole thing, his family gave in.

"If I had told you," said Hilda, "you would not have allowed me to do it. It was better my way."

"You could have been killed!" Sven said. It came out very much like a growl.

"Not with three strong men looking after me."

"But—I don't understand why she had to kill Miss Jacobs," said Erik.

The adults looked at each other, and then at Hilda. He was her brother. Let her explain.

"She is a criminal, Erik. She stole from the girls who lived in her house." And that was true enough, in a way. Stole their virtue, stole their reputations, stole a large portion of their money. Erik would grow up and understand, all too soon. "But Miss Jacobs was going to tell the authorities, so Mrs. Schmidt killed her."

"And what about that other girl who went missing?" asked Sven. "The one from the hotel—Nellie something."

"That was a mistake. She had gone to visit a cousin." Also true. Hilda didn't specify whose cousin. "She will come home tomorrow."

242 ∽

"What I don't quite understand is the Barnes angle," put in Colonel George.

"He was spying for Mrs. Schmidt," Hilda replied. "The police found your documents, sir, the ones he stole, in her desk. She had heard you were looking into vice in South Bend, and she wanted to learn what you knew. He broke into your safe, stole the papers, and went to give them to her, but when she found out he had been stupid enough to be seen, she thought he had become a risk to her, so she killed him, too. She is a deadly, ruthless woman and I am very glad she is in jail. I am glad, too, that you have been cleared of all suspicion, Mr. Barrett."

The old man looked sad. "Nevertheless, child, I bear some of the guilt for what happened."

They looked at him in disbelief.

"I saw them, you see. One of my upstairs windows overlooks that alley. I saw Mrs. Schmidt come out from a doorway and speak to Miss Jacobs, and then take her by the arm. I thought nothing of it—one woman walking with another—but I could have stopped it. I was tired. I did nothing. And then when the news of her murder came out, I said nothing. For that I blame myself most severely."

"But you could not know!" said Hilda passionately. "Mrs. Schmidt was her landlady. It was natural for them to walk together. You could have done nothing!"

"I could have spoken. I thought my information irrelevant, and I did not feel well. I was lazy. I sent you, a girl, to do a man's work." He shook his head, looking tired and hopeless, and Hilda's heart ached for him.

"And I suppose," said Uncle Dan, "that the—er—disarrangement of her clothing, and so forth, was to make it look as though she had been attacked by a man."

"And that is what everyone thought. Even I thought that, until we learned that the nephew was away. Then I was sure."

"Well, you were perfectly brilliant, Hilda, dear," said Mrs. Malloy, patting her hand, "and I'm sure everyone in town owes you a debt of gratitude. Decent women can walk the streets at night without fearing for their lives. And you've done a public service, too, in closing down that infamous house."

"There are others," said Colonel George heavily. "And gambling dens, and illegal taverns—a veritable sink of iniquity."

Erik, fascinated with the subject, opened his mouth to ask a question. Hilda popped the last cookie into it. "We must go, Erik. You are going to help me move to Mama's house, remember?"

"I'll help too, darlin'."

"And I," said Sven. They piled amiably into the Malloy sleigh, and as Hilda listened to the harness bells (restored now that there was no need for stealth), it seemed to her that they were the music ushering in her new life.

Afterword

ON MONDAY, APRIL FOURTH, the day after Easter, Hilda and Patrick were married in a very quiet ceremony at his mother's house by Father Faherty. They were also married in the parsonage of the Swedish Evangelical Lutheran Church by Pastor Borg, who had just come to town to take up the pulpit left vacant by Pastor Forsberg some months before. Since he did not yet know Hilda or her situation well, he was not aware of the earlier Catholic service, and no one bothered to tell him. Hilda was radiant in traditional Swedish bridal costume; Patrick wore a splendid new suit purchased at discount from Malloy's Dry Goods.

The happy couple held a reception after the second ceremony at their new house on Colfax Avenue. A Swedish smörgåsbord shared the dining room table with corned beef, soda bread, and several cabbage dishes. Huge bouquets of flowers were everywhere, early daffodils along with masses of white hothouse roses. The knotty question of what to drink had been solved with a delicious fruit punch, and if some of the Irish men strengthened it a little from flasks, they did it discreetly.

Both families were there in force, and for the most part they managed not to step on each others' sensibilities. Colonel and Mrs. George came, as well as Mr. Williams, looking a little pale still, but nearly his old self. Mrs. Clem sent her best wishes and an exquisite piece of old lace for Hilda.

Neither of the Barretts attended. Mr. Barrett had suffered a heart attack and passed away peacefully in mid-March. His widow, suddenly old and frail, was not expected to survive him by very long.

Erik and Birgit were given the day off school. Erik, by exercise of great self-restraint, did not fight with any of Patrick's young siblings or cousins.

Little Eileen O'Hara, eyes shining and step light, presided over the serving.

And Freya Johansson, eyed hopefully by Gunnar Borglund, caught the bride's bouquet.

Author's Note

I HAVE USED as the basis of this story a real murder that took place in January 1904, not in South Bend but in the southern Indiana community of Bedford. A Miss Sarah Schaeffer (or Schafer; the name is spelled variously in different accounts), a Latin teacher at the high school, was brutally beaten and murdered while walking from her boarding house to her rooming house. I have used many of the details of that historical murder in this book, the characters and plot of which are, however, either fictional or used fictitiously. I have no reason to suppose that my solution to the fictional crime has any bearing on the real crime, which was never solved.

I plan to research that crime more thoroughly and write an account of it. If anyone reading this book has any further knowledge of the Schaeffer family of Elkhart, Indiana, or the details of the murder in Bedford, I would like to hear about it. I can be reached through my website, www.jeannedams.com.

About the author

Jeanne M. Dams, of Swedish descent and a lifelong resident of South Bend, Indiana, holds degrees from Purdue and Notre Dame universities. A former teacher, she was in her forties before she decided what she wanted to do when she grew up. Her life ever since has revolved around her love of the mystery, the Victorian and Edwardian eras, and everything and anything old-fashioned. She is married with no children (unless you count her cats). Dams has been nominated for the Macavity and has won the Agatha Award. She welcomes visitors and email at www.jeannedams.com.

MORE MYSTERIES
♢ FROM PERSEVERANCE PRESS ♢
For the New Golden Age

Available now—

Paradise Lost, A Novel of Suspense
by Taffy Cannon
ISBN 1-880284-80-4
Appearances deceive in the kidnapping of two young women from a
posh Santa Barbara health spa, as relatives and the public at large try
to meet environmental ransom demands, and the clock ticks toward the
deadline.

Face Down Below the Banqueting House, A Lady Appleton Mystery
by Kathy Lynn Emerson
ISBN 1-880284-71-5
Shortly before a royal visit to Leigh Abbey, the home of sixteenth-
century sleuth Susanna Appleton, a man dies in a fall from a banqueting house. Is his death part of some treasonous plot against Elizabeth
Tudor? Or is it merely murder?

Evil Intentions, A Feng Shui Mystery
by Denise Osborne
ISBN 1-880284-77-4
A shocking and questionable suicide linked to white slavery and to
members of an elite Washington D.C. family embroils Feng Shui practi-
tioner Salome Waterhouse in an investigation that threatens everyone
involved.

Tropic of Murder, A Nick Hoffman Mystery
by Lev Raphael
ISBN 1-880284-68-5
Professor Nick Hoffman flees mounting chaos at the State University of
Michigan for a Caribbean getaway, but his winter paradise turns into a
nightmare of deceit, danger, and revenge.

Death Duties, A Port Silva Mystery
by Janet LaPierre
ISBN 1-880284-74-X
The mother-and-daughter private investigative team introduced in
Shamus-nominated *Keepers*, Patience and Verity Mackellar, take on a
challenging new case. A visitor to Port Silva hires them to clear her
grandfather of anonymous charges that caused his suicide there thirty
years earlier.

A Fugue in Hell's Kitchen, **A Katy Green Mystery**
by Hal Glatzer
ISBN 1-880284-70-7
In New York City in 1939, musician Katy Green's hunt for a stolen music manuscript turns into a fugue of mayhem, madness, and death. Prequel to *Too Dead To Swing.*

The Affair of the Incognito Tenant,
A Mystery With Sherlock Holmes
by Lora Roberts
ISBN 1-880284-67-7
In 1903 in a Sussex village, a young, widowed housekeeper welcomes the mysterious Mr. Sigerson to the manor house in her charge—and unknowingly opens the door to theft, bloody terror, and murder.

Silence Is Golden, **A Connor Westphal Mystery**
by Penny Warner
ISBN 1-880284-66-9
When the folks of Flat Skunk rediscover gold in them thar hills, the modern-day stampede brings money-hungry miners to the Gold Country town, and headlines for deaf reporter Connor Westphal's newspaper—not to mention murder.

The Beastly Bloodline, **A Delilah Doolittle Pet Detective Mystery**
by Patricia Guiver
ISBN 1-880284-69-3
Wild horses ordinarily couldn't drag British expatriate Delilah to a dude ranch. But when a wealthy client asks her to solve the mysterious death of a valuable show horse, she runs into some rude dudes trying to cut her out of the herd—and finds herself on a trail ride to murder.

Death, Bones, and Stately Homes,
A Tori Miracle Pennsylvania Dutch Mystery
by Valerie S. Malmont
ISBN 1-880284-65-0
Finding a tuxedo-clad skeleton, Tori Miracle fears it could halt Lickin Creek's annual house tour. While dealing with disappearing and re-appearing bodies, a stalker, and an escaped convict, Tori unravels the secrets of the Bride's House and Morgan Manor, which the townsfolk wish to hide.

Slippery Slopes and Other Deadly Things,
A Carrie Carlin Biofeedback Mystery
by Nancy Tesler
ISBN 1-880284-64-2
Biofeedback practitioner/single mom/amateur sleuth Carrie Carlin is up
to her neck in snow, sex, and strangulation when her stress manage-
ment convention is interrupted by murder on the slopes of a Vermont
ski resort.

REFERENCE/MYSTERY WRITING
How To Write Killer Fiction:
The Funhouse of Mystery & the Roller Coaster of Suspense
by Carolyn Wheat
ISBN 1-880284-62-6
The highly regarded author of the Cass Jameson legal mysteries ex-
plains the difference between mysteries (the art of the whodunit) and
novels of suspense (the hero's journey) and offers tips and inspiration
for writing in either genre. Wheat shows how to make your book work,
from the first word to the final revision.

Another Fine Mess, **A Bridget Montrose Mystery**
by Lora Roberts
ISBN 1-880284-54-5
Bridget Montrose wrote a surprise bestseller, but now her publisher
wants another one. A writers' retreat seems the perfect opportunity to
work in the rarefied company of other authors...except that one of them
has a different ending in mind.

Flash Point, **A Susan Kim Delancey Mystery**
by Nancy Baker Jacobs
ISBN 1-880284-56-1

Open Season on Lawyers, **A Novel of Suspense**
by Taffy Cannon
ISBN 1-880284-51-0

Too Dead To Swing, **A Katy Green Mystery**
by Hal Glatzer
ISBN 1-880284-53-7

The Tumbleweed Murders, **A Claire Sharples Botanical Mystery**
by Rebecca Rothenberg, completed by Taffy Cannon
ISBN 1-880284-43-X

Keepers, A Port Silva Mystery
by Janet LaPierre
Shamus Award nominee, *Best Paperback Original 2001*
ISBN 1-880284-44-8

Blind Side, A Connor Westphal Mystery
by Penny Warner
ISBN 1-880284-42-1

The Kidnapping of Rosie Dawn, A Joe Barley Mystery
by Eric Wright
Barry Award, *Best Paperback Original 2000.* Edgar, Ellis, and Anthony
Award nominee
ISBN 1-880284-40-5

Guns and Roses, An Irish Eyes Travel Mystery
by Taffy Cannon
Agatha and Macavity Award nominee, *Best Novel 2000*
ISBN 1-880284-34-0

Royal Flush, A Jake Samson & Rosie Vicente Mystery
by Shelley Singer
ISBN 1-880284-33-2

Baby Mine, A Port Silva Mystery
by Janet LaPierre
ISBN 1-880284-32-4

Forthcoming—

Face Down Beside St. Anne's Well, A Lady Appleton Mystery
by Kathy Lynn Emerson
Susanna Appleton's foster daughter, Rosamond, is certain her French
tutor has been murdered: Buxton, site of ancient Roman baths, is popular
with courtiers and spies alike. And the imprisoned Mary, Queen of Scots
is clamoring to pay another visit to the healing waters....

The Last Full Measure, A Katy Green Mystery
by Hal Glatzer
In November 1941, swing musician Katy Green joins two old friends in a
dance band on the *S.S. Lurline.* En route to Hawaii, the ship—like the
world at large—is riven by intrigues both political and personal, and by a
murder that might be a foretaste of war.